Praise for THE PARTED EARTH

A Georgia Center for the Bo   Read"
A Women's National Book Assoc   Selection"
Amerie's Book C
Most Anticipate
May 2021 Reads for the Rest of Us, *Ms. Magazine*
12 Must-Read Books for May, *The Chicago Review*

"I have read many books so far this year, but I can say unequivocally that *The Parted Earth* has affected me the deepest. For its
emotional honesty and insights, for its elegant craftsmanship,
and for braiding all of this through a cultural history most of us
know nothing about, this is a novel with the gravitas to transform.
Don't miss it."   **—Shannon Gibney, *Star Tribune***

"Both about firsthand trauma and inherited trauma...galvanized by the
modern belief that recovery and remembrance can help restore what
history has broken."
    —Sam Sacks, *The Wall Street Journal*

"When the puzzle pieces come together at the end...it's both a bittersweet relief & an opportunity for reflection on the complexity of interfaith relationships, the cost of sacrifice & what it means to be home."
    —The San Francisco Chronicle

"Like her characters, Enjeti ultimately reaches for hope. *The Parted Earth*
is a testament to the tremendous strength of the people of India and
Pakistan who found the courage to begin again."
    —Shelf Awareness

"An auspicious fiction debut."   *—Chicago Review of Books*

"When traditional family ties fray—here, a legacy of generational
trauma—other kinds of love and support often grow. As a result, chosen family becomes a strong influence in *The Parted Earth*. Through
the support of women like Chandani and Gertrude, Enjeti highlights
the unique bonds and challenges found within such intense, complex
friendships."   *—Chapter16*

THE PARTED EARTH

The
Parted
Earth

Anjali
Enjeti

HUB CITY PRESS
SPARTANBURG, SC

Design Lead: Meg Reid
Proofreaders: Kalee Lineberger, Kendall Owens, Stephanie Trott
Author photo: VKV Communications

Library of Congress
Cataloging-in-Publication Data

Names: Enjeti, Anjali, author.
Title: The parted earth / Anjali Enjeti.
Description: Spartanburg, SC : Hub City Press, [2021]
Summary: "Spanning more than half a century and cities from New Delhi to Atlanta, Anjali Enjeti's debut is a heartfelt and human portrait of the long shadow of the Partition of the Indian subcontinent on the lives of three generations."
Identifiers:
    LCCN 2020046269
    ISBN 978-1-938235-96-2 (paperback)
    ISBN 978-1-938235-77-1 (hardcover)
    ISBN 978-1-938235-78-8 (ebook)
Subjects: LCSH: India—History—Partition, 1947—Fiction. | East Indian Americans—Fiction. | Families—Fiction.
GSAFD: Historical fiction.
Classification:
    LCC PS3605.N54 P37 2021
    DDC 813/.6—dc23
LC record available at https://lccn.loc.gov/2020046269

"The Unbearable Whiteness of Mainstream, Canonical Southern Literature" from *Southbound: Essays on Identity, Inheritance, and Social Change* © 2021 by Anjali Enjeti. Reprinted with permission by the University of Georgia Press.

"'I'm a work-in-progress': A Conversation with Anjali Enjeti" originally appeared in *Catapult* (April 27, 2021).

Hub City Press gratefully acknowledges support from the National Endowment for the Arts, the Amazon Literary Partnership, South Arts, and the South Carolina Arts Commission.

HUB CITY PRESS
200 Ezell Street
Spartanburg, SC 29306
864.577.9349 | www.hubcity.org

In memory of my grandmothers
Dhyumani Subrahmanyam and Gertrude Angela Enzenebner Camacho

AUTHOR'S NOTE

This book is a work of fiction that contains violence and extremism, as well as miscarriage and suicide. The characters and many of the events are a figment of my imagination. But the 1947 Partition is not. After three hundred years of occupation, the British finally quit India. But before leaving, they divided the subcontinent into two nations—the Muslim-majority Pakistan on August 14, 1947, and the Hindu-majority India on August 15, 1947. More than one million people perished in the sectarian violence leading up to and following Partition. Fifteen million became refugees.

This is a tribute to those who died, those who survived, and their descendants.

Part
One

CHAPTER ONE
New Delhi
June 8, 1947

The afternoon air hung heavy and thick. In the classroom, it dwelled in the aisles between desks like phantoms. Beads of sweat dripped down Deepa's forehead and settled in the nests of her eyebrows, the curls of her sideburns. She fanned herself with her composition notebook but reaped no reward for her exertion.

Her fellow classmates scribbled the final lines of an essay on their favorite poem from *Gitanjali*. How unfair that she should have to choose only one to write about! Rabindranath Tagore's words swirled in her mind, seeped into her dreams. She could reach out and touch them, imbibe them like water. She finally settled on one of her favorite verses.

But I find that thy will knows no end in me.
And when old words die out on the tongue,
new melodies break forth from the heart;
and where the old tracks are lost,
new country is revealed with its wonders.

Tagore writes about the journey of change and creation, she wrote. *For Tagore, creation is life.*

Literature and composition was Deepa's favorite subject. Words spilled out of her. She loved the scratching of pen on paper, the curves and dots of letters. Oh, to write like Tagore, Kālidāsa, or Shakespeare. If only she could take in some of their gifts when she read them, pilfer just a tiny sliver of their styles, their voices, imbed them in her own writing.

Bells rang throughout the building, each one louder than the next. She pushed out her chair, dropped her notebook into her satchel, slung the bag over her shoulder. "Faseelah," she called to her friend three desks in front of her. "Can you come over later tonight to study?"

Faseelah pushed her glasses higher on her nose, adjusted the front of her hijab. "I wish I could, Deepa." Her gaze shifted to the floor. "Yesterday, some boys started harassing my mother and me. They said that we'd soon have to move to our prison in Pakistan and followed us all the way home. I'm not allowed to leave home anymore, except to go to school."

"Oh, Faseelah," Deepa said. "How terrible."

She walked over to her friend, embraced her tightly. Tensions had been steadily rising over the last several months, more so since Lord Mountbatten formally announced the Partition the previous week. Delhi was no longer safe for her Muslim friends and Deepa's heart felt heavy under the weight of it all, like it might plunge her into some kind of an abyss, the way a wave drags sand into the ocean. Was this grief? She had been lucky in life. She had never experienced it before.

"Please be careful, Faseelah," she said.

Deepa had once considered herself adept at offering comfort to her friends when they needed it, of always knowing the right thing to say. But these words were all she could muster, and in the midst of this crisis, they seemed shallow. Muslims were being forced to flee north. Deepa wondered how many more times she'd be able to hug her friend and how long it would be before she learned that Faseelah and her family, too, had escaped to what would become the new Pakistan.

"You be careful too," Faseelah said, squeezing Deepa's hand.

A sea of white salwar suits, hijabs, and bobbing black braids crowded the central corridor of St. Magdalene School for Girls. Here, and in the school's courtyard, Muslim, Hindu, Sikh, Christian, Buddhist, Parsi, and Jain students gathered together as they always did to study together or exchange gossip. It could be easy to forget that India was on fire when Deepa saw the love and laughter shared between her classmates regardless of their faith.

The Sisters monitored the commotion, wished students a blessed day with prayerful hands, bowed their wide, habited heads, hoped that some of the students might make their way to confession at the chapel, rather than heading directly home.

Outside, three-wheeled rickshaws lined up in rows. The rickshaw wallahs' arms slung over their eyes like blindfolds, their chests heaved in slumber. The edges of their white lungis waved like flags in the breeze. Upon hearing the rush of children, the drivers unspooled their limbs, mounted their seats.

Deepa scanned the grounds. When she couldn't find Sri and his rickshaw, her usual means of transportation to her parents' medical clinic, she sought shade under a harsingar tree. Its white petals framed her face like mogras on a bride's wedding day. She inhaled their sweet scent.

Another set of bells rang, another set of doors flung open, this time belonging to St. Francis, the boys' school adjacent to the girls' school. Students tore through the wrought iron gates, play-punched shoulders, knocked books out of one another's hands.

Father Michael in his long black cassock jabbed his finger at an older student who had wrestled a child half his size to the ground. He taught science at both schools and was a favorite instructor among the students. He didn't give too many exams, told jokes at the end of class. Lately though, he admonished, quite harshly, those who earned poor marks and instead sent rowdy children straight to Sister Louisa, keeper of the switches. Sister Ann, the music teacher, no longer sang cheery gospels in the mornings before classes started. All of the teachers at the two schools seemed on edge lately.

A page from a yellowed newspaper tumbled in the wind, caught onto the back of Deepa's chappal. She plucked it off, flattened the paper on her palm. The date was October 27, 1946. *Death toll high from latest riots in Bihar; citizens fearful of more bloodshed with upcoming Partition*, it read. A photo showed a pile of mangled bodies in the middle of the street. Several of the charred remains, including children, were missing limbs.

She shuddered, crumpled the paper, shoved it in her bag. She and her father had listened to the radio during the sectarian violence that broke out in Calcutta, Noakhali, and finally in Bihar late last October. He smoked one beedi after another as he adjusted the dial to quiet the static.

"How can we march together with Gandhi during the day and destroy one another at night?" he had cried between puffs. "How can brother kill brother? For thousands of years, Indian identity was never so inextricably tied to religion. The blood of Partition is on *British* not Indian hands."

Even if she agreed with him, Deepa often grew tired of her father's lectures. He was a deeply opinionated man, and his politics and personality were one and the same. "When one finds God," he always said, "one loses individuality and intellect." He sent Deepa to St. Magdalene for the quality of the education, not the indoctrination of a higher power. She was to keep her mind focused on her books, he'd told her, not on "silly bead prayers."

Her mother was not so rigidly anti-religion. She prayed, occasionally visited the temple, but had largely left the divine up to Deepa. And though Deepa had longed to believe in something—in a benevolent force that provided guidance, in the possibility of transcendence—only literature, the power of words, and ancient stories, had served as her anchor. She hoped they would be enough.

"Deepa," a soft voice said. "Do you remember me?"

Little Laila wore a white salwar kameez, maroon dupatta, brown chappals. Two long braids hung passed her shoulders. A dimple stretched along one cheek. Her top gums were missing her two front teeth.

"Laila, so nice to see you again," Deepa said, leaning over. "And how sweet you look in your uniform! Did you have a good first week of school?"

"Yes. I learned lots o' things."

Laila's brother jogged up, panting. "Laila, you're supposed to wait for me by the statue," Amir huffed. "I couldn't find you. I was looking everywhere." He was in the twelfth class at St. Francis of Assisi. He had a strong jaw, a toothy smile, a chest that filled out the creases of his school uniform shirt. Deepa noticed him for the first time a few months ago, found herself staring a little too long at his profile in the courtyard the two schools shared. Once or twice, he caught her eye. She looked away quickly, burned with embarrassment.

Last week, while still on school break, they formally met at the Taj Mahal in Agra. It was a pilgrimage her parents had wanted to make one last time before the imminent division of the subcontinent, before their beloved homeland became a fractured one. Her parents had gone inside the mausoleum. Deepa chose to wait for them outside on the terrace, willed the heavy, gray clouds to rain upon her, to wash away her sticky sweat. Suddenly, Amir and Laila appeared at her side. He had recognized her from St. Magdalene, he said, asked her how she was enjoying the school holiday. For the first time, Deepa had trouble producing words. When Laila eyed Deepa's tin, she finally found enough of her voice to offer the little girl a piece of jalebi. They talked for a few minutes before Amir and Laila left to find their parents in the gardens.

Amir let his satchel drop to the ground, rested his hand on his sister's shoulder. "Nice to see you again, Deepa. How was the rest of your time in Agra?"

Conscious of her slouch, Deepa straightened. "The bus ran out of petrol on the way back to Delhi. We waited on the side of the road for two hours for the driver to acquire enough to get us back home." She had not minded the delay so much. As she sat on the side of the road with Mummy-ji and Papa-ji, she replayed her conversation with Amir at the Taj Mahal, recalled what he wore, how he smiled, regretted that she had looked so disheveled during their first real conversation. "By the time we reboarded the bus," she added, "we were covered by so much dust we were the same color as camels!"

"That doesn't surprise me," he said. "Those drivers never fill up with enough petrol. They think they can complete an entire journey on prayer."

Laila laughed heartily. When her hands flew to her mouth, a beige paper drifted to the ground.

Deepa reached down and picked it up. It was shaped like a small oval bowl. But it came to a point at each end. Smudged fingerprints covered the folds. She balanced it upright in the center of her palm.

"What is this?" she asked.

"Origami," Amir said. "Japanese paper folding. A friend taught me how to do it. This one's a gondola. Do you know what that is?"

A painting of a gondola floating through the canals of Venice hung above her parents' bed at home. Its gondolier paddled a young couple through the shallow waters of the Grand Canal. The woman, mid-laugh, wore a dress with lace and ribbons. She held an umbrella over her head, gazed lovingly at the man across from her. When Deepa was younger, she wrote a story about the couple: a prince and princess who'd snuck out of the castle to escape the confines of royalty in search of a land where they could simply live together, as husband and wife, nothing more, nothing less.

"My parents have a painting of one in our flat. But I've never seen anything like this," she said. This paper gondola was sturdy. She peeked underneath one flap, imagined his fingers pressing and creasing it. "Did you use glue?"

He leaned in. His shadow cast over the boat. "See, here?" He pointed to the bow with his long, thin fingers. "The folds interlock to maintain its form."

She felt his stare gravitate higher, toward her face. She ran her tongue over her front teeth hoping to clear them of any food trapped from lunch. She hoped her breath didn't stink.

"May I have the boat back, please?" Laila said, rocking her body from side to side.

"Oh, certainly, Laila." Deepa had forgotten the child was with them. They had an audience of one, a precocious one at that. She handed it back. "It's really quite wonderful."

Laila tugged her brother's arm. "Amir, can you make one for Deepa too?"

"I'd be happy to. I can make you whatever you want, Deepa. How about a flower? Or a bird?"

"I don't want to trouble you," she said, though she instantly regretted saying it. She would give anything to have something Amir made with his own hands. "Actually, I would love a gondola. If it's not too much trouble."

"No trouble at all," he said.

She shielded her eyes, searched the street. Sri, with his white mustache, his long beard, stood on the pedals of the cycle and waved.

"I've got to go," she said.

"Don't you walk home like us?" Laila asked.

"I would walk if I were going directly home. But I go to my parents' medical clinic after school, so I take a rickshaw. Our home isn't far from here, though. Do you know Bassant Street?"

"Oh, yes. That's right around the corner from the market," Amir said. "I walk down Bassant all the time."

"We're the first bungalow on the northernmost side of the road," she said. "Our patio is filled with my father's plants. They're growing so quickly now, I have to prune them at least once a week."

Amir said, "There's a birdbath, too, yes?"

"Is that where we once saw the white mynahs?" Laila asked. "They were sitting on the edge and plunging their beaks in the water."

"Yes, that's it. We get the mynahs all the time." Deepa plucked a flower from the tree. "For you, sweet Laila." She tucked it behind her ear, secured it with one of the pins already in her hair.

Laila touched the petals. "Thank you."

"You're welcome." Deepa started toward the road. "Have a nice afternoon, you two."

"Goodbye, Deepa," Amir called out. He took Laila's hand. They headed in the opposite direction. For the first time ever, Deepa wished she didn't have to go to the clinic.

Cyclists sped by. When she reached the carriage, Sri helped her up. He was shorter than many of the boys at St. Francis, but so strong. "Hope you had a lovely day, Miss," he said.

"I did. Thank you." She pulled the carriage's hood over her head. "How is your newest granddaughter. Divya, is it?"

"Eating and sleeping well. A hearty child." He gripped the handlebars and merged into the street.

Motors of military trucks sputtered. Buses crawled with riders clinging to the outside of the doors, seated on rear bumpers. Donkeys poked their muzzles in heaps of trash. Women carried baskets on their heads. They overflowed with okra, cabbage, chili peppers. A little boy with a black pot wove between stopped rikshaws, coaxed passengers with chai.

Smog clouded the air. People blanketed the intersection. They carried small sacks and children on their backs. They appeared to be Hindu and Sikh refugees. Delhi's population was swelling with them. Sri's rickshaw came to a halt. He hopped off the seat, guided the bars to the side, searched for an opening between them to slip through.

"I'll just get out here, Sri. I can walk the rest of the way," Deepa said. She eased herself down from the seat.

"Yes, Miss," he said. "Probably faster that way."

She hoisted her bag on her shoulder, adjusted the dupatta around her neck. Turning down a side road, she passed the clock repair shop, the tailor who made all of her family's clothes, and the sweets shop that released scents of coconut and sugar. When she was little, her parents would send her every day to purchase kulfi or gulab jamin.

At the end of the road, she came upon the one-story building where she'd spent most of her childhood. The wooden sign read, MEDICAL CLINIC.

The front door squeaked as she opened it. She set her satchel down on a wide rosewood desk. A table fan groaned with effort. When she leaned in front of it, the air rushed against her neck. From a pitcher, she poured herself a glass of water, gulped it down. It spread like a liquid salve on the inside of her throat.

Her father's heavy, purposeful steps preceded him. He entered the room, dried his hands on a towel. "Hello, beta," he said. He was always buzzing about, always between tasks. His long days administering to patients often invigorated him. "How was your day?"

"Good, Papa-ji." She kissed his cheek, inhaled the lingering scent of the Chandrika herbal soap he bathed himself with every morning. He had been growing his mustache a little longer lately. It suited him.

He removed the mirror from his forehead, the stethoscope from his neck. "Your mother's helping John Uncle with another patient. She'll be out in a minute." He settled himself at a circular table, gestured to the desk. "Bala put your tiffin over there. She cooked your favorite dishes today. Go eat."

Deepa made her way to the large brown desk at the back wall. It was where she completed her schoolwork, where she greeted patients coming in for their afternoon appointments. From her chair, she witnessed the heart and soul of the work, how her parents, Aunty, and Uncle advised the community, bandaged their burns, took their blood pressure and temperatures. Drooling, babbling babies grew into walking, talking children. The elderly became frail, their stoops more pronounced with each visit.

Typically, Deepa manned the telephone in the afternoons, sorted through the stack of unopened mail, filed records. These tasks were not what drew her to the clinic, though. Her real interest lay in diagnosis, in taking histories, collecting symptoms, forming an opinion. People were stories, and every part of their stories influenced their physical and mental health. She flipped through the textbooks, perused indicators of the more common diseases plaguing the patients—ear infections, urinary tract infections, tuberculosis, bronchitis, malaria. When the process of elimination left her with a handful of potential diagnoses, she proudly presented the list to her father, like Sherlock Holmes solving a mystery.

She settled in, slid the tiffin toward her, removed each circular container from the wire holder, popped open the lids—first the sambar, then the aloo matar, the raita.

John Uncle's six-foot frame appeared in the doorway. He wore a doctor's coat over brown pants and a white shirt. Gray specks flecked his light brown hair. Unlike some Eurasians who only spoke English, John knew Bengali and Hindi as well. His great-grandfathers were British, his great-grandmothers Indian, and the children, grandchildren, and great grandchildren all married other Eurasians, himself included. John and her Papa-ji had been best friends since first meeting at medical school in London twenty years earlier. After completing their training, they returned to India to open the clinic together.

"How was school, Deepa? Learn anything interesting?" Uncle asked.

She finished chewing, swallowed. "I received the highest marks in my class on my maths test." Though of course she didn't really care about her marks in math. Only her performance in composition mattered to her.

"Good girl," he said, patting her head.

Her mother followed him, wearing a beige cotton sari, her hair wound tight in a bun. "I didn't hear you come in, beta," she said, kissing Deepa on the cheek. She poured water into a large ceramic bowl, lathered her hands with soap. Nora Aunty, John's wife, carried a box of bandages into the room. She managed the clinic's accounts, paid the taxes. Her sari was a pale peach, her reddish brown hair hung loose around her shoulders. Her father, a British diplomat, had met and married her Indian mother in Bombay. Nora was born in Paris and spoke French fluently but was happy to move to her mother's homeland to build a life with John. When the clinic was slow, she taught Deepa some simple French phrases and promised her they'd travel to Europe together someday.

A loud bang near the front door startled them. It sounded like a gunshot. Her mother ran to her side.

"What on earth?" Nora Aunty said. She set her box down.

Deepa's father held his hand out to keep everyone still. He picked up a cricket bat that he kept in the corner of the room, leaned it against his shoulder. "Who's there?" he shouted. "What do you want?"

The door flew open and a large man tumbled into the room. His shirt was half unbuttoned, his eyes red and raging. His long, wavy hair flopped over his face. He reeked of alcohol. It took Deepa a moment to recognize the intruder. It was Hari. She had known him her whole life. He had once been like a big brother to her.

When her parents worked late at the clinic, she and Hari used to play kho kho with all the neighborhood children, chasing one another through the streets. Hari would pretend he couldn't catch up to tag Deepa, letting her barely escape his arm's reach. He had given her her first taste of coffee when she was nine, taught her how to ride a bike when she was ten.

But Hari had become a stranger over the past few years. Papa-ji said he had joined the RSS, an organization whose members believed that being Indian was synonymous with being Hindu. Hari had helped organize a rally in Delhi recently, and in his speech he argued for the immediate expulsion of Muslims.

Papa-ji kept his calm. He stepped forward, held one hand up. "Hari, beta, please don't cause any trouble today. Your father is ill. He needs his eldest son home taking care of him. Stop making trouble."

"Uncle," Hari laughed. "*You* must stop treating Muslims at the clinic. It's against God's will. They are filthy swine! There will be serious consequences if you continue to do so. This is your final warning. And *you*," he pointed to John and

Nora, "you two suck the cock of the British Raj! You should be executed!"

Deepa gasped sharply and gripped her mother's arm tighter.

Her father stepped within inches of Hari's face.

"Hari, I don't want to see you or your band of RSS ingrates here again, do you understand me?" he said. "I know it was you who threw that bag of shit against our doorstep last week. It would break your father's heart if he heard you speak so horribly about our Muslim and Eurasian friends. Next time, I'll call the constable. Get out and don't ever return!"

Hari's eyes widened, his jaw tightened. He didn't budge. His fingers formed into fists.

Deepa bolted up from the chair. "Hari, what are you *doing?* Hari, *bhai,* look at me. *Look* at me!"

The sound of Hari's panting filled the room. He slowly turned to face her, blinked several times. His fingers gradually unclenched. For a moment, it was as if he suddenly remembered who she was, who *he* was from the old days. But then he closed his eyes. A grimace returned to his face. "This is a house of whores!" he spat as he ran out the door.

Papa-ji exhaled, shook his head. He carefully set the bat down.

"Beta, that was very brave of you," Mama-ji said. "Are you okay?"

Deepa nodded, even as her heart continued to race through her chest. She didn't know what had come over her. But in her mind, she had pictured Hari striking her father to the ground. She had to do something to stop it.

The truth was more complicated, though. Deepa had pretended all this time that the violence was elsewhere, that she and her family were safe. But it had now broken through her small sheltered world. She had witnessed the evil firsthand, and how it blossomed in someone who was once dear to her.

"What has become of our Hari?" her mother said. She made her way to a stool, sat on the edge, massaged her knuckes in her lap. "I remember delivering that boy as if it was yesterday. He was breech, remember, Nora?"

Nora nodded slowly. She couldn't seem to find her words.

"I couldn't turn him," her mother continued. "Sheila had been pushing for half a day. Within seconds of Hari's arrival, she took her last breath." She paused. "I don't think Hari has ever forgiven us. Is this why he harbors so much hate?" Sheila's death continued to haunt Deepa's mother. She had wondered, many years later, whether she was really cut out for midwifrey after all.

"You're not responsible for Hari's radicalism, Kavita," said John. "Besides, after Partition, many of these swayamsevaks will settle down. They'll go back to being boys playing cricket in the streets again."

Papa-ji wiped his face with his handkerchief. "I don't know, John. I worry they'll only get more extreme."

Deepa thought about Faseelah, about the taunting boys who followed her and her mother home. In Deepa's mind, their faces resembled Hari's. They weren't always bad people. But their rage and mob mentality now flowed through the streets like the monsoon rains.

"John, Kavita and I can manage the clinic by ourselves for the next few weeks," Papa-ji said. "You and Nora should go away until things settle down. I worry about your safety more than ours. These hellions consider Eurasians allies to the British Raj. They think your heritage betrays India."

Deepa hopped up from her chair. John and Nora were her family. And they were just as Indian as anyone else. She couldn't bear to see them go, even if it was only temporary. "Please, no, Papa-ji. We can't send Aunty and Uncle away."

"Don't be daft, Manoj," Nora said. "Where would we go?"

She draped her arms around Deepa's shoulders. "India is our home. *You* are our family. You're stuck with us, I'm afraid."

"Nora, we *want* you here," Mama-ji said. "But please, give it some thought. Even though we're not devout, this community still sees us as Hindus. We're more protected. People like Hari just want to threaten us. But they might harm you. Other Eurasian families we know, the Lloyds, the Bernards, they've already left."

"What about Deepa?" Nora said. "It's not safe for her, either.

Her mother sighed. "Nora Aunty is right, Deepa. You should go straight home after school, just until things settle down. Bala will be there with you."

"Oh, but Mummy-ji, I love coming to the clinic." She looked at John and her father, pleaded with her eyes, hoped they would intervene. What on earth would she do at home all afternoon by herself? Watch Bala chop vegetables for dinner? Follow Poonam around as she swept the floors? "Besides, you need me here."

Her father cleared his throat. "Your mother's right. Stay home until things settle down."

"If it's not safe for me here, it's certainly not safe for you or Mummy-ji," Deepa said. "Maybe we should just close the clinic until after Independence."

"We can't," Her mother said. She rubbed her forehead. "We have too many sick patients. But if riots start up in this area of Delhi, we'll all go south, far away from the new border."

"I'd certainly agree to that," Nora said.

Her father glanced through a short stack of files. "Kavita, the afternoon looks light. Why don't you and Deepa head home? Take the rest of the afternoon off."

Mummy-ji rose, adjusted the pleats of her sari skirt. "That sounds like a wonderful idea," she said. "Come, Deepa."

Deepa restacked her now empty tiffin cans, wiped her mouth. Her satchel fell open. The old newspaper article about the Bihar riot tumbled out. She picked it up quickly and tossed it into the wastebasket.

"What was that?" her mother asked, holding open the front door.

"Nothing," Deepa said. "I just didn't want to bring it home."

They turned down Bassant Street to number twelve. It was one among a row of whitewashed stone bungalows erected by the British Raj in the early part of the century. Her parents had purchased it last year from a Scottish family who, sensing the inevitability of Independence, packed up their belongings and moved to Edinburgh.

A concrete half-wall enclosed her father's garden—his leafy money plants, white star-shaped jasmine flowers, a curry plant, coriander, mint, and tulsi. The mint was triple the size of the other herbs. Deepa often plucked leaves off and chewed on them after meals to freshen her breath. A stone birdbath stood in the center. Carved lotus flowers encircled its base. She needed to clean it out, add some fresh water. It made her happy to know Laila had seen the white mynahs cooling off in it.

Inside the flat, the aroma of ginger wafted through the air. They kicked off their chappals, set their bags on a table. Pots clanged, spoons scraped against the bottom of the cast-iron pans. While her mother headed toward the bedroom to change into her housecoat, Deepa sought out Bala.

Bala squatted on the ground in front of the burners. She had wide-set, heavy-lidded eyes that turned down at the edge of her square face. Her white braid ran along her spine. Its end brushed against the floor. Silver bangles decorated each of her forearms, gold studs shined in her ears. She had worked for Deepa's mother's family since Mummy-ji was a young girl and cared for Deepa since *her* birth. When Deepa's parents married, and their parents disowned them for marrying outside of their castes, Bala quit working for Mummy-ji's family and followed Mummy-ji and Papa-ji to their new home.

"How was school today, Deepa?" Bala asked, stirring a bubbling pot of brown lentils.

"Good." Deepa removed the lid from a canister, popped a few almonds in her mouth. "Just going to water the plants. I'll be right back."

"Did you already have your chai?" Bala asked.

"Yes, on the way back from school."

"Good girl," she said. "Go check on the herbs, beta. The mint is looking a bit yellow."

On the patio, the money plant's dark green leaves curled around the lips of their clay pots. A vine from one pot twisted and turned to join a vine in the next, like little girls holding hands. She pressed her fingers in the soil. Dry. She lifted the can. Just as water emerged from the spout, she spotted something peeking out from between the leaves. She set the can down, pried it out.

It was a gondola, the exact replica of the sculpture Amir had made for Laila. He had hid it where he knew she would find it.

She traced the gondola's edges with her fingertip, spotted ink bleeding through the bottom. She turned it over. There was a message. *May your journey be calm and peaceful. Yours, Amir.*

She sat cross-legged on the ground and flicked off a few grains of soil from the gondola. She read the inscription again. *Yours, Amir.*

A warmth flooded her chest. She closed her eyes, imagined herself floating along in the gondola, her hair down, free from braids, whipping across her face in the wind, Amir sitting across from her in an English suit, a bow tie, cuff links like the man in the painting, his smile so wide his dimples fill his cheeks.

Bala's voice roused her. "Deepa, bring in some curry leaves please."

She slid the gondola in her pocket, plucked off a handful of leaves, and headed back inside.

CHAPTER TWO

Deepa tapped her pencil against the tabletop, slid her book closer to the candle. The flame disappeared as the wick charred to black, like the twilight eating away at the sun.

"Third outage in two hours," Bala mumbled. She lifted the candle, poured the excess wax into a steel dish, sliced the top of the wick off with a knife. Sparks popped as she struck the matchbox. Once, twice. Light budded, yawning awake.

"Remind me to buy more candles at the market," Bala said. She set the matches on the table, wiped her hands in her sari skirt. "I'll be in the kitchen."

Deepa put her pencil down, licked the froth off her chai. Flecks of ginger and cardamom seeds bobbed like fish in a pond. She took a small sip. As usual, slightly bitter. Bala never gave her enough sugar. Sugar would make her mind hold too many thoughts at once, Bala always said.

Deepa sat further back into her chair. She closed her book and instead thought about what she'd missed out on at the clinic over the past few days. One patient's ulcers had been flaring up again. He was supposed to have another appointment today. What to do with a patient who refused to cut out spicy foods? Another's right wrist would finally see daylight again after eight weeks in a cast. The croup had ignited like wildfire. The waiting area would be full of little bodies wilted over their mothers' laps, barking coughs echoing through the hallway.

She would miss it all in exchange for a quiet, boring evening with Bala, memorizing chemistry formulas and crouching over schoolbooks instead of patient files. She drank down the rest of her tea. Granules of sugar coated her tongue.

A soft thump sounded from the patio. Deepa nearly fell out of her chair. Was it Hari? She looked around the room for a potential weapon. All she had was a ruler. Had he returned, this time, to their home? Was he out for revenge against her father?

The sound was too soft, though. It must have been a bird aiming for the stone bath, narrowly missing it, colliding with the half-wall instead. This was a common occurrence at their home. When they first installed the bath, the area outside of the garden became a burial ground. Every few weeks they'd find another carcass of a bird that misjudged the space between the half-wall and the ceiling. After the fourth death, her father considered getting rid of the birdbath altogether.

The surviving birds wised up, though. They seemed to have learned, at the expense of their predecessors, the precise angle of flight needed to partake in the water.

A second thump. She pushed out her chair. Was it another bird who saw the fate of his friend but couldn't help itself?

"Bala, I'm going to go sit out in the garden."

"Let me know when you're hungry," Bala replied. "You can eat first. Your parents will be very late tonight."

Deepa opened the door. Pink and purple streaked the sky. Clouds layered like reams of cotton. The air smelled of freshly laundered clothes, hot oil from vendors selling chaat. On the street, men in trousers and stiff shirts swung briefcases. Stray dogs lapped at puddles. Chickens cornered an empty food stand, pecked at the crumbs on the ground.

She lit a fat, round candle. Diaphanous threads of cobwebs glinted against the stucco walls. The birdbath was a thick brown soup. She picked off a few leaves from its surface, tossed them over the half-wall. A white feather with gray specks stuck to the inside of the stone basin. She dried if off with her dupatta, set it on the stool. She'd save it for her collection.

She turned toward the plants.

An opaque stain lay at the base of the money plant pot. She stooped, touched it. Her fingertip turned red.

"Deepa."

Amir's face appeared just above the wall. It was streaked with blood. His right eye swelled partially shut. Dirt stained the front of his shirt.

"Oh!" Her hands flew to her mouth. Her clinic instincts kicked in. She began assessing his injuries, noting the depths of his cuts, the amount of lost blood. His wounds were ugly but seemed superficial. She was thankful for that.

"Climb over the wall," she said.

He rolled over the ledge. His feet smacked the ground. He propped himself up. "Can you help me get cleaned up?" He showed her his bloody palms. "I don't want my mother to see me like this."

"I'll be right back," she said. "Don't move."

She tiptoed back inside, peered into the kitchen. Bala squatted on the floor over the burners, hummed to the songs playing from the radio, throwing an occasional glare its way when static drowned out the voices.

Deepa crept down the hallway to her parents' bedroom, slid inside. She scooted toward the tall rosewood chest standing next to the window, pulled open the bottom drawer, rummaged around for a handkerchief, picked one she knew her father wouldn't miss—tea-stained with loose threads. She wet it with water from a pitcher.

"Deepa?" Bala called. "Are you back inside? Do you want to eat now?"

She hurried to the door, cracked it open. "Not yet. Just, uh, getting a book," she called. "Going back to the garden to complete my studies."

She closed the bedroom door, flung open a cabinet, extracted a bottle of alcohol, bandages, and tape. She slipped them underneath her dupatta, walked briskly down the hallway back outside.

Amir's elbows were propped on his knees. His head hung low between them. His fingers formed a steeple on his neck. She kneeled, set down her supplies, brought her hand to his face. "Turn toward me," she said.

It was just like at the clinic. She was just taking care of a patient. She *could* do this without her parents. She'd watched them often enough, had even assisted a few times. Her mother had shown her how to use the stethoscope, the blood pressure cuff, the otoscope (though she didn't use it often—she worried she'd poke patients' eardrums). She knew her way around superficial wounds.

It wasn't her lack of expertise that made her nervous, though. It was the caring of him, being so close to him she could hear his breath, see the slight chip on his tooth.

Touch him.

She raised her hand slowly. Her fingers connected with the

cleft of his chin. She slid her thumb underneath, along the stubble, the squiggled lines of a scrape, and angled his face toward the candle's glow. A thin stream of blood trickled from his nose to the chapped top edge of his lip.

"Judging by your expression, I must look terrible," he said.

Her neck flushed. He could never look terrible to her. He was handsome. Perhaps the most handsome boy she'd ever known. The way he carried himself—the way he moved through the world, talked with his friends—it was if he was unaware of his own beauty, his perfection. Or perhaps he knew and just didn't care.

She fumbled with the cap on the bottle. It dropped to the ground.

He handed it to her, smiled, his slightly crooked teeth peeking out of one side of his mouth, his pink gums from the other. With his eyes on her like this, it was as if she was the only person in the entire world.

"Thank you," she said. She folded the cap in her palm, twirled the corner of the handkerchief around her thumb, dipped it in the alcohol. "This is going to sting. I need to clean the wounds first. You don't want an infection." She chose her words carefully. She wanted him to understand that she would care for him. That she *could* care for him. That she cared, not in a silly, girlish way, like how her school friends giggled and covered their mouths when nice-looking boys passed by. She wanted him to see her as someone he could trust.

Gently, she dabbed the handkerchief along the length of his straight nose.

"I feel better already," he said.

She rolled the handkerchief to a fresh side, added more alcohol. The cut on his right eyelid concerned her. Its swelling covered half his eye.

"Are you able to see out of this eye?"

"Let's see," he said. He reached for the candle, brought it to her face, closed the other, uninjured eye. "There's a tiny dot just to the side of your mouth, too perfectly formed to be ink. It must be a beauty mark. A thin, delicate scar the length of a baby's fingernail sits above your eyebrow. Your irises are not dark brown, as I previously thought, but bronze. There are specks of gold in them too."

The mole, the one that looked, she felt, as if she hadn't properly cleaned her mouth after a meal—he had complimented. The "delicate" scar came from a particularly nasty fall when she was four or five. No one had ever described her eye color as bronze with golden specks—like one would describe a piece of art. It felt as if *he* was diagnosing *her*.

She cut a narrow strip of bandage in her lap, laid it over the cut, secured it with two pieces of tape. "Your vision's fine then," she said, with as steady a voice as she could manage. "Are you going to tell me how this happened?"

"You're the doctor. Are you going to *ask* me how this happened?" He laughed, touched his mouth as if trying to make sure he still had his teeth. He wasn't in pain. He wasn't afraid. He seemed to be enjoying himself with her, as she was with him.

"Then?"

He wiped his hands in his pants, picked at a few loose threads at the seam. "I was crossing a street, through a crowd. One minute, people were conversing peacefully, and another minute—pandemonium. People started calling one another names. *Vile Hindu! Idiot Muslim!* So childish! Not even Laila would behave in such a way. I don't even know how it started."

He rolled onto his knees, stood. "The crowd began to swell. I tried to go around." He walked the length of the patio, paused near the birdbath. His fingertips skimmed the surface of the water. "Someone started smashing bottles and hurling them through the air. One piece caught my face. Several people ran right over me trying to get away. No one stopped to help me up."

She saw him in her mind—his body, curled on its side on the ground, his face, bloody, his arms and legs pinned by trampling feet, his mouth, open, crying out for help. The scene filled her with a rage she'd never known.

The light drained from him. His body slouched. A shame seemed to wash over him, as if he suddenly realized what happened was his fault. She wondered if that night had been a turning point for him, as Hari's outburst was for her. If the moment *before* the violence he inhabited one world, and *after* another. This knowledge—that his mere existence inspired such hatred in others—seemed to have changed him.

"I'm so sorry," she said. Her words rang hollow. The same words had failed her father, too, who continued to wear his despair about Partition like a heavy overcoat, and they had failed her friend Faseelah. Surely, there were better words to express the agony of not being able to prevent or take away others' pain. Despite Deepa's "expansive" vocabulary (according to Madam Grover), she didn't know what those words were. Because words were no longer enough.

"Where were you trying to go?" she asked tentatively. She did not want to press him, but the way he was looking at her made her think he wanted to tell her more.

Her question loosened something. His face became more relaxed. "I was coming here again," he said. "I was delivering this." He reached in his pocket, held his hand before her, opened his fingers. "I wanted to add to your collection."

A swan. A long, curved neck, like the top of a question mark. Wings opened slightly, as if contemplating flight. A narrow, slight beak. She ran her fingertip from the top of its head, down the back of its neck, traced the four pleats of each wing.

"It's lovely," she said. "You risked your safety to bring this to me?"

His hand rose to her face. He touched her cheek, let his fingers linger on her skin. "It was worth it, to see your face light up like this."

She held her breath, slightly swayed. She'd never found it so difficult to stand on her own two feet. When he finally removed his hand, she exhaled. But he remained close. His breath was slow and deep.

"Deepa?" Bala called from inside. "Come eat please."

"I have to go," she said.

"Can I keep leaving notes for you in the plant?"

"You can't be wandering the streets at night, Amir. It's not safe. And if my parents find you here, they'll be so upset." Her parents were nothing like other parents she knew. They believed daughters should be valued and treasured as much as sons. They would never pay a dowry to Deepa's future husband upon marriage, should she decide to marry. Despite their own scandalous union, though, her parents upheld age-old taboos of etiquette and expectations. No visits with the opposite sex without a chaperone, and only in preparation for marriage.

Amir took her hand. His warm palm draped over her knuckles. "I'll be careful."

She wanted to freeze the moment in time, to suspend it in her mind. They had spoken for the first time at the Taj Mahal only a week ago, and yet, she felt she knew him better than anyone she had ever known in her life. How was it possible for her to feel this way?

"Besides," he said. "Look around us, Deepa. Look at what's happening to our people. This anger and distrust.... This could go on for days, weeks, months. What are we supposed to do? Stop living? Stop taking risks? Stop being who we are? I'm not going to do that. I'm not going to shrink in fear. That's what they want, isn't it? For us to … to cease to exist as we once did. To cease to be human beings in their eyes."

When he released her hand, she thought she might float away, as if he had been her anchor. She was not like him, though. She had, in many ways, already shrunk in fear. She wasn't sure any risk was worth this—this bloody though still beautiful face. "But why can't you just give the origami to me at school? Why must you risk coming here?"

His gaze dropped. "Laila and I won't be coming back to school," he said. "My mother was let go from her typing job this evening. Her boss said she was very skilled, but he could no longer employ a Muslim in this political climate. It was too risky for them both. And without her job, we can no longer afford the fees."

"Shameful," Deepa retorted. It was just like what was happening at the clinic. People were becoming enemies everywhere.

"Ammi's worried she won't be able to find another job," he said. "And my Abba's been sick for a long while. He's not been able to support our family for years. He thinks we should just move to Lahore to his sister's house. But I don't want to go. My aunt is very cruel. She's always blaming Ammi for Abba's poor health."

"I wish there was a way for you to stay safely in Delhi," Deepa said. "I'm sorry it's become so dangerous for your family."

"We have been lucky. Some of our Hindu and Sikh friends have been helping us out. They've been bringing by food, checking on my father's health. But others won't even look at us anymore. They hang out on their stoops. When they see us coming, they hush, stare us down."

It was a familiar scene. A river of apprehension flowed between homes not even one meter apart. Walls constructed with laundry hung out to dry. Windows half closed. Doors locked even during daylight hours. Detours taken around entire neighborhoods to avoid people of another faith. The families on her own street kept their distance, whispered, Deepa had heard, about her parents' insistence on treating Muslim patients at the clinic.

The wind chimes jingled in the breeze. A stray dog howled. The first stars in the sky twinkled as the sunlight grew dimmer with each passing moment. Her parents would return from the clinic soon. She leaned over the wall, looked north, toward the park, listened for the honking of Sri's rickshaw, the squeaking of his wheels.

She turned back to him. "Please, Amir, tell me what I can do to help. I'll do anything."

"There's nothing either of us can do, Deepa, except to wait it out," he said. "And not to succumb to the fear. That's what they want." He positioned his hands on the half-wall, jumped over it.

"Amir," she whispered. "How will I know if you leave Delhi?"

He turned around. "I'll tell you," he said. He gestured to the plants. "Just look before you water."

"Promise me you'll be careful," she said.

A chair scraped loudly against the floor inside.

"Quickly," he said. "Back inside."

She nodded, ran toward the door.

"Wait," he said. He leaned back over the wall. "Please, come close."

"What's wrong?" she said, returning.

He looked deeply in her eyes, lifted her chin, brought his soft lips to hers.

Her eyes fluttered shut. Her lips were still, too stunned to move. So he did this for her, slowly parting them with his own. He then skimmed her cheek, her forehead, her ear. She brought her hand to his chest. His heart pounded into her palm like Morse code.

"Good night, Deepa."

The breeze caused her to chill. She blinked her eyes open. His form faded to a silhouette and then diluted completely into the blackness of the landscape. She strained her eyes, willed his image to reappear before her, but he was gone.

She redrew his touch on her mouth, licked her lips to taste him again. She opened her hand. The swan. She'd almost forgotten about it. She wrapped it in her dupatta like a fragile package and went inside.

CHAPTER THREE

At the market, Deepa and Bala navigated through cyclists, small children tugging on their mothers' saris, carts dripping with yellow, white, red flower garlands. The acidic aroma of chilies infused the air. Food vendors stood in the shade, fanned themselves with newspapers.

Deepa brought the samosa to her mouth, folded down the brown paper around it, bit into the corner. Steam poured out of the aperture, burned her upper lip. She rubbed it with the tip of her tongue.

Bala tore ahead to forage for the family's meal. She was short, squat, but carried herself with such authority, such purpose, she seemed at least a meter taller than she really was. "Stop dawdling," she chided. She scrunched her doughy face. "I don't want to be here all day."

Deepa blew inside the pastry several times, shoved the rest of the samosa in her mouth, licked her fingers.

Finger-like buds of green okra blanketed a wooden cart. Bala approached it with suspicion, as she did all of the vendors' bounty. She picked one up, squinted, set it down. As she scanned the rest, she wrinkled her nose, turned away. Shopping with Bala was a far more arduous errand than Deepa had imagined, one she had become intimately familiar with ever since her parents quit allowing her go to the clinic in the afternoons.

Deepa rested her chin on Bala's shoulder. "I'm tired. Can't I just wait at home while you shop?"

"Eh. If you come quickly, we'll finish sooner."

Since her parents forbade Deepa from going to the clinic, she had become Bala's charge. She was forbidden from visiting friends alone, forbidden from strolling through the park, forbidden from even walking to the end of the street to purchase a daily paper. Bala chaperoned and monitored her every activity.

Bala's chappals slapped the dirt and left dusty clouds in her wake. She paused at the edge of a faded indigo blanket, lining her chappals along the border. A woman with streaks of white hair squatted behind it. Her crossed arms rested on her knees. The thin silver rings on her toes peeked out from her sari's petticoat. Star fruit, mangoes, and guavas were arranged in neat rows in front of her, their greens and yellows so bright they glowed. Deepa's mouth watered. She imagined the sweet juice of a mango coating her mouth, dripping along her chin.

As if reading her mind, Bala pointed to the mangoes. "Are they ripe?"

The woman held out the yellow-green fruit in her hand. "You see yourself."

Bala's fingertips lightly compressed the skin. She touched it to the tip of her nose, sniffed, rotated it in her hand, sniffed again.

Deepa sighed and shifted her weight. *Just purchase it.* Bala spent as much time diagnosing the ripeness of produce as Papa-ji did diagnosing the condition of a patient.

Satisfied, Bala placed the mango in her bag, counted out annas in the old woman's palm. "Come," she said, glancing back at Deepa. "We still need to buy rice and dal."

A group of merchants sat in a circle on the ground, puffed beedies. Smoke snaked out of their mouths, conjoined, floated across a basket stuffed with yellow peppers. At the next stand, buckets overflowed with toor and channa dal. When Bala sifted through them, they sounded like sheets of rain hitting the roof.

On a typical day, vendors waved their arms, called out prices to encourage negotiations, ushered prospective buyers to their goods with promises that their product was the highest standard. The market was a living organism with a snappy, syncopated rhythm. This afternoon it was sluggish. Vendors picked at their cuticles, yawned with wide-open mouths, conversed with other, rival sellers. No one seemed interested in making a sale.

"Here. The peppers," Deepa said. "Didn't you say we needed them?" She pointed to a wooden box containing red, yellow, and green orbs, all varieties of capsicum. A man with a thick, long mustache stood behind it, tapped his foot, glared in their direction.

Bala administered two sharp shakes of her head, beckoned Deepa to her. "He's refusing to sell to us," she said. "Can you imagine? I have always given him such good business. If my annas aren't good enough for him, we will take them elsewhere."

"Why won't he sell to you anymore?"

Bala pulled her close and off to the side. "Because the *fool* doesn't like that your parents see Muslim patients at the clinic. Pay the man no attention. Let's just keep walking."

Deepa spun around, flashed him a stern look.

"Deepa!" Bala quipped. "Please don't cause any trouble. Do you remember what Poonam said? Mind yourself! Don't provoke anyone!"

Poonam arrived every morning to shake out the rugs, wash the floors, and most importantly, deliver gossip to Bala. Two days earlier, as Poonam squatted and swept, she told them about the *terrible things*. One girl Deepa's age disappeared in broad daylight. She was returned to her family days later, badly beaten, her body defaced by many men. The girl's mother, filled with shame for her now unmarriageable daughter, soaked herself in kerosene and lit herself on fire. The story troubled Deepa so much she couldn't sleep that night.

The sun receded behind a blanket of dusk. Bala eyed the sky, pouted, resumed her mission. Shoppers filled in empty spaces between aisles, toted purchases in burlap sacks, sidled up to one another along the perimeter of carts. A shriek emitted from one stand, followed by gruff cursing, flung hands— an argument over the weight of rice. Accusations of cheating and fixed scales flew through the air. Such antics were a daily occurrence at the market. People argued. They fought. They tussled for the best quality items, stormed off in exaggerated tantrums when rebuffed. Today felt different, more tense, the kind of irritability inspired by a full moon. Bala took Deepa's hand, dragged her in the opposite direction.

Deepa slid her other hand into her pocketbook, wrapped it around the most recent origami note from Amir, a red paper heart, on which he'd inscribed, *You have mine, may I have yours?* She'd seen him only once since his injury almost a week earlier. He had been visiting his friends outside of the school he no longer attended. She was too shy to approach him.

They came upon a cart with rows of glass jars containing bronze, orange, black spices. Bala brought one close to her face, scrutinized its contents. The glass distorted her reflection, her dour facial expression. "This turmeric isn't the right color," she barked. "Four annas, that's all."

"I ground it myself, Madame," a man with a turban responded, puffing out his chest. "I know exactly what it is. Ten annas, nothing less."

They lobbed back and forth until Bala crossed her arms. "Come, Deepa," she huffed. "This man is trying to rob us."

Deepa's stomach growled. She wished Bala would tone down her dramatics for just one afternoon so they could return home more quickly.

Around the corner, a woman fried parathas while holding an inconsolable baby on her hip. The baby's two white lower teeth protruded awkwardly from her gums, saliva spilled from her lower lip onto the woman's shoulder. Despite the baby's constant squirming, the girl deftly captured the parathas with her fingernails, flipped them over in the pan. The baby must have been teething. At the clinic, her mother often advised the mother or father to soak a cloth in cold water and allow the baby to chew on it.

The clinic. How she wished she could be there instead of the market!

"Do you want another snack?" Bala asked.

Deepa nodded. "Yes, please."

"Just don't tell your parents I let you ruin your appetite for dinner."

Bala opened her wallet, counted out coins. In her periphery, Deepa spotted a little girl in a bright yellow salwar kameez carrying a basket of vegetables near a flower cart. When the little girl waved, Deepa's hand flew to her chest.

Laila.

Deepa touched Bala's sleeve, pointed. "I see a friend. Can I go say hello? I'll come right back."

Bala squinted her eyes at Laila, looked back at Deepa, and then to Laila again. She glanced at the line ahead of her. "Don't go far, beta. I promised your parents I'd keep you in sight at all times. From here, I'm going right over there to buy the rice." She pointed to a stand a few meters away. "Meet me there."

Deepa pecked her on the cheek. "I'll be quick." She hurried toward the flower cart, where she found Laila.

"Laila, I'm so glad to see you. Are you well?"

"Come." Laila shot out in front, disappeared around a corner.

Deepa turned back to look for Bala. She was engaged in an animated conversation with the woman standing in line behind her. Both women flung their hands up, flicked their fingers, complaining, most likely, about the prices at the market. Perhaps Bala wouldn't notice Deepa's temporary absence. She resumed following Laila.

When she turned the corner, she bumped into Amir.

"Oh," Deepa gasped. "Amir. Hello."

His starched white shirt was unbuttoned at the top. Rolled up cuffs exposed his strong forearms. His eyelashes were long and thick. She imagined them fluttering against her cheek. His wounds had healed nicely, but his face was pale, as if he hadn't slept in days. He laid a hand on his sister's head.

"Laila, be a good girl," he said. "Go sit down over there. I need to talk to Deepa."

Laila scrunched her face, propped her hands on her hips in protest.

"Please, beta. It won't be long," he said. "It's important."

She sauntered away with her basket toward a trail of flower petals.

His voice lowered. "This wasn't something I could write in a note." His eyebrows knitted together. The confidence that he had projected a few days ago, upon leaving her house, had evaporated.

"Amir, are you in trouble? Are you hurt?"

"I started working for a lawyer a few days ago. He's Hindu and lets me file his cases in the back room to keep me safe. But I can overhear the conversations with his clients who come by. They make me worry for your family."

"What do you mean?" she asked.

"Hindus aren't just targeting Muslims. They are making lists of other Hindus," Amir said, "lists of Hindu families who are hiding Muslim families and who are watching over their homes and belongings until they can return to India. There are lists of Hindu businesses that serve Muslims. They call these Hindus traitors to India, Deepa."

Traitor. The word vibrated through her eardrum. Her parents had devoted their lives to caring for the sick, risked their own health trying to manage outbreaks of malaria and tuberculosis. They visited the homes of the dying, held their hands, administered medicine, assured their last moments on earth were free from suffering. It was an absurd notion that her parents, who believed that the subcontinent should never be defined by caste, religion, language, or region, were traitors. They had devoted their lives to serving the land and the people they loved.

"You are the one who is in danger," Deepa said. "You and Laila, your family—other Muslims. I'm worried for *you*, not us. After Partition, everything will eventually go back to normal for us," she parroted with little conviction. "But this will not be true for you. You need to be careful. You and your family need to go somewhere safe."

Amir took hold of her shoulder. "Deepa, listen to me. Partition is filling people with a kind of rage I've never seen. Muslims are being targeted here the most but Hindus helping Muslims are also in danger. You must understand this."

A chill ran down her spine. Poonam's words—*the terrible things*—echoed in her mind.

"What do you want me to do, Amir?"

"I'm afraid—"

"*Amir*," Laila said. She ran up to him, tugged on his sleeve. "Can we please go home?" Her vegetable basket was now covered in flower petals.

"Laila, not now," he said. "Just go sit there like a good girl."

Her eyes darted between them. "Are you going to marry Deepa?"

"*Laila*," Amir sighed. His face flushed. "That's just...why would you—"

"*Of course not*, Laila," Deepa said. "We're friends. Just like you and I are friends. Do you understand?"

Laila's mouth twisted to one side. "No."

"Deepa, listen to me," Amir said, ignoring his sister. "These extremists, whoever they are—they're pinpointing businesses. Vandals have smashed in windows and stolen supplies from shops near Saravan Street. Isn't that where your parents' clinic is?"

Nora Aunty ordered most of their medical supplies from Vikram Pharmacy on Saravan Street—bandages, medications, cotton swabs, vials. If they ever ran out of anything, they'd send Deepa to pick them up. "It's a few streets away," Deepa said, swallowing.

"My new employer has been investigating some of the crimes—the looting, the assaults," Amir said. "He thinks it's going to get much worse."

A queasiness settled over her. She recalled an argument between her parents a few nights ago while trying to fall asleep. Mummy-ji had just received a post from Uma, an old school friend in Bangalore who begged them to come south for a holiday, far from the new India—Pakistan border. Mummy-ji pleaded with Papa-ji to close the clinic for just one month. Papa-ji said they couldn't leave Delhi. Their patients were too sick.

"My father won't listen to anyone," Deepa said. "He's determined to keep the clinic open."

"And *you* don't understand the forces I'm talking about."

Deepa huffed. "I'm not some naïve school girl, Amir. I have eyes. I live here too."

"But you don't—"

"Let's *go*, Amir," Laila whined, looping her fingers through Amir's belt. I want to go home."

"Laila," he snapped. "Please!"

Laila's mouth fell open. Her lower lip quivered.

Deepa bent low, put her hand on Laila's shoulder, eyed Amir. "Your brother did not mean to talk to you like that. He didn't meant to talk to *me* like that, either. He's just worried. Please give us a little more time, Laila. I'm going to make sure he calms down. Then he'll be ready to leave with you."

Laila nodded slowly, sulked to the corner, and draped herself over an upturned crate.

"I'm sorry, Deepa. I didn't—"

"Amir, I can't imagine what you and your family are experiencing right now," she said. "I want to help you. But if my parents decide to stay in Delhi, I can't change their minds. And I am frightened already. I don't need you to frighten me any more."

"I understand," he said. "I'm sorry, Deepa."

She stepped back, searched the crowd of shoppers. She spotted Bala inspecting grains of rice, her nose turned up. In her hand, Bala held a paper bag. The parathas, soaked in oil, stained the bottom. Deepa had been born and raised in Delhi, knew this city, this India, intimately. It wasn't so much that she didn't believe Amir—it was more that she couldn't understand how quickly things could change in such a short period of time. Or maybe things had always been changing. Maybe tensions had always been rising like the sea at high tide. *People are inherently good,* her mother had told her once, *they're just not inherently good all of the time.*

Amir had been right to some degree. Deepa *had* been naïve. She had been callous, even. She had bought into denial to push away the fear. India was on the verge of a war with itself. She could see this now.

"I have to go," Deepa said.

"Make your father understand things are worse than he thinks," Amir said. "Please, Deepa. I'm worried about you."

"And I'm worried about *you*," she said. "What will your family do? How will you escape this?"

"My mother found some temporary seamstress work, and together we're saving for the train tickets. As soon as we've saved enough," he said, "we're moving to Lahore."

Lahore. Less than five hundred kilmoters to the north. And yet, it might as well have been worlds away. Surely, she would never see Amir again. She searched his face, those lips that had brushed against hers, for a different answer, and blinked away tears. She wanted him safe, and yet, safety meant their separation. "Amir, please try to leave me a note to tell me when you go." Her response failed to capture how she really felt about him, how deeply her heart would ache when he left.

"I will." He took hold of her hands, squeezed them. His eyes lingered on her face. He touched her cheek. He then turned, lifted the basket of vegetables, and offered his hand to his sister. Laila looked back and waved. As they walked away, flower petals tumbled out of the basket. A few had already browned.

Deepa rushed back to Bala's side.

"There you are. Don't stay away that long again," Bala sighed. She handed Deepa the paratha. "I'm to watch you at all times, I—" she stopped short. "Why are you so pale? Are you not feeling well?" She laid her hand across Deepa's forehead.

Deepa removed Bala's hand, wrapped it in her own. "No, I'm not. I'm just tired. Please, can we go home now?"

Bala nodded. She clutched Deepa's hand, led her through the rest of the market, where at the curb, they boarded Sri's rickshaw and headed home.

Late that night, Deepa laid on her bed and stared at the ceiling.

After her parents' pre-sleep mumbling on the other side of the wall faded into light snores, she crawled out, opened her desk drawer, and removed a leather-bound notebook. Inside, Amir's origami notes were folded flat. She arranged them on her desk. Five perfect sculptures made with the most perfect hands she'd ever seen.

She selected the six-pointed star, traced her thumb over its fragile, narrow letters. A word on each point, it read YOUR SHINE LIGHTS UP MY HEART.

Tonight, as she drifted off to sleep, she would focus on *these* words, not Poonam's *terrible things*, not Amir's stern warning at the market. India, Pakistan, Independence, the world around her was crumbling and shaping itself anew. She would purge her mind of the chaos, fill herself only with thoughts of him.

She pressed the star to her chest, curled up on her side in her bed, and let her eyes flutter shut.

CHAPTER FOUR

D eepa's callus was bulbous and black, a lump of dough gone hard. She slid her thumb over the rough surface, the peeling edges. With every mark and dot, a blot of ink bled across her knuckle and nail. *A writer of intention*, her mother had once called her, *a messy scribe.*

Her teacher, Madam Grover, sat behind her desk and gazed out the window with the glazed eyes of a lost child. Her hair was pulled back in a loose bun. Her wide-framed glasses dangled at the end of her nose. She seemed not to notice they were about to fall off. She was much younger than the Sisters who ran the school and, according to the rumors, wore men's pants and danced holding hands with male partners—just like the Americans. Usually Madam Grover only pretended to be strict. Her scowling at misbehaving students often turned into the kind of laughter she failed to mute with the pallu of her sari. Sadness seemed to have settled over her lately, though Deepa found herself wondering whether the reason she excused herself to the toilet so frequently throughout the day was to cry.

Deepa twirled her pen, wiggled back into the seat. She read over her completed assignment once more, flipped the paper over. Her classmates continued to scribble.

The clock's ticking served as a metronome for the sighs of students. She glanced at its face. Five more minutes. She picked up a fresh sheet of paper, started a letter. *Dear John Uncle and Nora Aunty,* she wrote. *If you're reading this, you've reached Bangalore safely.* She strummed her fingers along her desk. *We're doing our best without you.*

The same day Deepa met Amir and Laila at the market, John and Nora received a disturbing note attached to their door.

Quit India like the British or you will pay for it. The note detailed John and Nora's routines, the days they'd shopped, the times they'd entered and exited the clinic, descriptions of the clothes they'd worn. Her beloved Aunty and Uncle were being stalked. And because they didn't want to risk the safety of Deepa's family or their patients, they decided to hurriedly leave Delhi.

On their last morning in Delhi, before making the nearly two-day train ride to Bangalore, they came to the house to say their goodbyes. John begged Papa-ji to temporarily close the clinic.

"We'll be fine," Papa-ji insisted. "We'll see you in a few weeks, when the worst has passed."

In their absence, the precise, clockwork routine of the clinic quickly unraveled. Patients spilled out in the street, unfinished paperwork draped every surface. Account balance sheets and inventory ledgers were neglected. Refugees from Punjab and the North-West Frontier filled their small waiting room. Deepa culled and updated what she could from the boxes of files her parents brought home and dumped on the floor, but she couldn't keep up. She needed to be there, in person.

Patri, a new girl who had just started at St. Magdalene a few weeks earlier, nudged Deepa with her elbow and slipped her a note before shifting away.

Poetry is boring, it read.

Smiling, Deepa set the note inside her desk. Her new friend hated writing. She could multiply four-digit numbers in her head in seconds but found the process of composing a sentence downright painful.

Deepa smoothed out the letter to John and Nora, added, *I wish we could have gone with you*. She signed her name.

Madam Grover's chappals shuffled toward the back of the classroom. The pleats of her light blue sari lined up like neat rows of desks. Three minutes until class ended. Then Bala and Anil, their family's new automobile driver, would arrive to whisk Deepa directly home after school. She would remain there for the rest of the day, trapped between the stuffy walls of their home. The garden was her only freedom, the watering of the plants her only unmonitored, unchaperoned act.

Two minutes left until the end of class. Too little time for recitations. Relieved, Deepa folded her poem in half. She leaned over, opened her satchel.

"Deepa," Madam Grover called. "If you have time to pack up early, then you have time to recite your poem to the class."

Deepa blushed. Muffled giggles erupted from the desks around her. Surya, Deepa's academic nemesis, turned around, snickered. She and Surya were always competing for first rank. As it stood, Surya was ahead of Deepa by two points.

"Deepa," Madam Grover repeated. "Please, stand at the front."

Deepa shut her eyes. Of all the things she had to read aloud! She pushed her chair back. It ground against the floor,

like pestle against mortar. As she made her way to the chalk-
board, she felt Surya's stare burrow into her back. Deepa
turned around slowly, unfolded the paper, lifted her face to
her classmates.

A sea of eyes blinked and settled on her. Relief swept their
faces. Deepa's reading would exhaust the last moments before
the bell rang. It would rescue them from doing their own
recitations.

A bead of sweat rolled from Deepa's armpit to her elbow.
The words on the page blurred, returned to focus. Her fingers
gripped the edge of the paper, trembled in her hand. She could
recite Emerson and Wordsworth in her sleep, recite them to
the entire student body with confidence. But her own poetry
was different. So raw and uneven and uninspiring, she thought.

Patri flashed Deepa a smile, nodded.

"Quickly, Deepa," Madam Grover said, leaning over her
desk. "Begin."

"Yes, Madam Grover," Deepa said. She cleared her throat.
"'Night Notes' by Deepa Khanna."

Pen to paper, paper to pen
coaxing my heart with ink
the shade of midnight.
Shapes shift
under the moon's glow,
unfolding
musical lyrics,
sweet sounds bringing
you to me, me to you.
Verdant leaves
cradle dew drops
in their veins,
our only witnesses.

She dropped her hand, looked up.

Silence engulfed the classroom. Patri's mouth hung open. Surya's eyebrows furrowed. Devi scooted her chair, causing her pen to roll off the desk and drop to the floor.

"Students," Madam Grover said, touching Deepa's shoulder. "This is a poem. This is how poetry sounds. This is how poetry feels. Very nicely done, Deepa," she said.

Madam Grover removed her glasses, pressed the frame against her chin. Her voice was so soft, only Deepa could hear it. "I had no idea you were a poet," she said.

The bells rang out. Students shoved their books inside their bags, burst into conversations across aisles. Deepa darted back to her desk, collected her belongings.

"Read the next two sections for tomorrow," Madam Grover announced as they filed through the doorway. "There will be an exam at the end of the week."

A collective groan echoed through the room.

"Excellent, Deepa," Patri said, lifting her school bag to her desk. "I could never write anything like that."

"Sure you could," Deepa said. "Just keep practicing."

"Deepa," Madam Grover interrupted. "Can I speak with you for a moment?"

Patri shot Deepa a look, shrugged her shoulders. "I'll see you tomorrow," she mumbled under her breath.

Deepa slung her satchel over her shoulder, slunk toward her teacher's desk. The muscles of her face tightened. There was no way Madam Grover could know what the poem was about. And yet, she worried that her teacher might have figured out something.

Her teacher wiped the blackboard with a wet cloth, rinsed her hands in a large glass bowl of water, sat in her chair. "Are you well?" she asked.

"Fine, Madam Grover. Thank you for asking."

"I wish your classmates could write poetry as thought-fully. I don't think some of them have even cracked open the *Gitanjali* yet. Actually," she said, "I was hoping to talk to you about something unrelated to your beautiful writing." She removed her glasses, set them on her desk.

"Yes, Madam Grover?" Maybe she'd performed poorly on her last maths test. Madam Grover hadn't given them their marks yet. She bet Surya bested her again.

"I saw you at the market last week," her teacher said, tilting her head. "With Laila and her older brother, Amir."

Deepa broke eye contact. She tried to keep her breath steady. She had no recollection of seeing Madam Grover that evening.

"Laila was one of my students last year, when I taught the five-year-olds," Madam Grover continued. She replaced the cap on an ink bottle, twisted it shut. "A bright little girl. I was very sad to know she had to leave school. I've had the pleasure of talking with her brother Amir a few times too." She leaned forward. "What a nice young man."

Deepa could not figure out where this was going. She fidgeted with her notebook, scratched the side of her face.

Her teacher reached out, touched her hand. "I'm not going to get you into any kind of trouble," Madame Grover said. "I just want to know if Amir and Laila are safe. I didn't stop to ask them at the market because the conversation between you two seemed...private."

Deepa tightened her grip on her satchel strap, tried to plot a safe arc for their conversation. "He's working for a lawyer," she finally said. "His parents need him to earn money so they can move to Lahore. They won't be staying in Delhi much longer."

In his last note, he wrote that they would be leaving at the end of the week. He would come by one more time, to give her one final note, containing the exact day of his departure and his new address in Pakistan.

Madam Grover's eyes drifted to the wilting green plant on her desk. Beads of liquid hovered among the dark, thick flakes of soil. In a few days' time, its leaves would turn brown and brittle. Madam Grover had overwatered it. Deepa knew this much.

"I'm sorry to hear that," her teacher said. She folded her hands across the desk. "But of course, they must do whatever they need to stay safe. I'm just sorry they have to leave their home to do it. Deepa, do you... do you have a way of getting something to Laila and Amir? Would you be able to give them something from me?"

Madam Grover didn't wait for Deepa's reply. She opened her purse, counted out several notes, held them out to her.

Deepa hesitated. If she took the money, Madam Grover would know that she and Amir were in regular contact. She might tell Deepa's parents. Not taking the money would make Amir and Laila's journey to Pakistan that much more arduous.

She opened her palm. "Yes, I will get this to them," she finally said. She stuffed the money in her bag, glanced at the clock. If she kept Bala and Anil waiting any longer, Bala might charge into the school looking for her and overhear their conversation.

"Thank you, Deepa. I appreciate it." Madam Grover reached toward the plant, plucked off a brown leaf. It crinkled when she enclosed her fingers around it. "My cousin, her husband, and their sons are trying to get out of Karachi. I haven't heard from them in almost two weeks." She sighed. "I'd like to think someone over there is helping them too."

So this was what had been troubling her teacher. Her own family had been trying to flee. The hasty departure of her own loved ones, the fraught journey from one point to another, the border-crossing, the loss of communication in the interim, the waiting for word as the moon moved through its phases. Northern and eastern India were undergoing a massive uprooting. The homes and businesses belonging to beloved friends and neighbors were emptied, the doors locked.

Faseelah had not shown up to school today. Was she ill? Or had her family, too, left in the middle of the night without telling anyone? Was she, too, crossing by foot or train over the border to a place where she had no family, no friends, no community?

"I hope your family makes it across safely, Madam Grover," Deepa finally said. "I *know* they'll make it safely. They must, Madam Grover. So they *will*."

Her teacher opened her palm. The leaf had disintegrated into crumbs and veins, its previous form unrecognizable. She looked back at Deepa with an expression of bewilderment, as if she suddenly had no idea why her student was there. She picked up her glasses, affixed them to her face, straightened her back. Her voice found its authority. "Don't forget to study for the exam. It's going to be a tough one."

Deepa backed away. Her hand clutched the notes inside her bag. "I won't. Have a nice afternoon, Madam Grover," she said, before exiting the room.

At home that evening, Deepa sat cross-legged on her parents' bed. Her mother, fresh from her bath, smelled of lavender soap and talcum powder. Her hair hung long and loose, formed a wet stain on the back of her light green housecoat.

She settled behind Deepa on the bed. Her teeth gripped bobby pins. She tugged on a section of her wet hair, started the brush at the crown of her head.

"One or two braids, Deepa?"

"Just one, Mummy-ji. Please."

The mirror above the vanity reflected the white hairs along her mother's forehead. Deepa had never known her mother's parents, her grandparents, but she had seen a few photos of their lined faces, tufts of their silver hair, their soft, veined hands. She could imagine what her mother might look like older, how age would make her even more beautiful, even more refined than she already was.

When the brush lodged itself on a tangle, Deepa contracted her back. "Ouch. Not so hard, Mummy-ji."

"Sorry, beta," she said. She spread coconut oil in her palm. Her slender fingers massaged it in Deepa's temples, along her ears. "It needed a good brushing today."

Deepa brought her knees to her chest, braced herself.

"We miss you at the clinic," her mother said. The brush started again at Deepa's forehead, down along her scalp, past her shoulders to her waist, in long, fluid movements, like the graceful arms of a classical dancer. "The patients ask about you all the time. Do you remember Shefali Aunty? She said your personality always brightened the office."

"When can I come back to the clinic?" Deepa asked. "When will Uncle and Aunty return from Bangalore?"

Her mother stopped mid-stroke, brought her hand to her side. "I don't know," she said. She set the brush on the bed, lowered her chin. "I don't know about anything right now."

"What's the matter, Mummy-ji?"

Her mother pursed her lips. She clasped Deepa's hands. "I need to tell you something. Papa-ji and I...made a decision this afternoon."

Deepa's eyebrows furrowed. "About what?"

Her mother's shoulders rose and fell with each breath. She looked at Deepa, turned her head back around, divided her hair into three, equal plaits. Her fingers moved quickly, rotating each section of hair to the inside, forming a neat, tight rope. "I told him we should have left with John and Nora to Bangalore."

Deepa hopped off the bed, turned around. The braid unraveled along her back. "What did Papa-ji say?"

"He said...he said he had taken an oath. That if we left, our patients would suffer. We'd be hurting the very same people we promised to help." Her mother twirled a loose button thread from her housecoat around her fingertip. "He's right, Deepa. He's right in so many ways. I don't want to leave our patients, either. We have the ability and the resources to help others who are not as lucky as we are, who do not have the means to flee Delhi, as we do. To turn our backs on them—it's just not right." She sighed. "But I wonder what the cost will be to us, if we stay," she said. "It's selfish, I suppose, to think this way, when others are suffering so much."

Deepa grasped her mother's hand. "Our absence would be temporary. Let's leave, Mummy-ji. Let's all go on a holiday together. What if Hari returns, what if—"

Her mother shook her head. "We can't, beta. We...we shouldn't—"

"We *can*," Deepa blurted. Her father was like a brick wall, so opaque he couldn't see what stood just on the other side. He had theorized and politicized the fallout of Partition on a state and local level, had worried about the risks to those who were poor and sick, Eurasians, like John and Nora, but had ignored the concerns of his own daughter and wife.

"Mummy-ji, please. He's being unrealistic. He's...wrong." Deepa had been foolish to dismiss Amir's concerns, to put so much faith in her father whose principles sometimes clouded his judgement.

"Deepa, do not talk about your father that way. He cares, very deeply, for others. This is what makes him such a good doctor." She looked down at her lap. "Besides, Delhi is our home." It was a statement that lacked any conviction.

"Delhi is not the same home it *was*," Deepa said.

During Deepa's quarantine, she could feel her bones calcifying from lack of movement, her lungs thirsting for more time in the fresh air. Meanwhile tension filled the streets outside of their home. Every honk of a vehicle startled Deepa. Every raised voice sent a chill down her spine. Most nights, Bala slept on the floor of the kitchen so she wouldn't have to walk back to her own home in the dark, just two kilometers away.

A pair of Papa-ji's reading spectacles sat on the bedside table. A thin crack ran the length of one of the lenses. He didn't have time to get it fixed, to do much of anything anymore. Last night, she found him leaning against the back of the sofa, his lips slightly parted. He'd fallen asleep. He was too exhausted to make a rational decision about anything.

Deepa could reason with him. She could do this tonight, when he returned from work, after her mother had gone to bed. She would convince him they should leave Delhi. She knew she could find a way to make him understand.

She rose, kissed her mother on the cheek. "I'm going to go finish my assignments, Mummy-ji. You rest."

"Wait," her mother said. She pulled her toward her. "I have something else I need to tell you."

Deepa searched her mother's face. "What is it?"

Her mother stroked the side of her cheek. "Tomorrow afternoon, Deepa, we're sending you by train down to Bangalore to stay with John and Nora. Bala will go with you."

Deepa stepped away so quickly she stumbled into the dresser. "No, Mummy-ji! You can't send me away!"

"You will be back before you know it. It's just temporary. They're so looking forward to having you."

"Mummy-ji," Deepa pleaded. "I don't want to go. Not without you and Papa-ji!"

"You'll enjoy it," her mother said, as if she was coaxing Deepa to try a new food.

Deepa's eyes burned. Her parents were casting her off. "Please. If it's dangerous enough for me and Bala to be sent away, it's too dangerous for you and Papa-ji to stay."

Her mother locked eyes on her. She straightened. Deepa knew she had lost the argument before the words came out of her mouth.

"Deepa, one of our new patients is having very high blood pressure this pregnancy. The baby will be born in a few weeks, but it will be a difficult birth. If I don't stay to help, I don't know what will happen." Her lips quivered. "We'll miss you, terribly. But it's for the best. Please, try to understand, Deepa."

Heat rose from Deepa's chest. They could not do this. They could not send her away and stay here without her with no one to protect them. Not when the violence had begun encircling their clinic like a kettle of vultures over a corpse.

She released her mother's hands. When she kissed her cheek, her lips met a tear rolling down her mother's face. Her mother seemed so small in that moment, helpless. Deepa had never seen her like this before.

"I'll just go finish my school work now, Mummy-ji."

In her bedroom, Deepa threw open the top drawer, grabbed the money from Madam Grover and the poem she'd written in class that day. She draped a dupatta over her shoulders, pushed her hair behind her ears.

"Deepa," her mother called from her bedroom. "I'll be there in a few minutes to help you pack your trunk."

In the kitchen, a pot of rice bubbled on the burner. Rows of okra lined up in the pan. Bala hummed. Her knife pounded the cutting board. Deepa turned away, slipped on a pair of chappals, entered the patio.

Darkness cloaked the skies. A faint glow from a candle across the way served as the only light. She folded her poem in half, slid the money inside. She then parted the money plant's leaves and laid the money and poem on the damp soil. She hoped Amir would come by later that night and find them both.

She then faced the wall, braced her hands on the top edge and heaved herself over. She would find Papa-ji and convince him not to send her away. It was the only way. Her soles slapped the dirt ground. Her eyes blinked in the darkness. She gathered her hair, shoved it inside the collar of her kameez, tied the dupatta under her neck.

She began sprinting in the direction of the clinic.

When she turned the corner, her chappal slid halfway down her foot. She tripped, careened forward. Her knees collided with the ground, skidded across sharp pebbles. Blood seeped through her thin cotton pants. Her palms burned. She pushed up to standing, hobbled a few steps, took off again.

In the darkness, her vision strained to translate the outlines of shapes into familiar markers. A tall square box with shutters—her mother's favorite sari stall. A pyramid glowing in the moonlight—the Sai Baba temple. A thickly veined mass—the wide trunk of the old banyan tree. She hadn't walked to the clinic in a while. It was farther away than she remembered. A trip she thought would take her ten minutes on foot would take at least twice that long.

She panted. Her calves pinched with every step. Her dupatta slid off her head, flopped against her back. At the market, she slowed down and tried to catch her breath. She cut through its deserted aisles, between clumps of rickshaws. The drivers were curled up on the benches, snoring.

"Hey, sexy girl," called one of them. He propped himself up. "Are you looking for me? Come," he motioned. "We'll have a good time."

She darted around him, the border of her dupatta just barely out of the reach of his fingertips. She turned a corner and dashed down the length of the alley where she last saw Laila and Amir. In a few days, they would board a train north to Pakistan. If she couldn't change her parents' minds, she would board a train south to Bangalore. The distance between her and Amir would stretch the length of the subcontinent.

At the end of the alley, she smacked into a vegetable cart. It knocked the wind out of her. The vendor, who'd been dozing on the ground next to it, woke. "Watch where you're going, filthy girl! Your father should beat you for being out so late by yourself!"

She bolted around, slowed when she reached the main road.

Sleeping bodies lined either side of it. More refugees. She leapt over skewed limbs, mothers nursing infants, children huddled into tiny balls against the sides of their fathers. A small boy wandered between bodies, searched for a place to rest his head.

She resumed running.

The dupatta's knot drifted up her neck, over her mouth. She yanked it off, cut diagonally through the park. She was almost to the clinic now. One hundred more meters until she reached her Papa-ji, until she could finally confront him alone, beg him to close the clinic and come with her to Bangalore.

In the final stretch, her other chappal slipped off her foot. She ran a few paces back, dropped to the ground, patted her hands in the darkness. Finally, her hand met soft, worn leather, a toe loop. She raised the pant of her salwar, slipped on the chappal.

She limped the last stretch.

A chorus of male voices shouted behind her. She turned around. Several silhouettes headed in her direction. Poonam and Amir's warnings returned to her at once. They were coming for her. She was finished. Just before they reached her, she moved out of their path, pressed her body against a wall, hoped the darkness would conceal her.

The men flew past. "Quickly, quickly," one man yelled to the group. They didn't even seem to notice her.

A parade of several women with hiked saris, jugs balancing on their heads swooped by. Water sloshed over the edges, drenched their hair and blouses. Deepa thought she recognized a few of their faces, but she couldn't place them.

She crawled along the wall in the shadows when she heard it—loud crackling sounds. A putrid smell surged through her lungs. Diesel. She pinched her nose, continued to hobble along. Voices, sharp, shrill, burst through the air. The memory of Amir's bloodied face surfaced. Something bad was happening.

She took a few tentative steps forward, peeked around the wall, blinked several times to bring what appeared before her into focus. Black, billowing clouds swirled in the night sky. A crowd congregated before a building. Women and men tossed buckets of water on flames bursting through doors and windows.

She had made a wrong turn somewhere. She reeled around. A small shop was shuttered. She walked toward it, spotted the awning. She knew this place. It was the chai shop near the clinic—the one her mother had brought her to last week on Deepa's last day at the clinic.

She spun back around, rushed toward the burning building, elbowed her way through the bodies, surveyed the sweaty, soot-covered faces. Sparks, smoke exploded out of the roof, knocking down at least a few dozen people on the front line. It was their clinic.

"Papa-ji," she screamed. "Papa-ji!?"

"Deepa," a woman called.

She frantically searched for the voice. Zainab Ali, an old beloved patient of theirs was lying on the ground, her arms streaked with blood.

Deepa ran to her side. "What happened, Aunty? Are you hurt? Where's my father?"

A man wearing a topi kneeled before Zaibab, lifted her head, brought water to her lips. She coughed a few times, sipped.

"Aunty, can you hear me?" Deepa took hold of her hand. "Where's Papa-ji? Did he make it out?"

Zaibab swallowed. Her gaze found Deepa. "Your parents," she moaned. "They may still be inside!"

Deepa dropped to her knees. "Papa-ji's still inside? He didn't get out?"

"A rock smashed through the window, hit your Papa-ji in the head. Others followed. Then there was fire. Your mother helped me outside first and went back in for your father. I'm so sorry, Deepa. I tried to help them!"

Deepa dropped her hand. *No. No. Mummy-ji was safe at home. Papa-ji must have made it out. Zainab Aunty must be mistaken.*

A group of men whizzed by with jugs of water. Deepa rose, bolted to the front of the crowd.

"Help me," Deepa screamed. "Somebody help me! Please! My father may be inside!" She tried to drag a few people toward the clinic. Flames shot within inches of her face, seared her skin. "Please," she begged. "Please, help my Papa-ji!"

"Deepa," a man yelled. Anil rushed toward her. Blood trailed from a cut on his forehead. "Thank God!" he said. "Where were you? Your mother and I were looking for you!"

"What? I don't understand? Where's Mummy-ji now? Where's Papa-ji?"

"I drove your mother here. She was trying to find you. I

was waiting by the car for her, just down the road, when I heard the explosion. I tried to get to them but I couldn't."

The ground quaked beneath them. Glass shattered. The clinic's roof caved in. The fire, finally freed, roared toward the sky. The crowd dropped back, set down their buckets. Their arms fell to their sides.

Deepa clutched his face. "Did she come back out? Did she or Papa-ji come out?"

His eyes widened. "I don't know, Deepa."

The police arrived, cordoned off the crowd. She abandoned Anil, rushed toward them. "My Mummy-ji and Papa-ji! Please, help them. They may be inside!" One of the officers gripped her shoulders. "Nothing we can do now, beta. Hopefully they made it out. Tell me their names and we'll look for them."

"But they're trapped!"

For she knew it now. Amid the black smoke and the stench of charred wood, the nightmarish narrative had taken shape. Mummy-ji would have searched for Deepa in the house, in the garden. She would have realized Deepa had gone to the clinic to convince her father not to send her away. She would have slipped on her shoes, run behind the house to Anil, sleeping in his car. She would have woken him, instructed him to drive her to the clinic straight away. They would have beaten her to the clinic.

They would have arrived a good ten minutes before Deepa.

"Please," Deepa cried. "You have to go get Mummy-ji and Papa-ji!" She knocked the officer's hands off her shoulders, dashed to the side of the clinic, searched for some opening she could force her way through. Blazes erupted out of every orifice. Shards, splinters, floated through the air.

Another explosion knocked her backward, to the earth. The last thing she saw were streaks in the sky lighting up like fireworks.

CHAPTER FIVE
June 30, 1947

Fingertips brushed Deepa's face, trailed warmth from her forehead to her ear. She inhaled the scent of cumin. A weight depressed the side of her bed. She rolled away from it, pulled the sheet up to her chin.

"Deepa, please. You must eat and drink. I've prepared chai and paratha," Bala coaxed. "Just a little bit, beta."

Sunlight colored the insides of her eyelids a golden pink. Deepa squeezed her eyes tight to keep out the light, to sleep for the next twenty years. Longer, if she could manage it, to terminate consciousness, to somehow pack it in the folds of her brain's cortex until her own death.

A thumb massaged her clavicle, kneaded her shoulder. A cool, soft cloth draped across her forehead. She shook it off.

Bala had hardly left Deepa's side over the past three days. She had entertained, on her own, the carousel of neighbors and patients who wailed and beat their chests and tried to outdo each other in grief. Deepa hid in her room, muted the hysteria with her palms flattened against her ears.

In the weeks leading up to Independence, fireworks exploded in the sky to celebrate the birth of the nation of India. Last night was no different. She huddled in the corner of her room, quaked in Bala's arms. Bala rocked her, thumped her back with a slightly cupped hand just as she once did to soothe a colicky infant Deepa.

"Deepa," Bala said more firmly. "I received a telegram from Dr. Davies."

Her eyelids, tempted, fluttered. She smeared her face in her pillow. Her cheeks were sticky with honey. It removed the sting of burns but failed to diminish the stench of charred wood and flesh from that night. Those odors had lodged themselves in her nostrils. Blisters covered her palms, her forearms. They bubbled up like suds.

"He and Nora will be in Delhi by tomorrow night," Bala continued. "They're going to stay with you here, in the house... until things are settled."

Until things are settled. Things would never be settled. John and Nora would stay with Deepa until they could figure out what to do with their best friends' orphan, who had no place else to go, no one else to care for her.

Two days earlier, Dev, Papa-ji's only sibling, had arrived just in time to light the funeral pyre. His thin skin hung loose from his bones, his back curved into a stoop. He was only eight years Papa-ji's senior but looked like a grandfather.

She'd never met him, had no idea how he even found out her parents had died. Probably Bala sent word. She still kept their estranged family's information in her address book. "I'm sorry, Deepa," he said from the doorway of the flat, on his way to catch his train back to Bombay. "But I'm not in good health and Aunty and I have four daughters to marry off. We can't afford another." Before stepping out into the night air, he looked at Deepa once more, wrinkling his nose. "Perhaps if your father had sent us money over the years, we could have taken you."

Bala quickly shut the door behind him. "How dare he? I *knew* your Papa-ji didn't like him for a reason. Terrible, *terrible* man!"

Deepa asked Bala why she couldn't live with her here, in the house.

"Oh, beta," Bala said, clutching her tighter. "I'm going back to my village. It's only a two-day journey by foot. I can't bear living here in Delhi anymore. This rotten, evil place."

Deepa inched further into the corner of the room, curled her body into a ball, willed herself to shrink, to filter between the cracks into the damp, crumbling stucco, the darkness.

"I'll put your meal on the floor by your bed," Bala said. "I have to go purchase more vegetables. There may be a few more guests coming this afternoon and evening to pay their respects. I need to go now, while I can." She paused. "Deepa? Can you go next door to Nina Aunty's house and wait for my return?"

Deepa shook her head. She'd never leave this bed again, hadn't even bathed since the priest performed the poojas for her parents.

"Shall I let you stay here then?" Bala said. She touched Deepa's cheek. "Beta? What do you think?"

"Go," Deepa mumbled. She rolled onto her stomach. Her braid flopped over her face. What could possibly occur in Bala's absence? The worst thing she could imagine, her parents' deaths, had already happened.

"Or you could come with me," Bala said, brightening. She smoothed Deepa's hair behind her ear. "Fresh air might do you good."

"No," Deepa said. "I just want to stay here. Please go."

"I'll be back shortly." Bala tucked Deepa back under the sheet. "Promise to take a bite of food while I'm gone."

She padded down the hallway. A few moments later, the front door opened and shut.

Deepa tossed from side to side, crossed her knees. She couldn't fall back asleep now. She needed to use the toilet. She pushed up to sitting. Gray matter and white streaks flecked her vision. Silhouettes appeared before her. Her parents, huddled together in a burning building, eyes locked on her. Gradually, they faded away.

She wobbled to her desk, braced herself. Blisters pinched her heels, the skin between her toes. Her kneecaps stung with scrapes that hadn't quite healed. Her head felt like lead.

In the bathroom, she squatted over the toilet, released a flood of urine. She pulled up her salwar, tied the cord. Over a ceramic bowl, she splashed water on her face, soaked her cheeks, her neck, drenched the front of her kameez, scrubbed her armpits with a washcloth. Water dribbled between her breasts, ran down in a stream to her navel. She cupped more water, tossed it back in her mouth, swished, spit. She popped open a tin, tapped baking soda onto her index finger, ran it over her teeth. Rinsed. Spit. Her face felt raw, tight. Burns and three days of tears had peeled off the outer layer of skin.

She unwound her knotted hair, raked her fingers through it, rebraided it.

The door to her parents' bedroom was closed. No one had opened it since that night. She tiptoed toward it, as if they might be sleeping, leaned the side of her head against the door. The gold hoop in her earlobe scraped against its surface. She held her breath, strained to detect even the slightest evidence of life—proof that the past few days had all been a nightmare from which, any minute now, they would all wake.

A sharp knock startled her. Seconds later, another knock on the front door.

"I'm coming," she called, her voice still hoarse and broken.

She rushed down the hallway and spotted a few coins on the kitchen table. Bala must have forgotten the money. She always forgot the money.

Deepa unlatched the door, pulled it open. "Bala, it's—"

Amir leaned against the doorframe, panting.

"I saw Bala leave," he said. "May I come in?" He didn't wait for her answer. He took hold of her face, brought his close.

She flinched. His touch felt like a slap.

"Oh, Deepa, I'm so sorry." He touched the scars on her cheeks, examined her fingers. "God, you poor thing. How horrible!"

Her shoulders tightened. She clenched her jaw. When she inhaled, the rage that had been building inside her for the last three days erupted like a volcano. "You *knew*!" she shouted. She pounded her fist into his chest. "You *knew* what was going to happen to them!"

"Deepa, no!" He grabbed hold of her fists, kicked the door closed. "I promise, Deepa, I didn't know anything more than what I told you. I wish I had done something more … to help you convince your parents to leave. But you have to believe me. I didn't know there would be an attack on the clinic!"

She broke free, collapsed to the floor. "I want to die. I want to die!" She clutched her stomach. "This hurts so badly, Amir. Oh, God, it hurts. I can't live without them! I don't want to live!"

She brought her forehead to the floor. Every cell in her body ached. Every breath felt as if it was ripping through her lungs. Every muscle and ligament knotted in a rope.

She knew how to end this kind of agony. A neighbor, four houses away, whose only daughter had run away and married a Christian, drank a whole bottle of bleach. A servant found her body the next morning. Deepa could do this tonight, while Bala slept. She could make this day her last on earth.

"Deepa, please, you mustn't say such things," he said.

"Why not?" she asked. "You're going to Pakistan. You're going away forever. I will be here, alone, in this godforsaken country. I will have no one."

"That's not true." He brought his hand to her chin. "I promise you will never be alone." He leaned over, touched his lips to her forehead. "Promise me, you won't hurt yourself. Please. I couldn't bear it."

He kissed her cheek. His lips were warm.

He was the only person left who cared about her.

She took his hand. "Don't go to Lahore, Amir. I won't survive if you leave me too."

"I have no choice, Deepa. I need to make sure my family has reached my aunt's house safely." He paused, glanced toward the garden where the plants, without her care and attention, withered in the heat.

He turned back to her.

His eyes lit up. An idea had taken hold of him. He leaned close, as if to confess his secret. His words enveloped her face like a gentle breeze.

"After I take my family to Pakistan, I can return here for you. We could be together. We could…if you want…we could get married."

For a brief moment, joy washed through her. *She could be with him. He would be her family.* But it would not be fair. He had not thought it through. He couldn't leave Laila, his sick father. He couldn't abandon his mother. It would break her heart. "Amir," she said. "We can't—"

He silenced her with a kiss, wrapped his arms around her waist.

She melted into him, ran her fingers along his collarbone, his jaw, his expanding and contracting ribs. The more she breathed him in, the less she hurt. He immersed her in a dream from which she did not want to wake up.

He broke away. "Marry me, Deepa," he said, more urgently now. His kiss ran down the side of her neck, back up to her earlobe. He traced her lips with his thumb, as if to pry the answer from her. "From the moment I saw you at the Taj Mahal, I knew we would marry."

She had known something then too. There had been something about him, how he stood in the twilight, smiled at his little sister, how his dimples folded into his cheeks. She hadn't known exactly *what*. Only that being with him made her feel more real, less like an actor in a film. She laid her hand on his heart, felt the force of its beat travel through her palm, up the veins of her arm. He would be her new family, her new home. "I knew it too," she said. "Yes, I will marry you."

"I will never be able to bring back your parents," he said. "But I promise I will always take care of you. I will make you happy again."

A dog barked in the distance. "I should go," he said. "Before Bala returns."

She grasped his shirt, pulled him closer. He could not leave her now. Not in this moment, when he'd just offered her a light, a reason to live beyond the next grueling second. With him near, she could replenish her lungs with oxygen, force out the smoke that continued to singe her airways. Besides, Bala would take a while. She was slow, picky. One hour at the market very easily turned into three.

"Amir, my husband. Don't go. Please stay," she whispered in his ear.

Her friend Kamila had told her what happened on the night the bride and groom married. Deepa hoped at least one part of her friend's revelation was true—that a physical act sealed a couple together, for all eternity, made them a family forever in the eyes of God. She inhaled deeply, took his hand. She led him to the sofa, placed his hand on her breast.

"Deepa, no."

She shut her eyes. How could she make him understand? How could she make him know that her life could only begin again with him, that he was the only person who could lure her away from her own death?

"Our souls are already married," she said. She opened her eyes. "That is all that matters. That we are husband and wife before God."

He touched her cheek, brought his mouth to hers. Lips, teeth, tongues connected. He lowered her to the sofa.

She slid her kameez over her head. His gaze took her in. She did not feel shy or embarrassed, like she thought she would. She only felt closeness with him.

He kissed her breasts softly, rose to kneeling, peeled off his shirt. When he lay back over her, the heat from his skin radiated through her body. She ran her hands along his shoulders, his arms. For three days, grief had suffocated her. She thought she would never feel alive again. But this, this she could feel. This felt real.

His kisses ran over her chest again. His fingers found her waistband, slid inside, probed between her legs.

"Deepa, is this...is this really what you want? Shall I keep going?"

She arched her back, tried to speak. The sensation robbed her of her voice. It traveled down her legs, to the soles of her feet, up through her spine, to her scalp. Her head dropped back. Her muscles clenched. Her clothes became damp.

"Amir," she gasped.

He removed his hand, pulled down her pants. His mouth found her waist, her hips. He slid out of his own clothes, pressed the length of his body against hers, laid himself between her.

It hurt the first time. That's what Kamila said. The husband would feel pleasure but the wife would feel pain, would bleed. Deepa had already experienced so much pain. She could not hurt any more than she already did.

He propped his hands on either side of her, rubbed against her. "I can stop," he said. "We don't need to do this. We will be married no matter what."

She shook her head. "Please," she said. She pressed her hands into his back. This would seal them forever. This would help her forget that night, the fire, the screams. It would help her forget, at least for a moment, that she had not been a good daughter.

When he pushed against her, she exhaled hard, rose to her elbows. A deep pressure, again. She bit her lower lip. The pressure became pain. She sucked in her breath. What once felt like a tiny crevice, opened.

"Amir," she whispered.

His breaths grew ragged, uneven. He said her name. He moved inside her until he shuddered, dropped from his hands to his elbows, laid his head on her chest. She could barely remember the first sixteen years of her life on this earth before him. She wanted to freeze this moment in time forever.

He ran his fingers through her hair. "How badly did it hurt, my wife?" he said.

She smiled. "I'm fine, my husband."

He kissed her forehead, moved off her, collected his clothes. "When I come back for you, we'll find a town that will accept our marriage, where people won't care I'm Muslim and you're Hindu. Not all of India is like this—this utter chaos. There are places that will accept us. I know it." He took her hand, kissed it. "My parents will forgive us. They must. I'll get a job and send them money. And maybe Laila can come live with us too." He lifted her chin, looked deeply into her eyes. "We will be together, soon, my wife."

She nodded. She knew it to be true. Knew it more than she'd known anything in her life. She picked up her kameez. "Bala will be home soon, Amir," she said. "You have to leave now."

He threaded her arms through the sleeves, pulled it down over her head. He kissed her again on the forehead. Let his lips linger a moment more. He stood, walked to the door.

"Wait," she said. She ran to the patio, threw open the door.

The light outside was harsh. She blinked to adjust her vision. She'd almost forgotten what daylight looked like after three days of darkness. She squatted next to the money plant pot, plunged her hands into it, where three days earlier, she'd hidden the poem and Madam Grover's money. She wiped off the excess soil, rushed back inside.

"This is from Madam Grover," she said, handing it to him. "When she found out you were leaving, she wanted me to give it to you. It'll help your family. Please take it."

He peered inside. "I can't accept this," he said. "It's too much."

"Don't be proud, Amir," she said, with the authority of a wife. "You can use this to purchase your ticket back to Delhi, back to me."

He slid it in his pocket. "That's very kind of her. Please tell her I said thank you."

"You can tell her yourself, when you return to Delhi."

He took her face in his hands, kissed her. "I will, my sweet. I will tell her myself, after I come back for you." He brought her to his chest. "Stay safe until I return."

"I will," she said.

He slipped on his shoes, brought his hand to the doorknob, looked back at her.

She tried to absorb every detail of him, to preserve his image in her mind, his soft eyes, the birthmark on the side of his face, his lips made redder from pressing against hers, the slight chip on his front tooth. It was if she was seeing him for the very first time.

He opened the door, hesitated, as if taking the first step out in the street would break the spell of them, of their union, would usher, too abruptly, the present to the past, begin, too quickly, the tenure of their separation. She knew he was thinking these things. She knew him as only a wife could.

He moved away from her, into another, more cruel world, and like the blinding flash of a camera, disappeared.

CHAPTER SIX

Deepa propped herself against the wall, knees bent, arms folded. Her chin rested in the crook of her elbow. A black ant near her feet stumbled along the living room floor, mounted the lip of a small rug, circumvented a folded newspaper. She gripped the newspaper between her toes, slid it over the ant, squashed it with her heel.

Nora stood above her, jaw clenched. She wore an ivory blouse with a stiff collar, a gray skirt that ended mid-calf. The narrow circumference of her skirt limited the length of her gait. She shuffled in short, awkward steps, like a baby learning how to walk for the first time, not the easy, languid pace that her usual salwar pants allowed.

She lowered herself to the ground, brought a cup of chai to Deepa's mouth. "Sip, beta," Nora said. "Just drink a little something."

Everyone wanted Deepa to drink something, as if a side effect of grief was dehydration. Their neighbors had practically pried Deepa's mouth open to feed her.

Deepa was too tired to explain to Nora she wasn't thirsty, that she'd gulped down four cups of tea already that day. Nothing anyone offered could make her feel better. It made *them* feel better. Deepa simply endured it.

She took a few sips, pushed the cup away. Satisfied, Nora dabbed Deepa's chin with a handkerchief, rose, set the cup and dish on the table.

The soles of John's shoes smacked along the floor, their laces dragged behind like wilted flowers. He traced a path from the patio door, through the living room, to the edge of the kitchen and back. His red-veined eyes darted around the room, as if he was looking for something he lost. Sweat plastered his hair to his scalp.

The ticking of the clock pounded through the room. When it struck four, brassy chimes echoed throughout the flat. Her parents had been dead and gone for five days. Deepa had somehow existed in their absence in tortured increments, breathing only when the pressure building under her ribs forced her to take in air. She'd lived what seemed like a lifetime without them. The night of their deaths played on an endless loop like a film. She rewound and replayed it, made mental notes of her culpability at crucial junctures. She altered the ending. A heroic rescue. She pulls them out of the burning building, mends their burns, feeds them spoonfuls of sambar while they rest in bed.

Further back in time. The three of them catch the train to Bangalore with John and Nora, far away from the new border. Papa-ji lifts their suitcases onto the train. Mummy-ji holds the tickets in her hands. As they board, the train whistles.

Deepa still felt their presence in their home. In the soft, rippling wind chimes, her mother hummed the melody to a Lata Mangeshkar song. Oil popping in a pan was Papa-ji cracking his knuckles. Images endlessly flashed through her mind: Mummy-ji raising her left eyebrow after catching a very young Deepa doing something naughty; Papa-ji ruffling his moustache while considering a troubling issue.

Deepa shifted her weight, slid her heels along the floor to ease the soreness in her seat. She refolded her legs, welcomed back the ache. She feared losing it, no longer knowing it, no longer having something of Amir. The bloodstained underwear from that night, the burning when she relieved herself in the toilet, reassured her, somehow, of his eventual return. At school, Deepa had learned about purgatory, the limbo after death, before redemption and renewal, the last stop on the journey toward heaven. Even though she believed, at least somewhat, in reincarnation, there was something about the idea of purgatory that appealed to her. These tortuous days between her parents' deaths and Amir's return were her purgatory. This is how she would survive her separation from him. Each minute that passed was one less minute she had to endure alone.

She crawled to the couch, curled up on her side, where he had laid her down, peeled off her clothes, touched her until she felt she no longer knew who she was, where she was, whether the life she was living was real or imagined, whether her parents were dead or alive. That was the best part, the part when her mind transported itself elsewhere, so that she was no longer an orphan, no longer alone. She belonged again, in those few minutes, to someone and something.

In the two days he'd been gone, she brought the feeling back. When she thought she might die in his absence, she slid her desk chair against the door of her bedroom, untied her salwar, let it drop to her ankles, and stood, one hand on her desk, the other between her legs, brushing lightly back and forth, waiting, as the folds of her skin grew wet, swelled, as her breath turned to a light pant, as her knees buckled, as her body, for a few, blissful seconds, released a tiny bit of its anguish into the hot, humid Delhi air.

"Deepa," Nora said. Her voice was raspy and thin. She approached the sofa, perched on its edge, gripped it so tightly it drained her fingers of color. She had spent all day yesterday, all evening, all night, shushing John as he sobbed in the living room. "Why? Why did this happen?" he had cried. "Why not me?"

"Deepa, John and I need to talk to you about something." She clasped her hands over her knees, released them, fiddled with the cuffs on her blouse, smoothed out her starched skirt. "As soon as we heard what happened, John and I made a plan." She looked at John, tapped her foot, waited for him to finish her train of thought, to join in the discussion.

John sensed his wife's watchful eye, paused. He raked his unclipped nails through his beard stubble. His hand wandered to his shirt pocket, patted something that wasn't there. His squint produced deep crevices in his face.

Deepa turned away, could hardly look at this disheveled version of a man she loved like a father. He moved about as if stumbling through a fog, responded in clipped, unfinished sentences, if at all. He was no longer the doctor who mended, who healed, who reassured. He, who had once talked so bravely, so confidently about Independence, had left her parents behind to their violent fates.

"We spoke with a lawyer," Nora continued. "About what happened to your parents."

Deepa cocooned herself tighter in the crook of the sofa. Despite the heat, she chilled. Her hands and feet were frozen like blocks of ice. She massaged the ball of her foot.

"John and I have decided to move to London permanently." She leaned toward Deepa, laid her hand on her back. "We want you to come live with us."

Deepa turned sharply. "What?"

Nora took hold of her hand, squeezed. "We'd like you to move to London with us. We're your legal guardians and we'd like to care for you there."

Deepa pulled away. She had a husband. She had to wait for Amir, to be here for his return. She didn't have his new address in Lahore. She had no way of communicating with him. If she didn't stay, he would never find her. "I live here," she finally said. "*This* is my home. India is *our* home. I can't go to London."

"Deepa, darling," Nora said. "You can't stay here alone."

John blinked, as if he'd just noticed there were other people in the room. He pulled out a chair, sat down at the table. He eyed the steel pitcher, dragged it toward him. Water sloshed over its sides. He poured some into a cup. His gulps resounded in the room. "She's right," he muttered.

Deepa uncurled her limbs, scooted off the sofa. Surely a man born and raised in India would never leave the only country he knew and loved. Surely he meant *Deepa* was right, not Nora.

"Uncle," she said. "You understand why I can't go to London, don't you?"

He grunted, gazed over at a family photo hanging on the wall, one of Deepa's favorites. Her parents sat in high-back chairs with wide arms like thrones. Two-year-old Deepa was propped on her Papa-ji's lap. Her hands were mid-clap, her smile wide. Mummy-ji and Papa-ji's mouths were tight lines, their backs stiff straight. Deepa used to tease them about the photo, about their serious faces. "You can't smile in photographs, beta," Mummy-ji said. "You'll attract the evil eye."

Her mother had believed in such things, that one could take certain actions to protect oneself from outside forces. In this, her mother had been foolish.

John picked at the skin on his lower lip. "You can't stay here, Deepa," he finally said. When he poured another cup, water spilled over the edge, pooled onto the table. He filled the cup to the brim again, guzzled, as if trying to drown himself. "None of us can."

She wrapped her arms around his legs, laid her head in his lap, just as she used to when she was a young child, begging him for more candy. If John and Nora had loved her as they claimed, if they wanted her to be a part of their family, they would not drag her away from her home. This was the only place she knew her parents, the place that rooted her to this life. "We *have* to live here. Please, we can't leave Delhi, Uncle," she sobbed.

Earlier that morning, she had crawled into Mummy-ji and Papa-ji's bed. It was the first time she had entered their bedroom since their deaths. Her mother's rosewater perfume and her father's musky aftershave lingered on the sheets. Strands of Mummy-ji's hair wove through the teeth of her comb. Deepa lay in the dip where the mattress had molded to their conjoined weight.

This house was all that was left of them, the couch where her father perused medical books, the kit that held Mummy-ji's needles and thread, the mirror where she had applied her kohl, the plants Deepa cared for. None of the items had monetary value, but their emotional value to her was incalculable. They told the story of her family, bonded to her memories like glue. If the items were packed away or sold, her memoires would dislodge, float away, like her parents' ashes in the Ganges River.

Nora tugged gently at her elbow. "Deepa," she said. "Please hear us out."

She shook her head. "No. I can't leave. I'm staying here."

"I'm so sorry," John said. His face contorted, as if he knew his apology made no sense, was uttered at the wrong time during the course of the conversation. "We should have brought all of you to Bangalore with us. It's our fault we didn't."

They were all to blame. If she had taken Amir's warning at the market more seriously, if India had stayed unified, if, if, a million and one ifs. Perhaps if Deepa could relieve John of the whole burden of their deaths, he'd let her stay.

"Uncle," Deepa said. "Mummy-ji and Papa-ji could have left with you. They chose not to."

"It's too dangerous for you to stay now," he said, with more conviction. "We have to take you away as soon as possible. The police don't even know who did it. What if it was Hari and his gundas? They know where you live, Deepa." His arm flinched, knocked over the cup. Water cascaded over the table. He ignored it, refused to right the cup. "I'm sorry, Deepa. Your father was my brother. India was my home too."

It was the most he'd said since his arrival.

He collapsed over the table, braced his head in his hands. The spill soaked the sleeves of his pale blue shirt, spread like a dark stain. Nora grabbed a towel, cleaned what she could. He refused to move. She could only work around him.

He began crying again. It vibrated through his body.

Nora laid her hand on her husband's head, stroked his hair, hushed him. All she could do was hush.

Later in the garden, Deepa faced a row of plants succumbing to neglect. The soil was dried and cracked, like faults in the earth. Her father had entrusted her to the care and maintenance of his plants. She had failed him. She squatted, pressed her fingers in the dirt of one pot, just in case it could be salvaged. It had hardened like clay.

Mumbled voices came from inside the flat. When the door swung open, Madam Grover greeted her with a hearty hug. "Oh, Deepa. Sweet Deepa."

She threw her arms around her teacher. "I received your lovely note, Madam Grover. Thank you for sending it. And

I'm sorry I turned you away the other day. I just...I wasn't ready to see anyone yet. I wanted to be alone."

"My heart breaks for you," Madam Grover said. Her eyes were swollen and red, as if they'd already dispensed of every last tear. "Bala told me you needed to see me. I got away as soon as I could."

Deepa peeked into the living room. Poonam scrubbed the floor while Bala stood over her, recounting the gossip from the last few days. Deepa was thankful Poonam had shown up at all. She had not wanted to clean and pack for a family with such bad luck, but Deepa had promised Poonam most of their furniture in exchange for her help.

Deepa shut the door, led her teacher to two wooden stools on the patio. The street was crowded with masses of people walking, sitting, standing. Autos and bike rickshaws attempted to maneuver between them. Their honks and bells would help to mask Deepa's voice. She slid her hand into her pocket, pulled out a piece of paper.

It was a huge risk, sharing her secret. But she had no choice. She needed a conduit. So many of her friends' parents wouldn't even let their daughters visit Deepa. They worried the attack on the clinic was proof that Deepa, too, had been a target, that being with her was too dangerous. Patri had written as much in a note that her family's driver had left at Deepa's front door.

"Madam Grover, I need to tell you something," Deepa said. "I hope I can trust you."

Her teacher glanced at the paper in Deepa's hands. "Of course you can. Always."

Deepa cleared her throat. "Amir and Laila have left for Lahore, but Amir is returning in a few weeks." She picked off flakes of skin that had started peeling from one of her blisters on her wrists, took a deep breath. Her teacher cared about

Amir and Laila, had given them money. Deepa hoped she would continue to help him, to help *her*. "Amir is coming back for me. We're going to get married."

Madam Grover's eyes widened. "Oh."

"I have to move to London with my Aunty and Uncle. There is no one here for me now. Even Bala, our cook, is returning to her village. But I hope...I hope that once Amir sees I'm no longer living here, he'll look for me at school. He'll ask around about me."

Deepa handed her teacher the paper. "This is my address in London. Please, give it out to the class. Tell everyone where I've moved. Ask them to write. When Amir looks for me, hopefully they'll tell him where I've moved, give him the address. Or if you see him, I hope *you* will. Once he writes to me in London, he and I can make a plan."

Madam Grover took the paper. Her eyes scanned the address. She folded it. "You two are so young, Deepa. How will you survive? How will you support yourselves?"

She had not yet figured out the details. But Deepa would find some kind of job in London to earn money, even if it meant delaying her return to school. She would use the money to purchase Amir a ticket to London. They would have a better life abroad than in India, even if they had to end their education to do so.

There would be danger, though, in Amir living in Delhi until she could send for him. She desperately hoped his friends would take him in, that they would help keep him safe until he left for England. She did not want to share these fears with her teacher. She worried Madam Grover wouldn't have confidence in her plan. Deepa had to believe it would work. "We'll find a way, Madam Grover."

Her teacher took her hand. "You should know, Deepa, that hundreds of thousands of refugees are stranded. Some are starving and becoming very sick. Typhoid fever is tearing through the camps. It might be too risky for Amir to return to Delhi. It might take him much longer to reach here than you think."

She had considered this. But Amir was strong, healthy. From what Deepa had read, it was families with young children and the elderly that were having the most difficulty making the journey. "Amir's just one person," she said. "He'll be able to take care of himself."

Madam Grover nodded, slipped the note into her pocketbook. "I'll give everyone your address, Deepa. And if I see Amir, I'll give it to him too."

"Thank you," Deepa said. Hot tears sprung from the corners of her eyes. "He's all I have left. I need to be with him. I need him to find me."

"He will." She took Deepa's face in her hands. "You've been through so much. You'll get through this too." She removed a paper from her purse, wrote something down, handed it to Deepa. "Here's my home address. Please write to me, Deepa. Let me know how you're doing. And keep up with your beautiful writing. It will keep your parents alive in your memory, preserve who they were, what they meant to you. In time, the writing will bring you some semblance of peace."

Deepa shifted in her seat. "I don't write," she said. "I just wrote that one poem for Amir."

"You wrote that poem *about* Amir. You wrote it *for* yourself, to process how you were feeling." Madam Grover rose, adjusted her dupatta.

"Madam Grover," Deepa said. "One more thing. Did you ever hear from your cousin? Or her family?"

Her teacher smiled, touched Deepa's cheek. "How thoughtful of you to ask," she said. "I received a letter just yesterday. She is safe. She and her family made it to Ahmadabad. I'm going to visit them over the next school break."

"That's wonderful," Deepa said. If Madam Grover's cousin had made it safely over the border, Amir could too. Such news gave her hope.

"It's a lovely city, Ahmadabad," Madam Grover added. "From what I've heard, Hindus and Muslims live in relative harmony there. If you and Amir choose to return to India, it might make a nice city for you both."

Deepa smiled. She did not know whether this was actually true, whether there really was a place in India where they could be safe as a married couple or raise a family some day. But she appreciated the sentiment. "Thank you, Madam Grover. Thank you for saying that."

Her teacher hugged her tightly. "I may no longer be your teacher, Deepa, but I will always be your friend." She kissed each of Deepa's cheeks, opened the door. When she looked back, tears filled her eyes. "Godspeed, Deepa," she said. She stepped back inside the flat.

Deepa picked up the watering can, tilted it. A stream of water trickled out of its spout, dampened leaves long past salvation. When she set it down, two small dark dots on the concrete, like teardrops, caught her eye. Old drops of Amir's blood from the night he first visited her. She brushed her fingertips over them, touched her lips.

"Godspeed," she whispered. "Godspeed, my husband."

Part
Two

CHAPTER SEVEN
Agra
August 10, 1985

S han maneuvered between elbows and knees, draw-
strings cinching loose cotton pants, khakis with wide
black belts. Purse straps, backpacks, fanny packs.
Bronze and silver zippers. Sweaty patches of armpits. Zoom
lenses, video cameras, sunglasses.

The tail of a sari swatted her face, grazed her parted lips.
Her tongue pushed away the gauzy cloth. It tasted like the sea.

"You okay?" her father asked. He'd been studying a map
of Uttar Pradesh, running his finger along its white weblike
creases, scribbling notations in the margins.

"Yeah," she huffed, though she wasn't. She was too hot, too
tired. She imagined collapsing into bed at the hotel, the street
noise outside lulling her to sleep, the fan overhead laboring
through stagnant air, the graciousness of it waging a war, for
her sake, against such an oppressive heat.

She wanted to act like the petulant child she knew she
could easily conjure, but resisted. In Seattle, she'd promised

her mother she'd be patient and well-behaved for her father. This wasn't the main reason she held her tongue. A small part of her wanted to deprive him of the means to comfort her, of the intimacy most fathers had with their daughters, daughters they hadn't chosen to abandon, like hers had.

A sense of urgency filled her, the need to know their destination, the need to get there, to rush toward something, to escape the awkward silences between them and the pauses that held the weight of everything.

She pushed forward.

He followed a half step behind, his hand on her shoulder steering her like a boat's tiller. The crowd moved in a wave, swelled and surged and retreated, funneled through the opening of a large stone wall.

On the other side, an open courtyard bestowed freedom. Rows of bushes were trimmed with the precision of cut-out paper dolls. Pink, white, and yellow flower petals whipped around in the breeze. She wandered off the walkway, plunged her feet into the manicured lawn. Her toes disappeared between thick blades of grass.

"We're finally here," he said.

He'd kept this trip a secret. Late last night, they climbed into the back of an Ambassador, bumped along a dirt road for six hours. She woke at dawn with an imprint of the leather seat on her cheek. She'd been enjoying Delhi, begrudged their short stay, her father's relentless itinerary.

He offered his hand, a hand that suddenly seemed small to her, as if in the year since their last reunion, it had shrunk. She let it hang in the air for a moment, to see if he might catch on, if he might realize she was too old to hold hands, that if she could walk five blocks to her elementary school all by herself, she could navigate herself here too. He probably didn't know any better. What he'd known of her childhood derived from static-filled phone calls, postcard summaries of her grades, Polaroids of her at bat at softball games. He still saw her as the chubby five-year-old who sucked her thumb, peed her pants when she got scared.

The same age as when he left her.

His smile was a dip that was wide and bright, gap-toothed, with eggplant purple gums. A silver filling peeked out of one side. The glint jarred something loose in her, the memory of his leaning over her bed, kissing her forehead, tucking the comforter tightly under her armpits, the click as he flicked off her unicorn lamp, the glow of the television screen lighting up his face. The memory quelled her quiet rage over the injustice of being dragged halfway around the world just to spend time with him.

His hand continued to linger midair, biding its time, begging for a reunion with hers. She let it be for another moment, long enough for him to understand her delay was a negotiation, that it had meaning, that he would have to earn her trust again.

Finally, she clasped it.

They followed streams of tourists down the walkway. Their shadows elongated, conjoined. When he squeezed her hand, she felt a tremble in his fingers. "I've really missed you, *Shanti*," he said.

She hadn't heard her birth name in a long time. Even on the plane ride over, during their one-night stopover in London, their connection to Delhi, he'd addressed her by her nickname, Shan. She'd adopted it at the beginning of the first grade, not long after he left them. She wanted something easier to pronounce, something that other kids wouldn't make fun of that sounded more in tune with her last name, her mother's name, Johnson. Shan could be short for Shauna. No one needed to know the truth. But she liked how he said Shanti right now, how it rolled off his tongue. How the *th* sound became something harder, sharper, something so different from the way her mother used to say it.

"I missed you too, Daddy." It slipped out by accident, *Daddy*. She couldn't remember ever calling him that, not even when she was little. He'd always been "Dad." Besides, she was almost eleven now, way too old for "Daddy."

His attention was elsewhere. "Take a look," he said.

A tall, red building the color of clay stood before them. Vines of white flowers twisted like serpents. It was nice, though nothing so impressive to cut their time in Delhi short.

He touched her chin. "Not this, here. See *that*? Through there?" He squatted, slid her on his knee. His arm extended in a straight line, like the needle of a compass, guiding her sight through the building's opening.

A castle the color of a cloud shone brightly in the distance. A king's rounded crown sat on top. Mama had taken her to Disneyland last year. They had seen Cinderella's castle, the turrets, the blue trim, the gold. This was different. Better, even.

"What is it?" Shan asked.

"The Taj Mahal. The Emperor Shah Jahan built it for his wife, Queen Mumtaz, after she died," he said. "It's been here for four hundred years. Can you imagine?"

He helped her back to her feet. "We have to leave our shoes here," he said. "They aren't allowed on the grounds."

"We're going *there*? To the castle?"

"To the Taj Mahal." He slipped off her flip-flops, spit on his hand, rubbed the dirt off the side of one of her feet. His thumb paused at a faint line. "I remember when you got this scar," he said. "It was just after your third birthday. You were wearing your green overalls. Your tricycle capsized on the uneven sidewalk in front of our apartment."

Her tricycle had a red, shiny frame, a bell strapped to the left handlebar. Or maybe it was the right. Silver streamers swooshed in the breeze, caught the sunlight. She loved that bike. When they moved last year to a new apartment, her mother gave it to a neighbor.

He looked up at her tenderly. A breeze flitted through his hair. A few faint lines kissed the outer corners of his eyes. She hadn't noticed them before.

"I was the one who found you upside down," he continued. "I lifted and carried you inside. You were so brave. You didn't shed a single tear, not even when the doctor stitched you up in the emergency room. Do you remember?"

His dark eyes searched her face for a hint of recognition. She felt sorry for him, clinging to his role in the rescue, the fear she now understood must have seized him. He wasn't seeking confirmation of her memory, but an understanding of how much he loved her. Adults did this sometimes.

She couldn't recall the fall itself, though she remembered the aftermath, lying on the couch watching Bugs Bunny cartoons with a big bandage taped to her foot. "Yes," she said softly. "I do."

He patted her head, kicked off his shoes, shoved them in the cubby. They stepped through the grand entryway.

A lush lawn, the size of several soccer fields. A path made up of different-shaped stones fitting together like a jigsaw puzzle. A pool of water, long, rectangular, shimmering.

Just looking at the water made her feel cooler. "Can we go closer?" she pointed.

"Sure," he said.

She broke free, dashed between tall narrow bushes. Her new gold chains shimmied against her shirt's collar. At the lip of the pool, she knelt on her cotton pants, peered over the water. Strings of algae drifted like the tentacles of jellyfish.

Mosquitoes the size of moths skated along the surface. The reflection of the Taj Mahal—the rounded dome, the four towers—glowed like a full moon in a dark sky. It spread to the edges of the pool. She swirled her finger. The Mahal remained unblemished among the ripples.

She leaned over farther. Her breath quickened. She could lose her balance, tip into the pool, head first. Still, farther. Her forehead erased one of the towers and then eclipsed part of the central arch. She raised her eyebrows, stuck out her tongue.

Her father lowered himself with a grunt. His hand dove beneath the surface, cupped, poured the water over his head. In his reflection, she spotted the matching depression in his chin, the similar squared angle of his jaw, the identical slight, straight nose. She traced the image of his cheek with her thumb. She had not noticed before how much she resembled him. His skin tone, a deep brown, perfectly matched her own.

Her mother's skin was a creamy white, like almost everyone's in Seattle. Shan had to claim or be claimed by her mother to prove their shared genes. Complete strangers would ask Shan, "Oh, are you adopted?" They asked her mother, "Is she your stepdaughter?" Here in India, Shan could see herself in her other parent, could match her skin to the skin of so many others around her. For the first time, she looked like everyone else, even though every Indian seemed to know she was an American.

She removed her hand from the pool, flicked off the beads of water. "Let's go," she said. "I want to see it up close."

They rejoined the crowd and followed along the path. With each step, the dome rose higher into the bright, cloudless sky. Its girth widened. When they finally reached the platform they began a steep ascent.

A chorus of bare feet slapped narrow, marble steps. Women hiked the skirts of their saris. Their bangles clanked along their forearms. Men stooped, clutched their hands behind their backs. Two small boys darted through the maze of bodies in a race to the top.

On the last step, she turned, leaned against the railing, shielded the sun with her hand. The gardens, the reflecting pool, and the entrance hall looked so tiny and ordered they appeared fake, like a landscape of Legos.

Visitors spilled onto the terrace, pointed to the monument, flowed toward the main entrance. She and her father fell in line, inched forward until a surge carried them through a short, narrow doorway of the building. She envisioned rows of armor, shields belonging to knights, scepters made of gold, red, plush carpet, portraits of royalty.

Instead, it was pitch dark. Cool. Shuffling feet echoed around her. She blinked her eyes, found herself in a single room with a vaulted ceiling. At its center, a marble lattice fence enclosed two long, narrow boxes. She wove her fingers through the grid, peered through the spaces.

"Here they are. The Queen Mumtaz and the Shah Jahan," her father whispered.

"What do you mean?"

"They're resting here together," he said, "for all eternity."

"These are coffins?" Her hand dropped. She stepped back. She pressed her face into her father's shirt, tried to shake the images of withering skin and bones from her mind.

"Shanti? Are you okay?" He raised her chin, narrowed his dark eyes. She saw in them the pain of disappointing her again, of falling short as a father.

"Can we please go back outside?" she asked.

He nodded. They worked their way quickly around the perimeter and exited where they entered.

"Let me show you something else," he said. He led her around the corner, pivoted her body, directed her gaze along the banks of a shallow river. "See there? It's called Agra Fort." In the distance, red cylindrical towers kissed low-lying clouds. Walls, like decorative curtains, strung them together.

"That's the palace where Emperor Shah Jahan ruled India," he said. "When Mumtaz died, he built the Taj Mahal here, so he could watch over her from Agra Fort. When *he* died, they entombed him here, with her." He paused. "Isn't that a lovely thought? He never wanted to be apart from his wife."

The truth of his statement stung. The Emperor had never wanted to be away from the Queen, but her own father had gone as far away from her and her mother as he could.

"I never knew my father," he said. His gaze locked on hers. "Did I ever tell you that?"

The words fell out of his mouth, landed with a thud between them. *His* father. *Her* grandfather. She knew this, though how she came to know it escaped her. She always seemed to know about this absence in her father's life, much the same way she always knew of her own father's absence in hers.

"I've no idea what he even looks like," he continued. "I think about him every day, though."

"Why don't you try to find him?" she asked.

"I can't. The only information I have is his name." He leaned over the railing, dropped his head to his chest. "He had a younger sister too. All I know is her name. Your grandmother refuses to tell me more."

Shan had just met her grandmother for the first time on their way to India. They had a twenty-four-hour layover in London and stayed overnight in her drafty apartment a few streets over from Big Ben. She was rail-thin with stark black hair. Her forehead wrinkled like an accordian when she raised her eyebrows. A lit cigarette dangled from her fingers. She held it like some kind of stylish accessory to her outfit.

Her grandmother had hugged Shan awkwardly, as if she hadn't quite known where to place her hands, patted her head a little too firmly. The next day, when she and her father headed out to catch the second leg of their flight to Delhi, their goodbyes had been just as awkward as the greetings. Shan couldn't imagine what it was like for her father to have such a cold mother, to never know his own father.

He had seemed oblivious to the fact that they shared this kind of sadness—of missing fathers. She wanted to shake him in that moment. His decision to move to India without her had been a selfish one. He still did not see it as such, five years into his relocation, was wholly unaware of how his absence continued to hurt her, how it made her feel so lonely. For her eighth birthday, he had mailed her a globe, the earth parted by latitudes and longitudes, oceans and continents. She had measured, with her hands, the distance between Seattle and India. Nine hands. The sun never shone on them at the same time. He had moved so far away from her he might as well have moved to the moon.

When he lifted his face, his gaze traced the horizon, settled back on Agra Fort. "Nothing makes me happier than having you here with me now," he said. "No one has ever meant more to me than you."

She smiled, her first of the day. If these rare moments were all they could ever have together, maybe it would be enough.

At Agra Fort, a flag waved from one of the towers. The Indian flag, she imagined. The flag of her father's new country, the country where he felt he belonged, instead of the one where she, his only child, lived.

She rested her chin on her forearms, squinted her eyes until the color of the Fort blurred into a burnt sienna sunset.

CHAPTER EIGHT
Atlanta
June 8, 2016

The radiology tech leaned closer to the screen. Her mouth contorted. Her lower lip swallowed her chin dimple. It continued its downward curl and suddenly, as if tasting something bitter, twisted to one side. She pushed the probe deeper into Shan's gel-slicked belly.

"I've been doing better lately," Shan said. Her mouth felt dry. She swallowed, cleared her throat. "I'm feeling great, for the most part."

The clock on the wall was the kind she hadn't seen in ages, a full moon, two big arrow-hands, a third hand ticking with each incremental step. She couldn't remember the last time she used anything other than a smart phone to tell time. "I guess that's what happens once you end the first trimester," she added, not knowing why she felt the need to keep talking.

Max laid his hand over hers. "She's even able to eat chocolate again."

"Uh huh," the tech said. Her blue eyes remained fixed on the image. Her black nails tapped a few keys on the keyboard, paused.

Shan flexed and curled her toes, fingered the hemline of her pilled cotton shirt, peered at her glistening belly. The nausea, the burning in her esophagus, the clenching and releasing of her stomach, had lasted the first few weeks. At her law firm, Walker & Associates, she'd tear down the stairwell to the bathroom on the third floor so her colleagues wouldn't hear her hacking into the toilet. She called out sick for a few days here and there (stomach virus, migraine), her excuses running thinner with each passing week. But she wanted to wait to tell her colleagues until her second trimester, once she knew the chance of miscarriage was small, and most importantly, *after* she was offered partnership at her law firm.

Just two weeks earlier, week ten of her pregnancy, on her seventh work anniversary, she patiently awaited the champagne toast offered to all new partners (she would only pretend to take a sip), the round of congratulations, the white, fluffy cake with the custard filling from the corner bakery, Shan's name scrawled across in blue icing script. It never came. Instead, Robert, the managing partner, slipped into her office at the end of the day and told her they couldn't make her a partner. The firm was still recovering from the last economic downturn. She needed to wait another year, possibly two, when the numbers were more in her favor.

That night, she sent Robert her resignation, effective immediately. She asked why they couldn't have warned her months earlier, said that the firm had humiliated her by leading her on for so long. His only response was to apologize, again, for how things turned out. But he didn't fight for her, didn't beg her to reconsider, which hurt almost as much. None of the partners did. Too bad no one at work knew she was pregnant.

If they did, she could have at least slapped the firm with a sex discrimination suit.

She inhaled deeply. Her spine grew longer. The paper covering the exam table crinkled as she released her breath. No matter. Her life had morphed into something else, something infinitely better. With this pregnancy, she felt whole again in a way she hadn't since losing her father, Vijay, three decades earlier, not long after her first and only trip to India with him.

"There!" Shan said, pointing at the screen. "There it is! Look, Max. Look at how much the baby's grown."

One, two, white, translucent threads. *Legs.* Tiny, delicate feet. She imagined them in the palm of her hand, those sweet, velvety soles. Two lithe, elegant arms bent at right angles. The subtle bump of a nose, the most delicate chin, like Max's. A tall forehead. Hers? Lips that would soon emit sweet breaths along her neck, part wide to take in her milk.

What would their child have from each of them? His blue eyes? Her dark skin? Her brown eyes? His olive skin? Would their genes alternate in their expression or blend? She hoped their child would have something she didn't have—a perfect amalgamation of DNA expression, an equal rendering of both parents.

Shan's hazel-eyed, red-haired mother had not bequeathed any noticeable traits to Shan. Her childhood had been defined by others' blunt judgments about their relationship. *You're so dark. Is that really your mother?* She hoped their baby looked like both her and Max, that their child wouldn't constantly have to clarify their relationship to their own parents, lecture others on genetics or on minding their own business. She did not want to be mistaken for the nanny.

Max leaned closer to the screen. His eyes lit up. "The baby is so beautiful," he said, squeezing her hand. Her husband's smile was full, the kind he freely offered her in the early days of their marriage, when everything about the prospect of being partnered for life was shiny and new. It had been so long since she felt this tenderness from him. The prospect of parenthood seemed to inch him toward a newer, healthier place. *He has changed*, she thought. *He has been working on himself, fulfilling his pledge to be a better husband, a better person.*

The tech removed the probe and wiped the end with a towel.

"I'm going to get the radiologist," she said. She rose, flipped on the light, exited. The door closed softly behind her.

Max squinted. "What was that all about?"

Goose bumps sprouted along Shan's skin. She pulled down her shirt, not caring that she'd get it sticky with gel. "I don't know. Why did she leave so suddenly? We didn't get to hear the baby's heartbeat."

"We did hear it, didn't we?" he asked. "I thought we heard it."

She closed her eyes. Twelve weeks, the bridge to the second trimester. They had heard and seen the baby's heartbeat just last month. They were safe. Weren't they?

The door flung open. A woman wearing gray slacks and a white blouse whooshed inside, parked herself on the stool, slid to the screen. "I'm Dr. Agarwal," she said. She adjusted her purple-rimmed glasses, smacked a few keys on the keyboard. "Let's take a look at your baby."

"Is everything okay?" Shan asked.

This question hung in the air and floated away, as if it'd not been spoken.

The doctor flared her nostrils, squirted the end of the probe with more gel, pressed it into Shan's belly.

"We've not had any issues with the pregnancy," Max offered.

Issues. The issues were plentiful, though not the kind she'd relay to the doctor.

Shan had always disparaged parenthood, and for over twenty years she actively blocked her reproductive cycle. Her accidental pregnancy at age forty-one was a shock. She scheduled an abortion during the sixth week. But when they arrived at the clinic, a familiar sort of sorrow had washed over her, like when her father had died. Ending the pregnancy felt like another end to him—the end of his line, of the possibility of his essense embodying another human being. She couldn't shake the feeling that took hold of her. She canceled the appointment and left the clinic.

Two weeks later, at the eight-week mark, she saw their adorable tadpole at the first ultrasound. Her fears about parenthood, her ambivalence toward the pregnancy, vanished. The baby was the future she now wanted more than anything.

The radiologist's lips drew a straight line. "I'm afraid I have bad news." She touched Shan's hand. "There's no heartbeat."

It couldn't be true. The charts and graphs in pregnancy books, the lofty what-to-expect expectations, the weekly emails she received about her baby's growth and development indicated that her pregnancy was progressing perfectly. She'd experienced all the symptoms—weight gain, tender, sore breasts, bleeding gums. New life inhabited every cell of her body.

"Check again," she said. "We heard it just last month."

The doctor replaced the probe, tapped the screen with the nib of her pen, traced the heart's outline. "I'm sorry, it's no longer beating. Given the measurements, the fetus stopped growing about a week ago."

Fetus.

Shan cringed at such a clinical word, its cruelty in this context. For the doctor, it was only a fetus, one of many she would see throughout her day. For Shan, it was her sweet baby. *Come, my little one, please, now, for Mama. Please stay with me. I love you so much.*

That's when she noticed the stillness. During the last ultra-sound, their baby had squirmed and flitted, had danced and waved. This time it resembled a leaf floating on the surface of the pond.

CHAPTER NINE

The two days after the miscarriage had been a fog. A comforter of used tissues. Half-drunk mugs of herbal tea. The cotton of an Ibuprofen bottle. Plates with peanut butter crackers, slightly burnt grilled cheese, just how she liked it. Except she no longer had an appetite. Her bedsheets stank of tears and sweat. Her hair knotted like a nest against the pillow. Because the ultrasound was late on Friday, the D&C to remove the baby had to be scheduled for first thing Monday morning.

The delay was agonizing.

A few hours after her ultrasound appointment, her ob-gyn had called to ask Shan if she wanted to know the sex. How odd it was to ask this question, under these circumstances—that one could even know the sex of a baby this small. Shan didn't think she could feel any more agony in that moment, but as the tears spilled down her cheeks, she said, "Yes."

"It's a boy."

The present tense had confused Shan, made her feel, for one brief hopeful interlude, that the baby was still alive, that the radiologist's initial diagnosis of a nonviable pregnancy had been false. But no, the baby, the boy, her *son*, was still gone. Her doctor may have thought she was being kind, allowing Shan to feel one second of happiness, of pride, affording her a fuller imagination of who their baby might have become. But possessing this knowledge that she was carrying a son gutted her even more. It made their baby less of a hypothetical, more real.

Shan sat up and dragged her legs off the bed. Early that morning, Max announced that he had to go into the office. "On a Sunday?" she asked. "Two days after our miscarriage?" He mumbled something about trial preparation and she let it go. He'd barely spoken since the ultrasound, had been lost somewhere in his mind as he puttered around the house. She knew the miscarriage had been hard on him, wanted to believe he felt the grief as deeply as she did.

But she also knew something else—that when things got tough, he immediately returned to bad habits. Ever since they decided to keep the baby, she'd done her best to ignore them, to let herself think only about the bright possibility of their family's future. She'd given herself the luxury of living in denial. She couldn't afford to do this any more.

Her laptop balanced on the edge of the nightstand. She reached for it, flipped it open. The password for their bank took its time to resurface from her cloudy mind—she had neglected to check the account since leaving her job, couldn't deal with being reminded that their income was slashed in half. She typed and hit enter. Rows and columns of the ledger appeared, debits and credits. She scrolled backward in time. The water company. The gas company. The trash company. The grocery store. At least he'd been paying the bills.

She logged out and pulled up the website for their joint credit card. She clicked on the most recent monthly statement.

The very first purchase caught her eye. The $8,000 Max needed for a new bike for an upcoming race had, in reality, cost $15,000. *He exaggerated by $7,000.* There were several withdrawals of large amounts of cash, including $2,500 he'd taken out just two hours ago. She inhaled deeply. She wanted to close the laptop, plug it back into the wall, walk away. But she couldn't continue to deny the numbers, to stick her head in the sand about their financial picture. She took a sip of water, swirled it in her mouth, swallowed.

The debits on the statement knocked the breath out of her. Thousands on clothes, shoes, a new computer. In a single month.

She shut the laptop, tossed it to the other side of the bed.

Every fear now materialized before her. Her husband had continued his binge spending, despite the fact that she no longer brought in an income, that they could no longer afford this lifestyle. With their massive student loans and mortgage, they could *never* really afford this lifestyle. For years, she begged him to go into therapy. He had refused. "You just need to learn how to relax," he'd said. When she became pregnant, he promised to curb his spending for their growing family.

She believed him, despite his history.

She liked to pretend throughout their marriage that other married couples were worse off, consoled herself with the fact that Max had a good job, was a kind, generous human being, worked hard, loved her hard, didn't abuse substances, had never been unfaithful. How easy it was to tick off so many good qualities so she could more easily bury his toxic ones. She saw it more clearly now—how the foundation of their marriage was her denial of the ways in which her husband let her down, the ways in which he lied to her, hid things from her, gaslit her when she complained his spending was getting out of control.

She picked up her phone and tapped Max's name. He answered on the third ring.

"Max, when will you be home? We need to talk." The sounds in the background were familiar. A symphony of chimes and beeps, ringing bells. She could picture where he was immediately. "Oh my God. Max, are you back in Murphy?"

"I needed some time to think."

"How could you do this Max? How could you do this, *right now*?

While she grieved their lost pregnancy, he lied to her about needing to work and drove two hours away to play the slots in North Carolina. He was gambling at his favorite casino, the place he swore last year he'd never go to again.

"Max, you have thrown us away. Do you understand this? Is this what you want?"

"It's been a rough few days, Shan. I needed to get my mind off things. Can you just give me this one day?"

"I'm always giving you *everything*, Max. That's the problem." She had longed to stay in Seattle after they married. But he'd wanted to move to Atlanta. She'd wanted to rent a small apartment the first few years so they could pay down their debt, but he pressured her to purchase a home that was too large for them, in a neighborhood further out from the city center. She wanted to take a job working with a nonprofit organization. He steered her to a position with a large law firm so she'd bring in more money (money that he spent on himself). And he lied. He could never stop lying.

"Don't come home tonight. Don't come with me to the D&C tomorrow. I want you out of the house, Max. This time I mean it. It's over. I want a divorce."

She hung up. Her heart raced in her chest. It wasn't until

she uttered those words that she knew them to be true. A few years ago, they separated for three months. Max stayed with a friend. When he returned, they drew up a budget, cut up a few credit cards. He promised to stay on track. But then he got his own credit card behind her back and started spending again. She had given him yet another chance, as she always did. But no more. Not even the prospect of bringing a child into the marriage had changed him.

She closed her eyes, took a few deep breaths. The urge for a brisk walk, a good, soaking sweat, seized her. *She needed to get out of the house, away from these four walls.*

She rolled off the bed and headed downstairs. In the closet, she yanked a hoodie off the hanger, slipped her arms through, pulled it over her head. The scent of Max's cologne lingered on the collar. She rolled up the sleeves, turned the doorknob.

The front door wouldn't budge. It warped in the frame whenever the season changed. Max had some sort of trick for dislodging it, but she couldn't quite remember it now. She wrapped both hands around the knob, braced her foot against the wall, yanked. The force of its release nearly knocked her over. She regained her balance, stepped outside onto the porch. A breeze kicked up leaves in a swirl, shimmied the branches of the maple tree.

"I guess he forgot all about me."

She whirled around. "Oh," she gasped. "I didn't see you there."

Chandani Singh, their neighbor three doors down the street, perched at the end of the porch swing. She pushed off the floorboards, rocked back, reveled, it seemed, in Shan's surprise at her presence. Her hair, dark and frizzy, resembled an unpruned shrub. Purple bifocals dangled on the tip of her nose. She was so thin Shan could practically see the blood traveling through her veins. Her voice was deep, throaty, outsized for her four-foot-ten-inch frame.

"Max said he'd be by to look at my lawn mower this evening," Chandani said. "It's broken. I waited at home for him, and when he didn't come, I came here. I guess he forgot about it. Perhaps he has more pressing matters to deal with and can't make time to bother with an old woman?"

"Uh, of course not. Max was...he was called into work, rushed out of the house. He must have forgotten. I was upstairs and couldn't hear your knocking. I'm sorry."

"All right then. I suppose I'll have to find someone else to fix it." She sighed heavily but didn't move. Waited, it seemed, for something. Shan glanced at her shoes, fiddled with her hands, sensed Chandani's stare burrowing into her.

Chandani was a widow, had lost her husband the year before, right before leaving New Jersey and settling in Atlanta. Shan would see her strolling through the neighborhood alone. Alone, again, watering her flowers, checking her mail. Shan couldn't recall a single visitor to Chandani's house. She felt sorry for her, and her pity gave her the grace she needed to be generous with her at the same moment Shan's own life had unraveled. "Can I offer you something to drink?" she said.

Her neighbor nodded, hopped off the swing, produced a smirk of victory.

Inside, Chandani scanned the surfaces of the tables, the walls, the floor, passed judgment, Shan assumed, on layers of dust, the absence of any wall décor, the several pairs of shoes haphazardly tossed on the floor—their less than stellar house-keeping. In the kitchen, Shan opened the fridge, brought out a pitcher, poured lemonade in a tall Atlanta Falcons glass for her nosey neighbor.

"Your skin is so splotchy and uneven. Why is it like that?" she asked, taking the drink. "I thought you were Indian. We don't have skin like that."

This was the first in a series of questions Chandani tortured her with upon each of their meetings. Each time, Shan gave the same answers. *My father was Indian. My mother was white, so I'm only half, even though I'm dark skinned. No, I don't speak any Indian languages. No, my father didn't grow up in India. He was born and raised in London but moved to India when I was five, died when I was eleven. My mother died a few years ago. Yes, my parents divorced. Yes, I went to India once as a child, a long time ago, haven't been back since, don't know of any family there.* Chandani would gasp at each of these revelations, as if she couldn't believe that such a tragic family existed.

Shan was in no mood to engage in this kind of exchange again. Not today. "I've been forgetting to wear sunscreen while planting bulbs. The sun's been taking a toll on my face."

Chandani shook her head. "You should plant bulbs in the evening." She set the glass down on the table, looked over the room.

Shan braced herself. Chandani's silences usually preceded pointed snark.

"How come you and Max don't have children?" she asked. "You should make it a priority. You're not young anymore."

The words were a knife to Shan's gut. She blinked away the tears forming in her eyes. Of all the things her neighbor could have said in that moment! But Chandani had no idea about her pregnancy, that her marriage had fallen apart. The remark, though extremely hurtful, was not made with ill will.

Shan took a deep breath. "Chandani, I...*we*...Max and I...we just had a miscarriage. We found out Friday. I'm having the procedure to...remove the baby tomorrow morning."

Chadani's hand flew to her mouth. Her face turned white. "I'm so sorry, Shan. I had no idea. I'm sorry for your loss. I'm so sorry, too, for asking such an intrusive question." She set her glass down. "What can I do to help? Where did you say Max was?"

Shan glanced at her hands, picked at one of her fingernails. "He's actually in North Carolina."

"Will he be home tomorrow? Is he able to take you to the hospital in the morning?"

"I...no, he's not. He can't," Shan said. "He *won't.* I asked him not to come." Her face crumpled. "We're breaking up."

Chandani cocked her head, clasped Shan's hand. It was warm, as if she'd just unwrapped it from a cup of hot tea. "Oh, goodness. Shan. This is too much pain all at once." She smoothed back a lock of Shan's hair. "What can I do to help? Please. Anything. I can take you to the hospital tomorrow morning. I can cook you food."

"Thanks, but I can get there myself," Shan said. This was something she wanted to do alone.

Chandani looked directly into Shan's eyes. "Please let me know if you change your mind. I'm here for you. Anytime. And I know what it's like to have the rug pulled out from under you, Shan. I've been there. And I can tell you from over four decades of experience that marriage is really, really hard. Oftentimes, unbearably so," she sighed. "We can all only do our best to make a marriage work, and sometimes...well, sometimes our best is simply not good enough."

Her words were laced with agony. Perhaps Shan had misjudged her neighbor. Behind that grating exterior was a person in pain who seemed to have the capacity for empathy after all.

She touched her neighbor's hand. "Thank you, Chandani. I appreciate you telling me this."

"Shan," she said. "You're Indian. So please call me Aunty."

CHAPTER TEN

At four a.m., Shan bolted upright, cried out to an empty room. The pain seared through her torso, spread to her sides. She breathed again only when it released its grip. And then, a few minutes later, it arrived again like a wave crashing over her.

The doctor said there was a chance her body might try to expel the baby before the D&C procedure. That if it happened, there would be cramping and blood. If she felt she could handle it, she could have the miscarriage at home. *Naturally.* But Shan didn't understand what that meant. What about the loss of a pregnancy was natural?

She whipped off the comforter. A red stain spread along her cotton underwear. Its mirror image appeared on the sheet. She made her way to the bathroom and collapsed over the toilet. Another tightening came with such power, she thought it might strangle her. This was a contraction. A natural miscarriage meant labor.

She felt no pain when her baby's heart stopped beating, had no idea, until the ultrasound appointment, that he was already dead. Wouldn't a good mother have sensed something wrong? It made no sense that such a loss would produce no physical pain, no wounds to dress, no scars to smear cocoa butter over. And now that the moment had come, now that her body was expelling her pregnancy, she didn't want to do it alone at home. She wanted to go to the hospital, early, and have the D&C.

She quickly changed her underwear and stuck on a pad. She yanked open her dresser, threw on a set of sweats and charged out of her room. At the bottom of the stairs, her belly tightened again, and this time the pain felt like something bigger. It reverberated down her legs.

She glanced at the time on her phone.

4:17 a.m.

She had rebuffed Chandani's offer to take her to the hospital, had decided instead to take a rideshare to and from the procedure by herself. She had wanted to do it on her own. She hadn't even told her friends that she was pregnant yet. Only Max knew, and, as of yesterday, Chandani.

With the pain came fear. It draped itself over her, the fear of it getting worse, the fear of enduring this all alone. The fear of no longer being someone's mother, someone's wife.

She tapped Chandani's number. She answered on the third ring.

"Chandani, it's Shan. I need you to come over, please. I need to go to the hospital. I think I'm miscarrying right now."

"I'll be there in a few minutes," she said. "And it's Aunty, remember?"

"Aunty," Shan said. "Please hurry."

Shan slipped her feet into her shoes. She reached for her wallet and keys on the hall table. She rose, unlocked the door, and slid back to the floor as another contraction came. She squeezed her eyes tight, moaned.

Knuckles rapped against the door. "Shan," a voice shouted. "It's me. I'm coming in."

The door opened. Chandani knelt next to her as the pain once again receded.

"I didn't realize it would hurt this badly," Shan panted. "The cramping. It's…it's really…I can't handle this…I can't."

"Not to worry. I've got you." Chandani wrapped her arms around Shan and lifted her. Shan would never have guessed she had such strength in her, that those little twig arms could lift anything heavier than a dictionary. She slowly guided Shan out of the front door, one foot in front another, an awkward dance in which Shan had to pause several times to breathe through the sharp tightening of her belly.

"My car's in the shop, so I called a Lyft. You lay in the back. I'll sit up front." In the back seat, Chandani laid a flannel blanket across Shan's body and tucked it around her.

"Let's keep you good and warm," she said. "We'll be there soon."

In the operating room, the anesthesiologist touched Shan's shoulder. "I'm so sorry for your loss," she said. "But we're going to take good care of you. Now, count backwards from ten."

Shan's gaze shifted to the ceiling. The numbers appeared before her in the air. *10. 9. 8.* She opened her mouth to speak them, but before she could, they shifted in form and floated away into something else, a memory of the very last time she was in the hospital.

"It hurts, Daddy," she cries, clutching her belly in the hallway of the hospital. "I want Mommy. I want to go home."

Her father rubs her belly in deep circles. "Be brave, my Shanti. It's going to pass. The doctors will come give you medicines very soon. They will flush out the bad germs, okay? Please be brave, beta."

She tries to focus on his face, his dark eyes. Every time she moans in pain, he winces. "I want to go to back to Seattle."

The cot isn't much wider than her body. Patients roam in thin cotton gowns. Some push metal rods holding plastic bags. An old man in a wheelchair is stranded in the middle of the hallway, hunched over.

Her father tussles her hair, clasps her hands. "I'm so sorry, Shanti. I'm so sorry this happened. Please forgive me. Please, please, forgive me. I promise I will take better care of you."

When his eyes water, a few tears spill down his cheeks. He is a grown-up. Grown-ups aren't supposed to cry. Mama never cries. Ever.

"I want to go home," she says. "I hate you. I hate India."

He turns away, presses a white folded handkerchief against his eyes, clears his throat. "They're bringing the medicines. You'll feel better very soon."

A woman in a plain dress makes her way down the hallway. "Nurse?" he calls. She doesn't look up, continues to scribble on her clipboard. "Excuse me, Nurse?" He has nearly jumped in front of her, blocking her ability to pass. "Please, I think my daughter is dehydrated. She can't keep liquids down. She's been having diarrhea and vomiting for over eight hours."

The nurse purses her lips. She speaks in a sharp, low tone. When she finishes her lecture, she darts around him, resumes her quick pace.

Her father turns back toward her. The muscles in his jaws clench. His face crumples. "I'm not going to let anything happen to you. I promise."

She shivers. He removes his shirt, lays it over her. A mole hovers at the base of his neck, like the one on her thumb. She has never noticed it before.

He leans on the side of her cot, closes his eyes, clasps his palms together. His lips move rapidly as he whispers, forming words to a prayer he says each night before he puts her to sleep: "Om, Shanti, Shanti, Shanti."

CHAPTER ELEVEN

A mint green pickup truck pulled to the end of the driveway. A small hand appeared in the passenger-side window, waved. Shan squinted but remained on the porch. The window lowered.

"It's me," Chandani called out. "Get in."

Shan jogged down the front walkway. "This is *yours*?" She opened the door and slid inside. "This is the car that was in the shop? I don't think I've ever seen an Indian sitting inside a pickup truck before—let alone *driving* a pickup truck." She buckled her belt.

It had only been a week since the D&C, but Shan had needed to get out of the house. She had been resting and bingewatching. But soon the four walls of her home, especially without Max there, felt as if they might collapse in on her. Chandani had suggested the Atlanta Botanical Gardens, a place Shan and Max had a membership to for years, until Shan started cutting back on nonessential expenses to put more toward their credit card debt. Well, *his* credit card debt.

Chandani flipped on her blinker and pulled away from the curb. She was propped up on a seat cushion, her hands at two and twelve on a steering wheel that looked disproportionately large given her height. Dark sunglasses with wide frames covered her eyes, a cotton scarf framed her face. She was an Indian Jackie O.

"Purchasing this was one of the first decisions I made after Harjeet died," Chandani said, patting the dashboard. "Actually, Harjeet made *all* of the decisions during our marriage, and before I was married, my father did. So if you think about it, getting this truck was one of the first major decisions I ever made for myself."

Chandani merged onto the highway, took a sip from a can of soda, and placed it back in the holder. "The used-car dealer kept pushing me toward a sedan. But this truck spoke to me." She removed her sunglasses and looked at Shan. "It feels good to call the shots, even if they are impractical."

The cloudy sky allowed Shan to more easily take in the view of the city. The skyline was nothing like majestic Seattle's with the Space Needle, the Puget Sound, and Mount Rainier in the background, but Atlanta's had grown on her over the years. The city was lush and green, with the Chattahoochee River running along the northwest perimeter. In the early years of the marriage, she and Max had countless picnics in Piedmont Park, which they could rollerblade to from their home. The sunshine is what she appreciated the most. Atlanta received more rainfall than Seattle, but it arrived in buckets, all at once, and then afterward the skies cleared and the sun shone. Seattle had a constant drizzle and grayness that she could never get used to.

Chandani found a spot on the first level of the parking garage, and they headed toward the entrance. She was a brisk walker. Shan could hardly keep up.

"Thanks for bringing me here, Aunty. I needed to get out of the house. I've been too much in my head lately."

"You're grieving. That's normal. And this place is good for grief. It's the first place I visited when I moved to Atlanta," Chandani said. "I was missing Harjeet and felt so lonely. As it turns out, spending time in nature, where things bud and grow, is a good reminder that one can begin again."

They followed a path that wound through the foliage. The crisp air smelled of cinnamon and soil. The clouds seemed to bloat with the next, imminent rain.

"Why did you move to Atlanta?"

"My niece lives here. After Harjeet died, she convinced me I needed a fresh start somewhere new. We get together on Sundays, but she has a family and a full-time job, so she's too busy to see me more often than that. So I got myself a membership here. I come here for clarity.

The loss of her baby, perhaps the only baby she would ever have, had given Shan the clarity she needed about her marriage. It was the kind of clarity that she had tried to push away for years, hoping Max would change. He didn't change, but she finally did.

If Chandani could survive the death of her husband, start her life over in her seventies in a new state where she knew only one other person, Shan could start over too. She could sell the house, move, look for another job, and build something beautiful on her own.

Their intended destination was just around the bend. *Earth Goddess.* A woman the height of a two-story home, her shoulders, left arm, and face aboveground, as if only the top part of her had sprouted from the earth. Her skin was a palate of lush green leaves. Thick plaits of hair in green and purple vines flowed down her back. She sat just behind a pool of water, eyes closed, face serene, her hand opened, palm up. Water cascaded from it.

"Sometimes, we need to give our heartbreaks over to some-one else. I bring mine here, to the Earth Goddess. You should try it. You have too many, if you ask me. Your baby. Your marriage. And you lost your mother a few years ago, and your father at such a young age." She shook her head. "Terrible."

"My father died so long ago," Shan said. "I hardly remem-ber him. I moved on."

"I don't believe there's any such thing as moving on, Shan. I think we simply rotate through cycles of joy and grief, like riding a carousel. Sometimes we are up, sometimes we are down. But we're always circling back, never getting too far away from where we started, from the source of our pain. We can never quite escape it."

Chandani had a point. After Shan's father died, she found a way, for a few years, to compartmentalize her sadness. But it erupted when she was a teenager. The summer she was fif-teen, she and her mother had forgotten to celebrate his birth-day for the first time since his death. It was the only day of the year her mother ever talked about her father.

When Shan realized it had passed, the first words that tum-bled out of her mouth were not about his birthday. They were about her mother's decision not to move to India with him. "If we'd joined him in India," she shouted, "we might have still been a family! We could have pressured him to go to the hos-pital sooner! The doctors could have discovered his aneurysm before it was too late!" Shan hadn't realized until that summer how much she blamed her mother for her father's death.

"Shan," Chandani said, "can I ask you why your parents split up?"

"They had nothing in common. My mother was twelve years older than him. They'd only known each other a few months before she got pregnant with me, so it's not as if they had a stable marriage to begin with. But what broke them was his decision to leave us. When I was in kindergarten, he suddenly got it in his head that we needed to move to India. And my mom wanted to stay and finish her PhD program.

"But he'd never lived there before, right? So why *India*?"

"My mom never knew the whole story. But she thought it had something to do with my grandmother, Deepa. She thought Deepa had planted some idea in him."

Deepa herself had little connection to the subcontinent. Her parents had died in India, tragically, it seemed. She hadn't been back in decades. That was all Shan knew about her father's family history. It was otherwise a vacuum, empty of details, names of places or dates, far more mystery than fact. Was this why Shan had felt so rudderless in life, because she had no family tree on her father's side to root her?

"Is Deepa still alive?" Chandani asked. "Are you still in touch?"

"After my father died, my mom left her several messages, wrote her a bunch of letters, sent her photos of me. She never responded. At least, that's my mother's side of the story. I have no idea whether Deepa's still alive. I wouldn't even know where or how to begin to look for her."

"Oh, I'm sorry to hear that Shan."

"Thank you, Aunty."

Shan took a deep breath. Exhaled. A breeze kicked up, brushed through the petals framing the pond. She took it all in, the gentle sounds of trickling water, chirping birds, the rustling leaves. The Earth Goddess's outstretched hand was an offering, a blessing, an absolution, perhaps, that Shan hadn't realized she needed.

A couple pushing a stroller walked by. The baby had black hair, fists pumping in the air. Thinking about babies the past several days had been so painful for her. The smile this infant brought to her face surprised her.

Chandani glanced at the stroller and then looked at Shan. "Have you thought about naming your baby? He was your son, and he will always be your son. A name might give you a little bit of closure."

The thought had never occurred to Shan—to name a baby she'd been pregnant with for barely three months. But naming her baby would mark his place in her family history.

"Just think about it," Chandani said, before Shan could answer. She then rose and offered Shan her arm.

Shan looped hers through it. They turned and walked slowly away from the Earth Goddess, toward another part of the gardens. As they did, a ray of light escaped between clouds and shined upon their faces.

Shan didn't realize how exhausted she was until Chandani dropped her off back home. She kicked off her shoes, climbed the stairs, headed down the hallway to the room that would have been the baby's. A full-size bed was pushed up against the wall. A small desk sat in front of the window. They'd planned on moving the furniture to the basement to make room for a crib and changing table. It would all stay put now, in the forever guest bedroom.

At the closet, she grasped the cold, metal handle, slid open the door. White, plastic hangers hung along the rod. Four pairs of footed pajamas, two white, two yellow. Six long-sleeved onesies unsnapped at the diaper. She imagined her son's downy head slipping through the opening, the tension during those few seconds her baby's face would be covered by a layer of cotton, the relief that would sweep over her when his chubby cheeks and drooling chin reemerged.

Three light green receiving blankets. For *swaddling*. The re-creation of the mother's womb. A new term, a new *world* for a first-time parent. *There's an art to it*, she'd heard, as if wrapping a baby in a blanket was akin to cross-stitching. She had imagined tucking her baby's limbs inside the blanket, the corner into a fold, the feel of him, bundled up against her chest. A sweet, beautiful cocoon.

A soft brown bear sat alone on the shelf. Its nose was black. A yellow ribbon was tied around its neck. Max purchased it the day they decided to keep the baby, the day their lives took a turn down an unexpected road. She lifted the bear from the shelf, pressed its body against her cheek.

She flicked off the light, shut the closet door. The few paces from the former nursery to her bedroom drained her of her energy. She crawled onto the bed, collapsed over the rumpled quilt. The bear laid next to her, its face directly in front of hers. An image appeared in her mind, her son, his head in the crook of her arm, his tiny toes pressed into her side, his blinking eyes staring directly into hers.

She rolled onto her back. Cracks and fissures ran across the ceiling. Her gaze followed them, each deep crevice sprouting new, thinner limbs. Their home wore its age proudly, demanded their time and attention. They had neglected it, assumed, wrongly, that it could hold itself together for them, even though they couldn't hold their own marriage together for their house.

Tears budded and burned, rolled down her cheeks, her jaw, her neck. She closed her eyes. Her dream last night had been the same as it had been almost every night since that horrible day: She was back in the ultrasound room. The black-and-white image of her son's heart blinked steadily on the screen. The doctor congratulated them. Max leaned over, kissed her cheek. She pressed her palm against her belly, felt, she thought, the slightest movement. She woke each morning with a smile on her face, though as soon as she came fully to consciousness, the sadness washed over her again.

Where to put the bear? She glanced around the room. She

needed it close, somewhere safe, but she didn't want to see it every day. She scooted to the end of the bed, knelt on the floor, lifted up the end of the blanket.

A few clear plastic containers stored clothes she never wore. Her hand caught the corner of one. She slid it toward her, popped open the top. Cable knit sweaters, the kind that went out of style in the nineties, were rolled up like sleeping bags. A pair of old sweatpants from the University of Washington was torn at the knee. Underneath was a plain, brown cardboard shoebox. She hadn't come across it since they first moved into the house eight years earlier.

It belonged to her father.

The mind was a strange thing. Ever since becoming pregnant, thoughts of her long-deceased father seemed to waft to the front of her mind. She would have never expected this, that a pregnancy, and the loss of the pregnancy, would form another connection to him, would resurrect his life, and the loss of him, all over again.

After his death, his worldly possessions, the few pieces of furniture he owned, his clothes, had all been donated to a local charity in Delhi. His landlord had discovered the box while cleaning out his apartment, found Shan's return address on a letter she had written to her father and mailed the box and its entire contents to her. It arrived with a note offering his deepest condolences for her loss. He described her father Vijay as one of his best, most timely paying tenants.

When she first opened the box thirty years ago, she hoped to find a message or sign that she'd been in her father's thoughts in the last days of his life, some manifestation of regret for leaving her and her mother. She wanted evidence that she'd meant more to him than India.

It was merely a haphazard filing system.

She lifted off the lid, spilled the contents onto the bed. The maps remained folded and creased, the guidebooks wrinkled and warped. There was the thin, gray paperback book. *Exodus* by Kavita Grover. She flipped through it. Words and phrases dripped down the page, segmented themselves into verses. Her father had been a lover of biographies, histories, *National Geographic.* She always wondered how he'd come into possession of a poetry book. In her teens, she read it a few times, even selected a poem from it, "A Folded Heart," to recite to her eighth-grade English class for an assignment.

The loose papers in the box were soft and grainy between her fingers. Pen marks, circular, light-brown stains, branded the margins. She selected one page, an old bank statement, brought it to her face, hoped the passage of time had somehow resurrected her father's scent—coffee, a hint of nicotine, Old Spice aftershave from a freshly razored cheek.

It reeked of mildew.

A photocopy of an article from *The Hindustan Times* was dated August 15, 1947, with the headline "India Independent: British Rule Ends." In the body of the article, India's first prime minister, Jawaharlal Nehru, shook the hand of Liaquat Ali Khan, Pakistan's first prime minister. In another photo, a defeated looking Gandhi stood alone in his dhoti, propped up with a cane.

Beneath it lay a city map of Delhi. As she opened it, its folds released clouds of dust particles. Her father's notes filled the white margins. Her own shaky penmanship encircled a few monuments. It was the map from their trip together, the one they used the very last time she would see him alive in New Delhi.

Among the grids of roads, the green squares for parks, the noises of those busy streets returned to her now, the revving of auto rickshaws, the chiming of bicycle bells, the blaring honks of long-bodied Ambassador cars. Unlike the sterile gridded coordinates of American urban centers, the streets of India breathed and moved like a living organism. She missed the sounds of India the most, had discovered something beautiful in them, the feeling of never having to be alone, of never having to be left behind.

A light green hexagon identified India Gate. She remembered the military officer stationed in front, unsmiling, stiff straight, in a dark brown uniform. To the southeast, just beyond the national zoo, sat Humayun's Tomb, the blueprint for the Taj Mahal, her father had said. They guzzled juice boxes of Frooti there under the shade of a nearby palm tree.

She began refolding the map. A small sticky note was stuck to the opposite side. She hadn't noticed it before. She tugged it off, tried to make out her father's faded black penmanship.

Lahore Trip—
June 14, 6 nights, Himalayan Hotel. Confirmation # 645.

He had planned to take a trip to Pakistan, one month after his death, only nine months after she last saw him.

Why?

She set it down, searched through his papers again more carefully. She found a familiar index card with a name and address. *Gertrude Enzenebner, 84 Foster Street, London.* Years earlier, she had asked her mother about the name. Her mother couldn't recall her father ever mentioning a woman named Gertrude. Shan had hoped she was an old friend of her father's—not a lover who may have played a role in breaking up her parents' marriage.

An old pamphlet of the Taj Mahal lined the bottom of the box. Its edges were warped. On the cover was the monument as she'd remembered it—white, glowing. They stood on its terrace, overlooking the Yamuna River, as the red turrets of Agra Fort in the distance kissed the purple peaks of clouds.

She'd remembered how the weight of his sorrow draped

over her then. She'd assumed he was invincible, didn't quite know how to comfort a man she had come into contact with only once a year since kindergarten.

This longing to know him, to understand him, had only intensified over the years. She often wondered, if he had lived, how his life would have shaped hers. When she was teased in school for her brown skin, would having her brown father there to console her have made her feel less alone than a white mother who simply told her to ignore it? Would Shan have placed so much importance on getting married and staying married? Would she have turned down the job offer at Walker & Associates and pursued more meaningful work? Her relationship with her father since his death consisted of a decades-long, one-way conversation from which she had no answers.

She sighed, picked up the maps, the guidebooks, the book of poetry, the slip of paper, and laid them back inside her father's box. She squeezed the teddy bear once more, laid it inside, and as she did she pictured a world that would never exist, one where both her father and his grandson would know each other. The loss of her son now embodied the loss of a chance at redemption for her own fractured father–daughter story.

It came to her then, the name that she'd held so closely to her heart all of these years, the only name that could help her make sense out of her grief, that could ground her in both the past and her future, that could bring back a piece of her father.

Vijay, she said, closing her eyes.

My son's name will be Vijay.

Part
Three

CHAPTER TWELVE
London
September 9, 1954

The young woman forged ahead, a quick, purposeful march along Brower Street toward Wallace Hall. She had dark skin, shoulder-length wavy black hair, wore a wide-collared plaid dress, an ivory cardigan, hugged a stack of books in the crook of her left arm. Her long, slender legs took two steps at a time. She paused halfway up, visored her hand from the light cast by silver, low-lying clouds, surveyed the concrete stairs filled with dozens of students. Their knobby knees lined up like rows of apples, textbooks splayed open on their laps.

Gertrude caught a glimpse of the woman's profile, her long, elegant nose, her short chin, lips pointed, pursed. The woman shifted her weight, scanned again. Dissatisfied with her view, she climbed higher. She tried and failed to button her cardigan with one hand, settled for pulling the wings of her sweater tighter around her chest. A book slid off her forearm. She caught it before it fell.

Gertrude was so focused on the woman, her heel caught on the edge of a step. Her foot slipped, her arms shot out to her sides to regain her balance. A sharp pain pulsed through her ankle. She lifted the skirt of her dress, looked down. Her T-straps cut into the top of her feet, molded themselves in her ballooned flesh. She lowered herself, adjusted the hooks into looser eyelets. Her light brown hair dislodged from behind her ear, fell into her eyes. She shook it out of her face, continued her pursuit of the woman.

She knew the woman was new, new to London University, new to Gertrude's apartment building, though they hadn't officially met yet. The woman stuck out in a neighborhood made up of aging Jewish refugees, just as Gertrude did, who was Catholic. But everyone in the neighborhood had lost someone, or several someones, during the war.

Gertrude's father had died in prison. Or so they thought. No one knew exactly when or how, or why he'd been arrested, though rumor swirled through Linz that Otto, the baker, had turned her father in to the Gestapo for listening to Radio Free Europe. Gertrude had been helping her mother in the kitchen with dinner when the door was kicked in, when her father, who'd been napping on the sofa, was tackled and beaten by three SS officers. They wrapped a blindfold around his eyes, tied a rope around his hands, dragged him outside. She and her mother pled for mercy, chased after him down the stairwell. They didn't even get to hug him one last time. *Pass auf deine mutti*, he shouted to Gertrude, as they tossed him into the back of a truck, as clouds of exhaust erected a barrier between them. *Look out for your mother.*

After, she and her mother stuffed whatever they could into two suitcases and boarded a bus to Steyrling, a tiny town in the Alps, to hide out until the end of the war. Three months later, her mother died giving birth to a premature boy, who Gertrude named Gerald. A week later, Gerald passed away in Gertrude's arms. In a blink of an eye, her entire family had evaporated from the earth. She was an orphan, in a continent of orphans, who developed a knack for identifying other lost souls like themselves.

After liberation, Gertrude was shipped to the only relative who would (begrudgingly) take her in, Great Aunt Hedwig in London whose actual blood relation to the Enzenebner family was tangential at best. When Aunt Hedwig passed away, at an age twice Gertrude's mother's, Gertrude found herself the sole heir to her two-bedroom apartment and a bank account flush with enough money to pay for her living expenses while she completed her education, a degree in history.

The woman paced back and forth along the step, checked her watch, frowned.

Each morning, the woman waited for the 803 bus outside of their building. Gertrude watched her from her third-floor window, still in her nightgown and slippers, while nibbling her tea and toast. She would see the woman standing at the curb, cloaked in a long, dark trench coat, hair in a tight bun. The woman kept her gaze southward in anticipation of the bus's left turn on their street. She spoke to no one, not even chatty Mrs. Lockhart who wore her overcoat even in the dead of summer. In the late afternoons, while Gertrude poured over her school books at the table, the woman would step off the bus, walk over to the red cylindrical pillar box, drop in a letter. She did this once a week, sometimes twice, that Gertrude could see. Gertrude often wondered who was on the other end of those letters, perhaps relatives in India, where the woman was unmistakably from. She wondered if the letters arrived in chronological order, or if the letters from past weeks bypassed the most current ones. The post could be so unpredictable.

Gertrude mounted a step of equal elevation, traversed its narrow surface. The woman's gaze continued to sweep the area. She didn't see Gertrude until she was nearly upon her.

"Hello there," Gertrude said. "I'm Gertrude. I believe we live in the same apartment building on Foster Road."

The woman relaxed her face when Gertrude mentioned their shared domicile. She appeared older than Gertrude initially thought. Her athletic gait had belied her hollowed cheeks, the dark circles under her eyes. A raised mark the size of a coin bordered her jaw line. It was several shades lighter than the color of her skin, a scar of some sort. Her forehead looked plastic, as if the skin could barely stretch enough to cover it. Still, the woman was quite beautiful with her pen perched above her ear, the lovely mole near the corner of her mouth. She had thick eyebrows, long lashes. "Yes, we do," she said. "I've seen you in the building."

"And you're a student here at the university?" Gertrude asked.

"In the graduate English department. I'm teaching this term. My name's Deepa." She offered her hand, fingers with short, utilitarian nails, a cold palm. "Very nice to meet you, Gertrude."

"Are you originally from India? Do you mind me asking so?" Gertrude did her best to restrain herself. She had a way of pouncing on others to make friends, of trying far too hard. She was the woman others looked past. "A little too plain," her mother used to say. Gertrude had made some friends in London, had someone to sit with at lunch at Collins School for Girls, English girls of pedigree, with family trees of means, but had never felt particularly close with any of them. They made fun of her accent, how she couldn't make the *th* sound, pinched their noses at the vinegary smell of her sauerkraut.

"I don't mind at all," Deepa said. "I'm from New Delhi, though I've been in London for more than seven years now. I quite like it, except for the dreariness. The weather, I mean, not the city itself." She looked out again over the steps. Something caught her eye. Her face brightened. She raised her hand up, waved. "Oh, thank God. There he is."

Gertrude followed her gaze. A little boy held the hand of an older woman with bouffant hair. The boy broke away, charged up the steps.

So the boy belonged to Deepa. Gertrude had seen no sign of him in the building, no bike parked in the foyer, no ball in the hallway. He never got on or off the bus with his mother.

Deepa extended her arms. He rushed into them. She lifted him, sidled her face next to his. "Oh, my sweet boy. I was so worried. I couldn't find you."

"I was playing at the park, Ma. I made a friend."

His voice was high-pitched, gravelly in that out-of-breath, little-boy way. He was a wisp of a thing but had strong, bright eyes, a tiny little pug nose, thick hair with a curled cowlick on one side of his forehead. He was handsome, like his mother. Gertrude guessed he was a few years younger than Gerald would have been, had Gerald lived. She wondered if the boys might have been friends had they grown up in the same building together.

The older woman eyed them from the bottom step, set her hands on her waist, as if her time with the child had been some sort of a punishment.

"Vijay, this is my new friend, Miss..."

"He can call me Miss Trudy. Enzenebner, my last name, is a mouthful."

His eyes darted to Gertrude. He offered her a slight smile. "Hi," he said.

Gertrude stepped a little closer, touched his elbow. "How old are you, dear?"

"Six years and four months. How old are you?"

"Vijay," Deepa gasped. She shifted him to the other hip. "Mind your manners."

"Oh, I don't mind sharing it. I'm twenty-two and, let's see," Gertrude counted out her fingers, "six, seven, eight months."

"Ma says adults count age only in years, not months."

Gertrude's jaw fell open in feigned shock. "Well, *I* certainly do. There's nothing like counting down to the next birthday, is there? I can't wait for mine. I love to bake cakes. Maybe you can come over next time and help me eat them."

"Yes, please!" he bellowed.

Deepa set him down, handed him a few crisp bills. "Be a good boy and give this to Mrs. Darrow." She patted his head. "Go on, she's waiting."

Vijay took off. His feet barely connected with the surface of the steps. Gertrude supposed she hadn't been around little children enough to know how nimble they were, sprightly, energetic, like pogo sticks, the perfect blend of balance and power.

"Deepa, if you ever need me to watch your little boy, you can drop him off at my place anytime," Gertrude said. "Most of my classes are in the evenings. I'd be happy to keep him during the day."

"Thank you, Gertrude, I appreciate the offer. I'll definitely think about it. Mrs. Darrow is a sweet lady, but she doesn't seem to have the energy to keep up with Vijay. She's always canceling because of her migraines."

Gertrude opened her bag, pulled out a sheet of paper, a pencil, wrote down her contact information. "Here's my phone number." She folded it in half, handed it to Deepa.

"Thank you," Deepa said.

Deepa didn't wear a ring on her finger, though Gertrude wasn't sure whether Indian women wore wedding bands. A bindi, certainly, and Deepa had a red one painted between her eyebrows. But Gertrude wasn't sure about rings.

"I've got to get Vijay home. He's had a long day. But I'll call soon," Deepa said. "Perhaps you can come by later in the week for tea, spend some time with us so we can get to know one another. Vijay's quite an active little boy. If you're really interested in the job, I'd like to make sure you understand what you'd be getting yourself into."

"Looking forward to it," Gertrude said. She fingered the pencil in her hand, slid it above her ear. "See you soon."

Deepa smiled. She glided down the steps. The skirt of her dress billowed in the wind. She approached Vijay and the sitter, took her son's hand, guided him away, toward the street where, Gertrude imagined, they would catch the 803 bus home.

CHAPTER THIRTEEN
Atlanta
August 12, 2016

From her mailbox, Chandani Singh watched Max load his last few boxes into the back of a U-Haul. He pulled the door shut, wiped his hands in his pants. When he came around to the driver's side door, he spotted her, waved. She wanted to run over to give him a piece of her mind, but she didn't want to make things any harder on Shan than they already were. Chandani had always considered herself a good judge of character, her friends had always consulted her to help find their children matches in marriage. She hadn't gotten to know Max that well over the past year but had deemed him a decent, patient, and kind human being.

She'd been flat-out wrong.

All marriages, she supposed, looked one way on the outside, another way on the inside. Just like her own.

She headed up the walkway, tapped Shan's name on her cell phone. "He's pulling away. You can come home now," she said. "Why don't you stop in for chai?"

"Sounds good," Shan said. "I'm running an errand. I'll be there in a few minutes."

Shan had worn a brave face over the last two months, told Chandani she was excited to start a new journey, to look for a job that meshed better with her interests, perhaps do a little traveling. She was even considering moving back to Seattle but would have to hang around until the divorce was final, until she and Max completed the division of their assets, sold the house.

Chandani had once known that same kind of forced, fake bravery she now saw in Shan. She projected it, too, during the long years of Harjeet's depression, his darkness, his days spent alone in the bedroom. Ever since he returned from his father's deathbed in Amritsar, her formerly funny, exuberant, gregarious Harjeet had been like a spirit haunting their house, inhabiting an alternate world, parallel to hers, one she could see but not reach. She was forced to feign normalcy when she ran into friends who casually asked what Harjeet had been up to lately. *The flu! Second time this winter!* Or, *Busy with consulting work! Business has taken off!*

When he died by suicide, Chandani felt as if the earth had split open. She'd roll over to his side of the bed, and when she didn't feel his arm wrap around her waist, his hot morning breath tickling her cheek, when she awoke enough to realize that her fingertips were running along the pills of cotton on his pillowcase, not the locks of his hair, she found herself freefalling into the abyss all over again, with nowhere to plant her feet.

Her healing began the day she realized she needed to escape Jersey City. Some of her dearest friends, some of the first people they met when they immigrated to the States, had insinuated that Harjeet's death was her fault, that she'd not been a good enough wife. *Maybe if you had just...* Just what? They had no idea what all she had done to try to help her husband.

Few of her friends believed in mental illness. They condemned therapy and medication. She knew how they talked, how they whispered about someone having "issues in the head." Indians, at least the ones she knew, didn't believe depression was a disease, like cancer. They considered it a character flaw, a sign of a bad marriage, a lack of faith.

A younger niece had convinced her to come to Atlanta to make a fresh start, to get away from the cliques, the wives who centered their lives around their husbands, children, and grandchildren, who didn't know what to do with a widow.

Chandani's "fresh start," until recently, had been a lonely one. She found it difficult to make friends. She knew she could be abrupt, but she wasn't always this way. It wasn't until Harjeet fell ill that she became so defensive, so judgmental. Her niece invited her to parties, but Chandani didn't gel too well with her wealthy Buckhead clique. She couldn't relate to this second generation of Indian Americans. They drank too much alcohol and flirted openly with other people's spouses. She'd declined the last few invitations to dinner parties.

At home, she talked with her sister in Amritsar on WhatsApp, gardened, discovered a love of poetry. Khalil Gibran, Maya Angelou, and Sarojini Naidu were among her favorites. Naidu, in particular, captured the depth of Chandani's grief in "Autumn's Song." *My heart is weary and sad and alone. For its dreams like the fluttering leaves have gone.*

She settled on the steps to her porch, watched Shan slowly pull into her garage. Her neighbor emerged a moment later carrying three bags of trash, set them out in a row on the curb. She paused, set her hands on her hips. A wistful look settled over her face.

Chandani imagined the contents of the bags, what parts of her marriage Shan had disposed of, what she might have needed to purge from her life in order to move forward—receipts from romantic dinners, utility bills for their marital home, checkbooks with both of their names printed in block letters.

"Shan," she called. "Ready for chai?"

"Be there in a few. Just going to wash up first."

Chandani stepped inside the house and headed to the kitchen, where she filled a small cast iron pot with enough water for two full cups. She spent so much of her life married, forty-three years to be exact, she could calibrate water in a pot for two people down to the last drop. How strange it had been to live alone, to relearn food portions. She hadn't noticed how much her husband used to eat until she started halving her own recipes. Even just half lasted her three full meals, though after eating the same thing two days in a row, she'd grow tired of it and simply toss it out.

The chai seemed to replenish Shan a little, or so Chandani thought. She knew her neighbor needed something strong, so she made sure to boil it for a full fifteen minutes, added whole milk, a couple of cinnamon sticks, cracked cardamom seeds, a touch of fresh grated ginger. Feeding Shan, nurturing her was all she could think to do to help.

They sat together in the formal dining room, a room Chandani had decided to reserve for special occasions, dinner parties and such, and as a result, had not used once since moving to Atlanta. She'd purchased the rosewood table and chairs from a furniture importer in Jersey City, who said he got them from the woodshop of a renowned carpenter in Mumbai. Who knew whether this was true? Origin stories, she found, rarely had any truth to them. No matter. She didn't need authenticity to appreciate the set.

In the good years, she and Harjeet loved to entertain at this table, routinely opened their house to the local South Asian community, usually new families who'd been transferred to New York or New Jersey for work. Every Friday night, some thirty, forty people milled about their home, snacked on treats Chandani prepared, usually pakoras and chaat. They sat down to a full dinner around nine, a dinner that Harjeet had spent days preparing. He was a magnificent cook, and not just of traditional Punjabi food. He made lasagna, several kinds of quiche, chili, burritos, hearty soups and stews, and, under the close tutelage of an Ethiopian neighbor, mastered shiro wat. Their guests dined on Harjeet's international menu well past midnight, topped their bellies full, and then pushed all the chairs and tables to the walls of the room so they could dance until the wee hours of the morning.

Chandani picked up a set of matches, lit the candles. Wax budded along the sides forming a column of beads. The flames bobbed and danced whenever Chandani or Shan moved. Either the table or the floor was uneven. Chandani hadn't noticed it until now.

Shan set her cup down. It rattled against the dish. She picked up a pakora, inspected it, nibbled. "Hmm...this is so, so good."

"Shan, do you ever cook Indian food?"

"No. When my dad was living with us, he sometimes cooked it at home. A simple dal, paneer. That's what I remember. But after he left, my mom and I would just get takeout from local restaurants."

"I see," Chandani said.

Shan had lost not only a father but a culture. It made Chandani unbearably sad. One's heritage and traditions kept the ancestors alive long after they'd gone. Chandani still had her grandmother's receipes saved to a file on her computer, her gold earrings in the safe. She had memories, too, of long walks with her grandfather in the evenings, riding on the handlebars of her uncle's bike, the cousin who taught her how to sew. What had been passed down to her, on both sides of her family, was what made Chandani who she was. No wonder Shan seemed so unmoored in life. She was genetically and biologically Indian but had no other Indian roots to speak of.

The silver candlesticks drew Shan's attention. She reached forward, ran her fingertip along the square base of one, and then along the engraved vine that wound around the stick until it morphed into a serpent. The serpent's eyes were rubies. Sapphire and garnet stones encircled the nozzle.

"These are gorgeous," Shan said. "Where did you find them?"

"They're heirlooms, probably at least two hundred years old," Chandani said. "They belonged to my husband Harjeet's mother." Such an odd coincidence that Shan would admire the two items in the entire house that held the largest significance in her husband's life.

"Did she give them to you when you got married?" Shan asked.

"No. She passed away soon after she gave birth to Harjeet. He never knew her."

"How sad," Shan said. She dragged her hand back away from its base, laid it in her lap.

The mark of a child who's lost a parent young is unmistakable. Chandani wondered whether Shan's father's premature death affected her the same way Harjeet's mother's death had affected him. In the early part of their marriage, before the darkness, Harjeet always seemed to be searching for something, for someone, never quite knowing what he was looking for. He'd step out the front door to go to work and walk right back in. "I feel like I'm leaving something at home," he'd tell her. He would retrace his steps through the kitchen, the living room, down the hallway to the bedroom, scanning table surfaces, couch cushions. "Huh," he'd finally say. "I guess I have everything I need."

Shan seemed to have some memories of her Indian father, and from what Chandani could tell, some sort of a relationship with him before he died. Still, she could sense his absence in her gaze, in the way her words hesitated to form.

It must have been hard to grow up in the States with deep brown skin and a white mother. She hoped Shan's mom had been sensitive to this. Her son Kush had a hard enough time as it was. The kids called him Raghead even though he'd never worn a turban. Kush quit believing in God years ago, only dated white women. She blamed the childhood bullying on his abandonment of his culture and faith, wished he could find a way to get back to it. Did bullies know this, she wondered, how their abuse could alter the very identity of their victims, could erase thousands of years of ancestry via incessant humiliation? How they could really break someone with a few cruel comments?

He was a good son, Kush. But the distance between them had grown long and wide since Harjeet's death. He'd not yet visited her in Atlanta.

She dabbed her mouth with a napkin. "There's quite a story behind these candlesticks," she said, clearing her throat. "The Singhs were Sikhs who lived in their home for generations and had planned to return after the chaos of Partition died down, but that's not what happened. The candlesticks, along with some gold and jewelry, were the only things Harjeet's family could carry with them when they fled Pakistan to Amritsar, a city on the Indian side of the border."

Shan raised her eyebrows. "Where in Pakistan were they from?"

"Rawalpindi. Harjeet's family home had already been ransacked and robbed once. His father, Akal, worried that they'd be killed the next time."

"How did they make the journey?" Shan asked.

"They took the train," Chandani said, "at least for most of the trip. They had to stay one night at a refugee camp." She stopped herself there. She promised her husband she would never tell the story. Doing so now would betray his memory, wouldn't it? Didn't promises between spouses outlast death?

Chandani skipped further ahead. "Anyway, they lost everything at the camp except for the candlesticks."

The heater kicked on. The drapes ballooned open from the air rushing out of the vent. Shan ran her index finger around her cup's rim, took another sip. "How did you meet Harjeet?" she asked.

"My family is Hindu and has always lived in Amritsar," Chandani said. "But Harjeet's family and my family became close soon after they came to India. I've known Harjeet since I was a baby."

"So you were born after Partition?" Shan asked.

She nodded. "I'm the youngest of four girls, the only one born after Partition. But I felt its aftermath. Amritsar was a border city, the rope in a tug of war between two new nations. Pakistan insisted that Amritsar belonged to it, just as India wanted to keep Lahore. My mother's sister, Ekta, lived on the opposite end of Amritsar. During a riot, her infant son was knocked out of her arms and trampled upon. He died that night."

"Oh, how awful."

"It was," Chandani said. "Apparently before Partition, my aunt was the funniest person in our family. I'd heard she was always telling jokes, playing pranks on others. She laughed with her whole body. After she lost Geet, she was never the same again."

Chandani gazed at the bottom of her now empty cup and the formation of the remnants of leaves. She'd heard once these patterns told fortunes, predicted the future. As her own future shrunk before her, she seemed to understand less about life with each passing year, how little control anyone had in its ultimate direction. Perhaps there was a freedom in this kind of ignorance, in the not knowing or speaking of all things.

Shan rose, and picked up both teacups and the two plates. "The chai was delicious. Thank you. It was just what I needed."

Chandani wouldn't have normally let a guest clean up in her own house. But over the last few minutes, a fatigue had settled over her. If she was to lay her head on the table, she might fall asleep.

Shan flipped on the faucet in the kitchen, squirted soap onto the dishes, rinsed and set them in the drying rack. "Chandani," she called, "do you mind if I use your bathroom?"

"Not at all. It's down the hallway, the last door on the left."

Chandani rose, blew out each of the candles, plucked the candles from the sticks. She imagined them swaddled inside layers of clothing, tucked deep inside a bag, little Harjeet lugging them through the camp in the dry heat, dust coating his face.

She set the candlesticks in a drawer, paused in the doorway of the dining room. It had been good to sit at the table again, to break the spell of not using it, of not entertaining because Harjeet wasn't there with her. She supposed she had just surpassed another milestone in her life as a widow.

On her way to the living room, she glanced down the hall. The bathroom door was wide open, the light switch off, but there was no Shan. She walked down the hallway, passed her bedroom, which she'd painted lavender, her favorite color, and then the office, with its small desk and folding chair. She arrived at her pooja room, the door ajar. She peeked inside.

Shan was standing in front of the dresser, holding a picture frame. Above her was a painting of Guru Nanak. The peppery scent from incense sticks Chandani lit that morning lingered in the air. She pushed the door all the way open.

Shan turned to face her. "Is this Harjeet? What a handsome man he was. It's a gorgeous photo."

It was Chandani's favorite. She'd taken it herself. In northern New Jersey, she had been a professional photographer. She shot weddings, sari ceremonies, anniversaries, had taken publicity photographs for temples. She hadn't touched her cameras since moving to Atlanta, hadn't even removed them from the bubble wrap. Their cardboard boxes collected dust in the office.

In the photo, Harjeet was young. The first specks of white glinted in his thick beard. His smile was warm, full. It reminded her of his laugh, how he threw his head back, how the sound of it boomed throughout the room. The love and light—this was Harjeet before his illness.

"He *was* handsome, Shan. All my friends were jealous that I ended up with someone with such good looks. But he was so kind and compassionate too. He was always the first to arrive at someone's front door during a crisis. That's what I loved about him most. And he was so much fun. Goodness, we had some wonderful times together. How I miss him!" She had missed their long hikes in the Poconos, the weeks every summer they spent at Cape May. They were long ago, those good years with him, but her memories of them now flooded her with joy.

"How did he die, if you don't mind me asking?" Shan said.

Chandani averted her gaze. The window against the far wall was the only bare window in the house. She liked to keep it uncovered so the full sunlight could shine on her husband's face. No one had asked her how he died. She supposed they didn't care. Once you reached a certain age, people assumed that how one died was irrelevant, inevitable. *Old age.*

Except Shan. Shan seemed to sense there was something more to it.

What was the point of keeping Harjeet's story a secret now that he was gone? In the eighteen months since his death, she'd lived with the burden of his sadness, alone. Kush refused to talk about it. He harbored so much anger toward his father, not just from his death but for the twenty years preceding it, the years Harjeet was simply a man moving throughout their home, not a parent.

"Let's go to the living room," Chandani said. "I'll tell you about my husband."

CHAPTER FOURTEEN
Attari
August 28, 1947

H arjeet's eyes popped open. He turned and buried his face in his sister's armpit to block out the bright afternoon sun shining through the window. Simran flung her arm around him and they found a conjoined position against the bench seat. The hum of the train's engine began to lull him to sleep again, but this time his mind refused to succumb to slumber. It awoke fully, and when it did, so did the numbers. They leapt before him, spun like spokes on a wheel, swirled around him in clouds. All he had to do was reach to pluck them out.

The first few years of his life, he didn't speak. Shortly after his fourth birthday, when Papa-ji had finally become alarmed, he said, "You're four years old, Harjeet. You need to be talking." It was only then that Harjeet decided to open his mouth. "No Papa-ji, I'm four years, three weeks, and two days. 1,483 days, total."

He'd been talking ever since. At seven years old, he knew several thousand words. He wanted to know infinity words, though this was impossible according to Simran. Infinity wasn't an end point or a destination. It could never be quantified. It would always remain just beyond his reach.

Their train journey *was* quantifiable, though. It was two hundred seventy-six kilometers from their home in Rawalpindi to the train's next stop in Attari, just inside the new Indian border. Two hundred seventy-six kilometers equaled 276,000 meters. With another 28,000 meters from Attari to Amritsar, they would have traveled a total of 304,000 meters by their journey's end. The numbers floated around until he could picture them, the multiplication and addition symbols, the numbers encircling and swelling.

They began this morning well before dawn, carrying only a few small bags. "You'll have everything you need at Aunty's house, Harjeet. Irfan Uncle has promised to watch over the house for us and send some of our belongings later." Aside from food and water, they packed their gold, Mummy-ji's wedding jewelry, which would someday become Simran's wedding jewelry, and Mummy-ji's silver candlesticks. They'd never taken such things on other holidays. Those items had always remained behind, locked away safely. But this holiday, Papa-ji had said, was not like other holidays.

Harjeet wanted to ask why but he didn't want to be any more of a nuisance. Three days earlier, when Papa-ji woke them to begin the trip, Harjeet's body was burning up. He had chills and fever, couldn't keep food or fluids down. Papa-ji had to bribe the sales ticket agent at the station to switch their passage to today.

Simran rubbed her eyes. "Harju," she said. "Have we reached Attari? We should be there soon, yes?"

"Must be, bhenji."

His sister gently nudged Papa-ji. On the other side of him, Harjeet's older brother Lacchman snored like a great beast, a monster, something out of the *Panchatantra*. His bhraji could lift Harjeet up with one arm, toss him effortlessly over his shoulder like a bag of rice. Before Harjeet knew it, he would be upside down, the blood rushing to his head, his feet kicking in the air. His bhraji had told him that on this trip he would need to be brave. Harjeet *was* brave. When a small black snake entered the house a few weeks ago, he picked it up, let it loop itself around his arm, freed it in the courtyard, all without calling anyone for help. He'd not let his fear control his actions. "That's *real* bravery," Lacchman had told him.

The train slowed. Harjeet peered out the window, and in the distance, he saw the dot of the station. Already bodies filled every centimeter of space inside of their car. They stacked the bench seats, packed the center aisle. He wondered how many additional passengers would try to board. When he looked up and outside the window, dozens of bare feet dangled over his head. He wondered whether his family should have sat on the roof so they could watch the clouds move across the sky and feel the full wind against their bodies.

"We're at Attari," Harjeet announced, bouncing on the seat. "But there's still 28,000 meters after that."

Lacchman groaned and opened his eyes. He leaned over and ruffled Harjeet's hair. "Thank you, Einstein."

When the train stopped, the passengers jerked forward. The crowd outside on the platform swelled and jostled. Arms extended to every opening. Ahead, Harjeet spotted several train agents walking the length of the cars, blowing whistles, waving their hands. There were shouts coming from inside of the train. Passengers began spilling out of the doorways.

"Something's happening," Harjeet said.

"What is it, Harju?" Simran said.

"Lots of people are disembarking here."

"Some are probably staying here," Papa-ji said, "now that we've crossed to India."

An agent with a white curled mustache pushed the platform crowd back, and addressed the passengers in their car. "Train to Amritsar is canceled," he shouted. "The next one leaves tomorrow morning. Everyone must get off."

They erupted in protest. "We paid to go to Amritsar," a man with dark long beard shouted. "We have no place to stay here."

"I have no control over this decision, Sahib. But you must exit the train now. It needs maintenance. And there's a camp a half kilometer south of here. You can stay there for the night."

"What about tomorrow? When is the train?" Papa-ji asked.

"First one is at seven a.m. Get here early."

A collective groan echoed throughout the car. It startled a small baby whose face crumpled into a frown. Gradually, masses of feet shuffled to one of the doorways. Mothers positioned children on their hips and backs and trudged off the train.

"Will we go to the camp, Papa-ji?" Simran asked, when they could finally move.

He slung a bag over his shoulder and rubbed his temple. "Let's see this camp. Come. Lachhman get the other bag."

They joined the hundreds who spilled onto the platform and fanned out around the station. Some remained on the platform, settled in the shade, and opened sacks of food. The others flowed in the direction of the camp.

Lacchman charged ahead. "Lacchman," Papa-ji called, "let's make sure to stay together. I don't want us to get separated." He nodded and fell back.

Simran tightened her grip on Harjeet's hand. It was warm, strong. Like the one he imagined their mother must have had. "You go in front of me, Harju," Simran said. "Bhenji will follow right behind you."

At fifteen, Simran had always mothered him the best she could. She fed him with her own fingers, drilled him on his math skills, blew on his tea when it was too hot, comforted him at night if he woke with a nightmare, helped him in the bath, scrubbed hard behind his ears, his back, all of the places he couldn't reach himself. He knew real mothers did these things, saw his friends' mothers do them. His sister completed these tasks as well as any mother and probably as well as their own Mummy-ji would have, were she still alive.

The ground was lumpy, uneven. His ankle twisted in the pits in the ground. The skin between his two biggest toes pinched. He would need to wait until they made it to the camp before he removed his chappals.

He focused on his father's shoulders, straight and strong. Papa-ji had been a respected commissioned officer with the British Indian Army. His Papa-ji's Papa-ji, also a soldier, received the Victoria Cross for his bravery. And *his* Papa-ji received the Indian Order of Merit for his bravery during the Battle of Saragarhi.

Harjeet would make make them all proud now. He pretended to be marching with his own regiment, a rifle propped against his shoulder.

They came upon rows upon rows of brown tents. Harjeet tried to do a quick count but had to stop at forty. The number of tents seemed to stretch to the horizon. Hundreds. Perhaps even thousands. When he had a better vantage point, he'd count them all. Travelers milled about, slept on heaps in the ground, squatted in the shade where they could find it. A few children about Harjeet's size chased one another between tents. They were smiling, laughing. Harjeet wondered if this was their new life, here, in this camp, if they, too, had left behind their homes, their schools.

They waited in a line for what felt like hours. Finally, an older gentleman dressed in a white shirt and dark pants with a stack of papers approached them. "I'll help you find a place to sleep tonight. We also have some rice for children but not enough for adults."

"Thank you. But is it safe to stay here?" Papa-ji asked.

"Cholera and typhoid are the biggest risks. A few weeks ago, many fell sick."

"But what do you hear of raids?" asked Papa-ji.

Raids. This was a new word for Harjeet. He would ask Papa-ji what it meant later.

"We've not been disturbed, though the raids are becoming worse in Punjab. Where are you trying to reach?"

"We're boarding the early train tomorrow to Amritsar," Papa-ji said.

"Very good," he said. "It's a quick journey."

That evening, at dusk, Harjeet and Simran sat on the trunk of a fallen tree. A group of children had tried to tempt him in a game of tumbleweed kickball, but he waved them away. Simran squished together balls of rice between her fingertips, placed them in Harjeet's mouth. "Just eat something, Harju," she said. "I know you're hungry."

He opened his mouth. "Look, Simran, the stars! They're starting to appear."

On some hot nights, Harjeet, Papa-ji, Simran, and Lacchman slept on the roof of their home. Simran taught Harjeet how to read the sky, to identify the big dipper, the little dipper, Cassiopeia and Hercules, the Greek myths that inspired the constellations' names, the distance from the earth to the moon, the earth to the sun, the order of the planets, their sizes, from largest to smallest, how the Vedic verses, thousands of years old, first introduced the concept that the sun was the center of the universe, the earth was the shape of a sphere.

He never met anyone as smart as his sister.

He tilted his head. The stars were specks like tiny particles of dust, flames just catching on a wick. It comforted him to know that the sky looked the same here, from this camp, as it did at home, where they were surrounded by friends they'd known and loved their whole lives. How small the earth was, a mere drop of water in an infinite ocean of universe.

He yawned, held up his hand when Simran tried to bring more food to his mouth. "I'm tired, bhenji. Can we go to sleep now?"

Simran set the food down, wiped her hand on a towel. "Yes, Harju, let's get you to bed." She picked up a lantern, lit it. He followed behind her to their tent.

She helped him find a spot to sleep in, made him a small pillow out of her scarf. He waited for her to lie down herself so he could tuck his head in the crook of her shoulder. That's how he slept every night at home, to the rise and fall of her chest, her breath sounds. It was the only way he knew how to sleep anywhere.

Simran leaned over, kissed his forehead. "Get some rest, Harju. Tomorrow, we'll be at our new home with our mother's family. How wonderful will that be?"

He woke to high-pitched screams, the sounds of snapping wood, what felt like an earthquake or a stampede. He bolted up, strained his eyes in the darkness, rubbed his face with the heels of his palms. He searched for movement or shapes in the tent, patted the ground next to him. "Bhenji?" It was cool, flat.

Another scream jolted him out of the fog of sleepiness. A faint, irregular light drew jagged shapes on the outside of the tent.

"Bhenji?" he whispered. "Papa-ji? Lacchman?"

A baby cried out. His spine pricked with fear. He rolled onto his hands and knees, crawled to the tent's flap, slowly lifted it from the bottom.

Columns of smoke spun in the sky like tornados, extinguished the glow of the stars. A small boy huddled next to a tent. His cheeks were coated with tears. An older woman with outstretched arms, a white braid, called out a string of names. A man about Papa-ji's age collapsed on the ground near Harjeet. He was covered in red. It looked as if someone had painted him with a dripping brush.

Harjeet rushed out, crouched near his head. It was the relief worker who had found them a place to sleep. "Uncle, what's happening? Why are you hurt?"

He lifted his head off the ground, spit. "Run!" he said. "Run, my son, now!"

"But my bhenji is here, my Papa-ji and bhraji. I need to find them."

The man's eyes closed. His head fell back.

Harjeet scooted away, stood. He scanned the tents, the frantic, waving limbs. People flew past him. He tried to stop them, to ask if they knew where his family was, but they pushed him aside, yelled at him to hide. A chorus of dogs barked and howled.

"Simran!" Harjeet yelled. "Simran!"

Nearby, tents collapsed. Flames replaced their peaks.

Harjeet jumped inside their tent, scooted across the ground, tossed items in every direction until he found it, the bag with the silver candlesticks, his mother's favorite possession, or so he'd been told. He tore back out, ran away from the camp, up the side of the dune. His feet sunk in the sand with each step. He held his hands straight out in front of him, waved them in the darkness to avoid colliding into trees or other people.

"Papa-ji! Where are you?" he called.

He tripped, crashed to the ground. The bag flew out of his hands, thudded on the other side of a large boulder. He crawled toward it, bumped against something small, soft. A doll. Its tiny hand bunched into a fist. It was spongy and warm, wet. The fingers gradually fell open, like the petals of a flower.

He gasped, recoiled.

The shouts grew louder. They were getting closer. He grabbed the bag, took off.

At the top of a hill, he looked down below. Fires lit the camp. Backs arched, voices raised, fists knocked down those attempting to flee. Some of the residents held their prayerful hands up in surrender, pled for mercy. Others were dragged by their hair along the ground, kicking and screaming. Dozens of men swung bats and wielded swords. They stormed through the makeshift city, deflated the remaining tents, hunting down, Harjeet imagined, more victims. One after another, weapons pummelled heads, torsos, and limbs. The attackers were like an army of ants smothering a piece of food. They mowed down everything and everyone they came across.

Harjeet turned around, crawled behind a tree, clutched his sister's bag. His family would find him. They were looking for him right now. He would wait here. He stayed awake for as long as he could, until the wails from the camp grew softer and the smoke faded in the sky. When the only sound left was the panting of his own breath, he gave in to the weight of his eyelids.

He woke to a violent shaking, a dawning light. He blinked his eyes at the familiar form in front of him, the broad shoulders of his brother. Lacchman's clothes were torn. His eyes were bloodshot, wide, like a mad dog. He thrust Harjeet to his chest, sobbed in his hair.

Harjeet pushed off his brother. "Where were you, bhraji? Where are Papa-ji and bhenji?"

Lacchman's face froze. He turned away, ran his hand over it. "Papa-ji was hurt very badly. Someone is taking care of him now."

"Is Simran with him?"

Lacchman squeezed his eyes tight, flung his arms around his brother. "Oh, Harju."

"Tell me where she is," Harjeet said flatly. "I have the bag with the candlesticks. See?" He opened it, took one out. "She will be so proud I saved them."

Lacchman collapsed on the ground. Tears streaked his dirt-stained face. He buried it in Harjeet's shoulder, choked on his own sobs.

"Lacchman, are you hurt?" Harjeet asked. "Where does it hurt?"

Lacchman touched Harjeet's cheek. "Harjeet, Simran, your bhenji...she died, Harjeet. She didn't survive the raid."

Lacchman made no sense. Bhenji wasn't in the tent during the attack. She had gone somewhere, escaped. She might be at their home in Rawalpindi right now, waiting for them to find their way back. "No, Lacchman. That's not true. She is waiting for us. We must go find her."

Lacchman rolled onto his knees, grabbed Harjeet by the shoulders. "Harjeet, you must listen to me. She's...she's gone. Our sister is gone. I saw it, Harjeet. I saw it with my own eyes. I saw them kill her."

Harjeet grew cold, chilled. He had seen the bad men with his own eyes, had seen them strike people down. He had not seen Simran among them, had not heard her screams. Lacchman was wrong. Their sister was safe.

"Take me to her, bhraji. Please."

Lacchman turned away. "No, Harjeet. She's with God now. She is with our mother."

Harjeet threw down the bag and spun away toward the smoldering heap of the camp. He tore off down the hill, away from Lacchman, toward the charred tents, over limbs detached from bodies, babies crying out for mothers, men beating their chests, women bent over praying.

The stench of death hit him like a slap. It eroded the lining of his windpipe. He choked on it, felt the bile begin to rise in his throat. He tore on, his bare feet thudding against the ground. He would run until he found his sister, until he could nestle himself next to her again, name the constellations with her. If Lacchman's words were true, if she was dead, if her body was here, somewhere on this earth, he would lie down right next to her and never leave. They would still have each other. They would still have the nights, the stars.

CHAPTER FIFTEEN
London
March 17, 2017

Gertrude didn't remember it was her birthday. She hadn't remembered her last few birthdays, couldn't tell if this was because, as an octogenarian, the years passed by so quickly they felt like pages in a flipbook. When she received her breakfast tray this morning, pink carnations lay alongside her silverware with a note wishing her a happy birthday from Pretoria Homes. She thought she was given the wrong tray, called Rachel to retrieve it. Rachel directed Gertrude's gaze to the calendar hanging on her wall, the box indicating the date.

It really *was* her birthday.

With most of Gertrude's friends and family long gone, birthdays had lost their significance. Her parents had died over sixty years ago. How was that possible, to have been separated from them for so long, to have lived a lifetime triple their own?

Clumsiness had aged Gertrude more quickly than she could have ever imagined. Ever since she fell out of her bed two years ago, hit her noggin on the corner of her nightstand so hard she wound up in an ambulance, memories felt like sand slipping through an hourglass. Time no longer seemed concrete, tangible. It floated around her in a bubble, popped as soon as she tried to reach out to it. She'd wake from what she thought was a nap, only to realize it was morning. She'd fall asleep, certain she slept through the night, only to realize it was the middle of the afternoon. The sun and the moon do-si-doed around her in a dizzying dance and she was always two steps behind.

Two knocks sounded on the outside of her door. It couldn't be time for her pills yet. Those damn pills clouded Gertrude's mind, made her see ghosts—her father, in prison, his rail-thin body starved of all nourishment; her brother Gerald, swaddled in a blanket, his body gray and still. She told Carolina, the night nurse, about the apparitions, how they appeared so real she felt she could reach out and touch them. Carolina would simply pat Gertrude's arm, hand her a paper cup, coax her to sip water to wash the pills down.

Gertrude raised the head of her hospital bed higher, shook out the folded flannel blanket wedged in her side, covered herself up. Not that it mattered whether any of the staff saw her in her pale pink cotton nightgown, the one she wore every day, all day. These were the same people who showered her once a week, lifted the pale folds of her sagging, naked skin, scrubbed her inner creases red raw.

There was another knock. "May I come in? You have some mail today."

. Kathy, with the high-pitched, singsong voice, was the third-floor day nurse who always felt the need to talk to Gertrude and all of the other patients as if they were preschoolers during circle time. She meant well (didn't they all), but her sunny countenance grated on Gertrude.

The door cracked opened before Gertrude could respond. She never understood why anyone here asked permission to enter her room when they did what they wanted anyway. Gertrude could answer no to every question they asked her for the rest of her life, and the staff at Pretoria Homes would still go about their business, oblivious to her objections.

Kathy slid inside, squinted at the dim light, flicked on a few switches. She wore pale blue scrubs with pink elephants, had a different set for every day of the week. Gertrude could picture Kathy at her closet every morning contemplating the decision to wear the elephants over the scrubs with the smiling frogs. The dilemmas of some people!

"Miss Trudy, you got some mail! It's been *ages*, hasn't it? I can open it for you. Do you want me to open up your mail for you? Maybe it's a birthday card!"

Gertrude had corrected Kathy on more than one occasion about her name. There had only been two people in the world allowed to call her Trudy. Kathy wasn't one of them.

"Must be a bill of some sort," Gertrude mumbled.

Kathy walked over to the bed, handed her the envelope. She smelled like melons. Not the melons that passed for the peaked fruit salad here, but the honeydew Gertrude's mother used to grow in her garden in Linz. Gertrude remembered being barefoot as a little girl, getting her toes tangled in the vines as they twisted in the ground, the cool, fertile soil under the soles of her feet. She thought of these memories often, the ones from before the war. Those old memories made her feel less alone, not so far away from the country of her birth, the homeland she hadn't visited in over a decade.

She took the envelope, studied its exterior. Her few senile friends had conveniently lost her address over the years, somehow removed Gertrude from their holiday card lists after she landed at Pretoria. It was as if moving to a nursing home was akin to moving to a cemetery.

The envelope had been forwarded from her former home on Foster Street, the apartment she'd lived in for her entire adult life, had inherited from her aunt. The return address was USA. Georgia. Her second cousin's children lived in Virginia, but they'd never mailed her a letter before. They sent her emails, which she checked and responded to the few times she could remember her password.

Kathy eyed the letter, waited for Gertrude to open it in front of her. Gertrude had given up any semblance of privacy living in this place. She wanted to preserve at least this.

"Thank you for bringing it, Kathy. But I can take it from here."

Kathy flashed a pout before stepping away from Gertrude's bed. "Alright, Miss Trudy. I'll be down the hall if you need anything." She hung on the doorknob a moment longer to see if Gertrude would change her mind, if she wanted a companion to open a letter with a foreign address. There was so much drab routine here, so little to look forward to, the staff and the patients brightened at the most mundane of things. Gertrude almost felt sorry for her.

She waited for Kathy to shut the door, for the squishy footsteps of her sneakers to fade down the hallway before she reached for her glasses on the side table, perched them on the edge of her nose. Her red manicured nails maneuvered into the corner of the envelope, slid along the flap. It held a single paper folded into thirds, squared letters in black ink. Penmanship she didn't recognize.

Dear Mrs. Enzenebner…

The author didn't know her well. Gertrude had never been anyone's "Mrs." (This unexpected reminder stung). "Ms." had always sounded too drab. She'd chosen "Miss," clung to the title long after she'd outgrown it, longer still, after her usage seemed uncouth. "Miss" embodied the younger, fun aunt who imbibed a little too much schnapps at family gatherings. It fit her perfectly.

I'm trying to find out some information about my father, Vijay Khanna. I think you may have known him. Or at least, he knew who you were. He had this address for you among some of his old papers.

Her hands opened. The paper dropped into her lap. She slid her fingertips underneath the lenses of her glasses, kneaded the skin. She located the name again, grazed it with her nail to make sure what she read was real, that the words in the letter were not yet another hallucination.

Vijay.

The sweet little boy she once loved as her own.

The memory came to her in a flash: Vijay in a baseball cap, the lid grazing his thick eyebrows, a head that didn't quite fill it, hair that peeked out from the side, curled around his ear like a hook; two slightly buck front teeth, a gap between them; a small, hard fist pounding into a baseball mitt she'd given him for his eighth birthday.

A later memory: Furniture, dozens of boxes, Vijay's bike, Deepa's plants loaded into a moving truck. Their empty apartment. Scraps of packaging paper tumbling in the cross breezes, swirls of dust covering the hardwood floor like beach sand shaped by waves. That raw, hollowed out feeling in her gut.

Gertrude had lost her first family to the war, her second family, the one she created with Deepa and Vijay, to betrayal. If she could go back and relive those last days with Vijay, how different they would have been!

She glanced back at the letter. *I don't know what kind of relationship you had with my father, or when you were last in touch with him. Perhaps you know he passed away thirty years ago.*

Gertrude sucked in her breath, read the words aloud to fully take them in. Thirty years ago, Vijay would have been so young, not even forty. He would have hardly had a chance to live, to father this woman writing to her now. What a cruel God, to snuff out the lives of so many so young—her parents, her brother Gerald, Vijay—while she sat here with over eight decades under her belt.

I was wondering if you had any contact with him during the last years of his life. If you were still in touch with him while he was living in Delhi. If you knew why he moved there.

Delhi. So Vijay made it to the subcontinent, after all.

She slid her legs to the side of her bed to begin a slow motion dismount. Her socked feet stretched toward the vinyl floors until they made contact. She shuffled to her rocking chair by the window, the only piece of furniture she'd been allowed to bring with her here, to this place, with its thousands of "safety" regulations. She bent her body in half, walked her bottom backward until it connected to the seat cushion. The runners crackled under her weight, as if they might snap, squeaked as she rocked back.

She knew Vijay as well as if he'd sprung from her own womb. In the hours he spent in her apartment working on his homework, the afternoons he napped on her couch, in the meals he consumed right across from her, in their walks to and from his school, she came to know what he was thinking before he said it. In four years, she taught him enough German they could converse in her mother tongue.

It was in this language that he finally opened up to her about his mother, how she moved through her life as if the past never existed, refused to talk about the deaths of his Granny Nora from cancer, and Granddad John, just two years later, from a stroke, refused to answer questions about his first set of grandparents, who died years earlier in Delhi. He begged Gertrude to tell him if she knew anything about his father, who he was, his name, where he lived, why he never made contact with them.

At the time, she had only recently come into this information herself. Despite her promise to Deepa, when Vijay crumpled at her feet, cried into her trousers, she had to tell him *something*.

Gertrude stopped the movement of her rocking chair, closed her eyes. She'd hoped, when Vijay was older, he might search for her. She envisioned a teary-eyed reunion, one where she finally got to apologize to him, tell him how much she loved and missed him. No call or letter ever came.

After a few years, she did what she could to push the Khannas out of her mind.

She opened her eyes, straightened in her chair, reread the last line of the letter again.

If you knew why *he moved to Delhi.*

Of course she did.

A pressure deepened in her chest. She slowed her breathing, expelled all of the carbon dioxide before taking in clean oxygen, just the way her respiratory therapist had taught her.

Shan Johnson signed the bottom of the letter. It was a strange name for the daughter of Vijay Khanna. There was a physical address, an email address, and a telephone number. Gertrude wondered what this Shan really knew of her grandmother, understood what trauma could do to a person, how it could make them unknowable. She assumed, given Shan's questions, that Deepa had shut Shan out too.

Gertrude leaned over to the wall, tapped a blue button.

Kathy's voice came over the intercom. "Yes, Miss Trudy? What can I get you?"

"Would you mind coming by my room, please?" Gertrude asked. "I need help dialing an international number."

CHAPTER SIXTEEN
London
November 8, 1958

W hen his mother's voice rose sharply on the other side of the wall, Vijay startled in his seat, spit the straw out of his mouth, set his orange soda down on the kitchen table. He closed his *Eagle* comic book, the latest one in the series, which Miss Trudy had bought for him the day before.

The exchange grew more heated. There were whisper-shouts, like the sound the television made with white squiggly noises when the programs were over. He strained to listen. His mother's heels pounded the parquet wood floors. It was the first argument he'd recalled Ma and Gertrude having.

He broke off a piece of a blueberry scone, chewed it slowly, thoughtfully, wiped the crumbs on his pants. He crept to the door dividing the kitchen from the living room, leaned on it, pressed his lobe against it. It was warm from an afternoon of baking.

He couldn't make out individual words but his mother's voice was shrill.

She was not the most affectionate person. Her tenderness was doled out in small doses, like medicine for a cough. She administered tight hugs and cheek kisses once in the morning, before heading off to work, and again at bedtime, before flicking off the light, and otherwise moved through the world with a sort of impersonal calm, a formality that made her seem immune to anything.

He pushed on the door slightly, until the opening was wide enough for him to hear them at full volume.

They faced each other by the coffee table, his mother in her long dress cinched at the waist, stockings, Miss Trudy still in her apron, bare feet. He watched the rises and falls of their chests. They hadn't noticed him yet.

"He doesn't *have* a father, Trudy," his mother spat.

"He does, Deepa! And all Vijay wants is to know who he is!"

Ma pivoted, moved to the lacy curtains, the window overlooking the street. She crossed her arms. "His father disappeared."

Miss Trudy sighed. She took a few tentative steps toward his mother, rested her hand on her shoulder. "Vijay is almost eleven, Deepa, practically a man. He wants to know who his father is, where he comes from. What if he's been out there looking for the two of you all these years?"

It was Vijay's fault for pestering Miss Trudy for information, for begging her to find out what she could. Miss Trudy was the only person his mother ever let into their lives. She was the only one who could get through to Ma, make her see that pretending the past didn't exist was lonely. It hurt.

He walked over to them.

They locked eyes on him at the same time, stiffened at his sudden presence. Miss Trudy lowered herself to the edge of the couch, laced her fingers over her lap. Mummy-ji returned her blank gaze to the curtains, pushed her hair behind her ear.

"Ma, *please*. This is *my* fault. *I* wanted to know who my father was. I wanted to know how I could find him."

Deepa shifted her weight, dragged her fingernails along her knit sleeve. "You're just a child, Vijay. You don't understand."

"How is keeping information from Vijay about his father helping things, Deepa?" Miss Trudy leaned forward, pushed her sleeves up to her elbows. "It's only natural for the boy to want to know where he comes from. Please, don't deprive him of that."

Mummy-ji furrowed her eyebrows. "You don't have a child, Trudy. You don't know what we've been through, what it's like to raise a child alone, with no family, no help or support."

"*I'm* your family, Deepa. You and your son have *me*. You've had me for the past four years." Miss Trudy stood, walked to Vijay, laid her hand on his shoulder. She smelled of cinnamon and butter. Flecks of flour dotted her apron. "I know what it's like to lose parents too," she continued. "You're not the only person who grieves for family."

Vijay hadn't known this, that Miss Trudy had lost loved ones. He never thought to ask about her family, whether she had siblings, parents. She made him the center of her world, so much so that he never once considered her life before him. He'd been selfish, wholly consumed by her love for him.

It ached to see Miss Trudy, his second mother, upset like this. Ma made sure he completed his homework on time, praised him for his high marks at school, ensured his school uniform was pressed, his tie affixed neatly to his collar. She assigned him extra math problems every night, extra books to read, made his bed every morning, tucked the corners of the sheet tightly

Miss Trudy taught him how to make dough rise for bread,

how to sew on a button, how to draw a dragon, kick a football. She took him on his first Ferris wheel ride, bought him a pink tuft of cotton candy. She tended to his skinned knees, comforted him when his classmates called him a half-caste bastard.

Miss Trudy let him be weak, so that when his mother picked him up in the evenings, he could pretend to be strong.

When he first asked Miss Trudy if she knew anything about his father, she fumbled with the seam on her skirt, encouraged him to ask his mother. But over the next few weeks, he wore her down. She finally said his mother loved his father, that Partition separated them. When Vijay asked for his name, she claimed she didn't know it.

Vijay never believed her.

Still, he'd at least gotten somewhere. Ma had insisted his whole life he never had a father, scolded him for even asking. He couldn't understand why Ma wouldn't tell him this. If his father had loved her, maybe his father would also love him. And he wouldn't know unless they tried to find him.

Ma wrapped her hand around the doorknob. Her breath slowed. Her eyes flitted between him and Miss Trudy. Her face wore an expression of betrayal, reflected a sudden understanding about the special closeness her son shared with his babysitter, instead of his own mother.

"Vijay, get your coat," Ma said softly. "We're leaving right now."

"Deepa, please," Miss Trudy said. "Let's step out in the hall and talk this through."

"I trusted you, Trudy. You were my friend."

"I'm still your friend, Deepa!"

Ma rushed toward him, grabbed his hand, yanked him through the doorway, down the stairwell to the building's foyer. Miss Trudy tore down the steps behind them, one hand grazing the banister, the other hiking up her skirt. "Wait, Deepa. Please. Please, hear me out. I'm sorry. I told him what I did out of love. I thought he should know the truth."

Ma's fingers dug into his wrist. "Trudy, I'm trying to protect him from the truth."

"What truth is that?"

"That his father didn't want me!"

"Deepa, you don't know that!"

Their voices echoed in the foyer, ricocheted off the windows. A first-floor doorknob rattled. An old, bald man stuck his head out, narrowed his eyes, slammed the door shut.

Miss Trudy took his mother's hand. "It's not too late to try to find him, Deepa. He could still be out there, looking for you. If he knew he had a son—"

Ma opened the door. A gust rushed in, flung the door open so hard it bounced on its hinges. A sideways rain splattered their clothing. She stepped into the sheets of rain, squinted as it soaked her lashes. Drops ran down the length of her nose, trailed along her jaw. Her head dropped to her chest. Her own tears mixed with the rain.

He'd never seen his mother cry before, not even at Granddad John's funeral when Vijay was in kindergarten. At the funeral, her face was as smooth as a stone. He'd mistaken it for strength, but understood now it was a mask, a disguise for the feelings she needed to hide in order to survive, to be able to raise him on her own. Vijay had been wrong about his mother. She had never been strong. Only determined. There was a difference that he understood now.

Miss Trudy looked at Vijay, pleaded forgiveness with her eyes. But something had shifted inside of him. It was as if he'd suddenly grown from a boy into a man, a man who needed to take care of the woman who needed him the most.

He stepped back inside, wrapped his arms around Miss

Trudy's waist, and squeezed her tight. "I love you, Miss Trudy," he said. He then turned away from her, pressed his hand against his mother's back.

"Ma, come," he said. "It's time for us to go."

CHAPTER SEVENTEEN
Atlanta
March 17, 2017

Her cell phone vibrated through the empty house like a dentist's drill. Shan abandoned a vase half entombed in bubble wrap, wiped her hands on her pants, jogged toward the foyer. The soles of her sneakers crunched over loose staples, stray nails, crumbs of stale food, debris she uncovered when she rolled up the hallway rug.

She found it leaning just inside the front door, against the glass of the transom. The screen, with a long string of numbers, reflected in the beveled glass. She picked it up, flipped it over.

"Hello?"

"Is this Shan? This is Gertrude from London."

Shan pressed the phone harder against her ear. "I'm sorry, who did you say you are?"

"Gertrude. You sent me a letter."

Shan leaned against the banister. This *couldn't* be. She assumed the name and address would be a dead end, had forgotten completely about mailing the letter, when was it? Three, four months ago?

"I'm sorry, I'm a little stunned. I didn't expect to hear from you," Shan said. "I didn't know if the address was still current."

"It wasn't current. The post forwarded your letter to me here, at this godforsaken place." She sighed heavily. "I'm sorry for your loss, Shan. I knew your father a long time ago, when he was a little boy. He was very dear to me. I'm so terribly sad to hear he's gone, and has been gone for such a long time."

"Thank you. I appreciate that."

Gertrude had an accent, though not a British one. It sounded German, slightly guttural, breathy. The thought had occurred to Shan, when she first discovered the index card with Gertrude's contact information, that Gertrude had been a former lover of her father's, the woman he left her mother for, his overseas mistress. But it was clear her affection toward him was maternal.

Shan had been searching online for Deepa Khanna too, for about a month. But she hadn't gotten anywhere. She wondered why she bothered chasing a grandmother who had never wanted anything to do with her. She wondered whether she was replacing her grief over her broken marriage and miscarriage with a fresh wave of grief for her long-dead father and her estranged grandmother. Her identity had begun to be defined by the holes family members left behind. Perhaps she needed to move forward, not backward.

So she quit searching completely, concentrated on her next steps—putting the house up for sale, finding a place to live, looking for another job. She had placed her father's box of personal affects into a larger moving box, sealed it shut.

And yet, here was Gertrude.

"You said he was living in India at the time of his death?" Gertrude asked.

"Yes. He and my mom separated when I was five," Shan said. "We stayed in Seattle, he moved to Delhi. Mrs. Enzenebner—"

"Gertrude. Please call me Gertrude."

"Sorry. Gertrude, can you tell me how you knew my father?"

The rhythmic creaking in the background on the other side of the line now went silent. "I was his babysitter," Gertrude said. "Though that title doesn't adequately convey what Vijay meant to me. I came to love him like a mother loves a son," she said tenderly. "I never had children. He was it for me."

"Oh," Shan said. Her father had never even mentioned a Gertrude to Shan. She felt sorry for her, how vested she had been in him emotionally, how it didn't appear her father returned the affection equally. It seemed the list of people her father had abandoned was a long one. There had been many broken hearts in his wake.

"So, you must have known Deepa too," Shan said.

"She was my friend, my best friend. She and Vijay moved into my building soon after Deepa's adoptive parents passed away. Deepa had been trying to raise Vijay by herself while teaching full time. During those four years, the three of us formed a sort of makeshift family."

Something didn't add up. Deepa and Gertrude were friends, but not good enough friends for Gertrude to know that Shan's father died three decades earlier.

"When was the last time you heard from either of them?" Shan asked.

Gertrude sighed again. "Vijay was eleven. Your grandmother and I had a fight, a serious one. They moved out of my building a few days later."

Shan made her way to the kitchen, sat down at the table.

"Why would my father have kept your name and address with his personal papers if he hadn't been in touch with you since he was a child?"

There was a pause at the end of the line.

"I have no idea, Shan. I never heard from him again. But I would love to think that perhaps he'd been thinking of finding me after all of these years," Gertrude said. "Or, perhaps the real reason he kept my contact information has something to do with the question in your letter. You asked me why Vijay moved to India. I think he wanted to try to find his father, who might have been living in Delhi at the time. I was the only person, aside from Deepa, who knew anything about him."

Shan shifted the phone to her other ear. "You knew who my grandfather was?"

"Shan, have you had this conversation with Deepa? I interfered once and hurt her very badly in the process. I won't do it again."

"I haven't seen my grandmother since I was ten," Shan said. "She disappeared after my father died. I've spent hours searching for her online. There are a million Deepa Khannas living in London."

"You're probably looking in the wrong place," Gertrude said. "A long while back, right before her book was published, I heard she moved out of the UK. But I don't know where."

"She published a book?"

"A collection of poetry," Gertrude said. "As far as I know, it was her first and last one. I have a copy of it here somewhere. It's one of the few things I brought with me here to the nursing home."

Shan heard several thuds, items colliding into one another.

"Here it is. *Exodus*, by Kavita Grover."

"Who?"

"Kavita Grover. Deepa's pen name. Kavita was her mother's name. Grover was her favorite school teacher's name."

"Hold on a minute, Gertrude."

Shan dashed into the living room, unstacked several of the boxes, found the one marked, BEDROOM. She ripped off the tape with her fingernails, opened the flaps, tossed the clothing to the side. Her father's box sat at the bottom. She exhumed it, lifted off the top. *Exodus* sat just inside. She flipped to the back cover.

In a stunning debut collection of poetry, Kavita Grover recounts India's Partition. Below the description was the author's brief, bare-bones bio.

She was born and raised in New Delhi and moved to London at age sixteen.

This was why the book was among her father's things. It was *his mother's.*

Shan picked up the phone. "I found it! I have a copy of the book too. I don't believe it."

"I don't know what transpired between you and your grandmother, or why you two are estranged," Gertrude said. "But if she's still alive, you need to do what you can to reach out to her. Before you know it, you'll be as old as I am, shut up in a nursing home somewhere, your life dependent on the call button next to your hospital bed."

A voice emerged in the background, urging Gertrude off the phone. "Shan, we'll need to continue this another time. I'm being told I'm tired, even though I'm not, that I need to get some rest, even though I don't."

"Wait, Gertrude, one last thing. If you lost touch with Deepa, how did you know about her book? How did you know she was Kavita Grover?"

"I didn't, initially," Gertrude said. "I found the copy of the book waiting outside my door the year it was published. It was wrapped in brown paper, tied with twine. There was no return address, no other identifying marks. It wasn't until...oh, here it is, on the third page. It wasn't until I read the dedication that I knew, with certainty, that Deepa had written it.

The voice in the background grew more persistent. "I've got to be going now, Shan. Good luck on finding Deepa, and please, keep in touch."

The line went dead.

Shan set the phone down, opened the cover of the book. She flipped past the copyright page, a blank page, to the dedication, to another name she'd never heard of before but one she seemed to know, intimately, as soon as she read it.

For Amir Rahim.

CHAPTER EIGHTEEN
Atlanta
April 15, 2017

S han sliced through the packaging tape of the large cardboard box with an X-Acto knife, winged the flaps open,
removed a layer of sweaters, sweatshirts, a few scarves
she'd never worn in winters never cold enough. She lifted
out picture frames shrouded in bubble wrap, set them on the
coffee table of her new, temporary abode, a small, one-bed-
room apartment a few miles from her former marital home.

She stood, stretched her legs, walked over to the desk. In a
single relocation, she'd downsized decades of her life, reverted
to the postcollegiate living quarters of a cramped apartment,
minimal furniture.

Before her laptop, she considered, briefly, following up on
the twenty or so resumes she submitted to potential employ-
ers, all law firms of various sizes and specialties.

The truth was she didn't actually miss practicing law.

She needed an income eventually. She and Max had amica-
bly worked out the division of their property. She would keep

all of the money in the investment account, all of her retirement (an amount far more substantial than his), her share of the proceeds from the sale of her home.

The money gave her wiggle room.

She thought about traveling for a bit, perused the old India travel guide she'd come across in her father's box. The memory of her day with her father at the Taj Mahal returned to her full force. She wished she'd been more grateful to him for taking her there.

Exodus perched nearby. She cracked it open, perused the poems. Kavita, the sentient poet, seemed to be the polar opposite of Deepa, the impenetrable grandmother. In "Engine," she wrote:

I will lay railroad tracks across continents, one plank after another in perpetuity. Look for my reflection in the rails, listen to the vibration of my voice.

Why must words fail me now, when only syllables can bridge the distance, the gap of our sorrow, the abyss between our entwined souls.

How different would her grandmother's life have been—would Shan's father's life had been—if Deepa had learned to open herself up to others in the same way she opened herself up in her poems?

She pulled her laptop closer. In the search engine, she typed *Kavita Grover writer*.

Several entries appeared. Most of them belonged to journalists. She tried again with *Kavita Grover poet*. Then *Kavita Grover Exodus*. Nothing of significance appeared. This was not surprising. The book's copyright, 1986, predated the internet. It seemed Deepa would continue to elude online, as she had in real life.

Shan leaned over the desk, picked out a few dead leaves from the plant pot on the windowsill, turned it slightly, so that it received more light. If Deepa—a woman who lost her parents, her adoptive parents, her son, who dispensed with her only friend—was still alive today, how would she be moving through the world? What would her life look like?

Shan imagined the meals eaten alone at the kitchen table, the nights curled up on a bed without the body heat of another, holidays spent in solitude. To lose so much, to endure so many consecutive losses in isolation was something she couldn't quite comprehend.

She flipped to the dedication page in *Exodus*.

Amir Rahim.

If Deepa was so keen on never being found, on never being known, she would never have dedicated the book to Amir. Despite using a pen name, she couldn't resist leaving a clue to her past in her volume of poetry.

She turned back to the screen, typed *Deepa Khanna Partition*, scrolled through the results. Nothing on point. She then tried *Kavita Grover Partition*.

A few pages in was an entry for an organization called the Partition Project. A header in black cursive spread across the home page. A yellow box highlighted its mission statement. *Since its founding in 2004, the Partition Project's mission has been to collect as many stories as possible from firsthand witnesses to the 1947 Partition of India and Pakistan and upheaval in the the years that followed.*

Shan scrolled a little lower to a heading entitled "Delhi." It listed several photos with names and links to testimonies. A Kavita Grover stood against a wall in cotton pants and a long, loose blouse. A casual salwar suit. Her hands were behind her back, her legs crossed at her ankles. Shan magnified the photo. Her mouth turned up at the corners in a slight smile. Her wide-set eyes stared off to the side. She had a short forehead, thick eyebrows.

She was young, and familiar. Her profile matched Deepa's, Vijay's, and even Shan's—a perfect continuity of gene dominance. *This was her grandmother.*

Shan tapped on the link. Deepa's life story appeared. She had submitted it in late 2014, less than three years ago. Which meant she could still be alive today.

Deepa had written about her home in New Delhi, her parents' medical clinic, her father's political views, his marches alongside Gandhi for a unified India. She described the increasing hostilities in their neighborhood as Independence approached, the raging fire that had consumed their medical clinic, the moment she realized both of her parents were trapped inside.

I regret, some days, that I didn't force my way into that building, not so much to rescue them, but to die with them.

Shan gasped. She knew her great-grandparents had died tragically. She had no idea how or why, that Deepa, their only child, had witnessed their horrific end. She wondered whether her own father had ever known this.

At the end of her statement was her bio.

Kavita Grover teaches poetry at Amsterdam College, the Netherlands.

Gertrude was right. Deepa *had* moved out of London. And now Shan knew exactly where she was.

She took screen shots of the entire passage and returned to the organization's home page. *Over the past three years, the Partition Project has collected over 2,000 testimonies from people in their seventies, eighties and nineties. Time is running out to record as many surivors' stories as possible.*

She clicked on the header, *Map*. It listed all of the regions of the subcontinent. Her cursor moved over Bangladesh, Pakistan, India. The numbers reflected how many stories the Project had collected from each region to date.

What if her grandfather's story lingered here in the database alongside her grandmother's?

She clicked on Delhi. Typed *Amir Rahim* in the search bar. *0 results.*

She remembered, then, her father's box and the trip he planned on taking to Lahore.

She clicked on the Pakistani city, typed *Amir Rahim.*

3 results. None of the survivors had a birth year that would have made them a teenager during Partition.

She checked the time. She had fifteen minutes before she had to meet Chandani for lunch. She picked up her wallet, grabbed her keys, swung the door open. She paused in the doorway. There was one more person she knew who had a Partition story. He was from Rawalpindi. She knew both his first and last names.

She sat down before her laptop, opened the search bar for Rawalpindi, typed *Harjeet Singh.* Seven results appeared. Halfway down the page, she came across the exact same black-and-white photo from Chandani's pooja room.

Her beloved husband had recorded his story.

CHAPTER NINETEEN
Amritsar
August 12, 1996

H arjeet wiped the sleep from his eyes, peered out of the dusty, oval airplane window at the new Sri Guru Ram Dass Jee International Airport. The last time he came to Amritsar, he had to take a train from New Delhi. Now the bustling city had its very own airport.

The tarmac teemed with airplanes, passengers, rows of luggage. Businessmen and women filled every seat in the airplane, their briefcases perched on their laps, black pens scratching yellow steno notepads. The plane's engine cut off and with it the air conditioner. Amritsar in August was a fiery sort of hot. He felt it immediately, the way the heat seeped into the seams of the plane, how it rushed through the cabin when the flight attendant propped open the door. Each inhale brought a lungful of burning air.

He'd grown accustomed to life in the United States, to indoor spaces cooled to near frigid temperatures, to the endless stream of electricity with no interruptions. He had forgotten what it was like to bake, to steep in sweat, to soak through layers of clothes in mere seconds.

Seven years had passed since his last trip to India, when he came to say goodbye to Lacchman, who was dying of end-stage hepatitis. His strong-as-an-ox older brother, who sired four sons with his wife Neema, had taken his first drink soon after Simran's death, and spent the rest of his life attached to a bottle of some sort. At the hospital, Harjeet knelt by his side, kissed his hand. Lacchman forced open his mouth and uttered the last words he would ever speak, before he slipped into a coma and passed away three days later.

I should have protected Simran.

It wasn't merely the words that haunted Harjeet on his way back to New Jersey. It was his brother's anguish as he spoke them. The raid in Attari was not Lacchman's fault. And yet, his brother's very last emotion before dying was guilt over that night.

Harjeet's home in Amritsar looked nothing like he remembered it. The awnings were gone. Heavy opaque wooden doors replaced the wrought iron. Greek columns framed the entryway. His father was always trying to improve on the house in some way, to recreate their former home in Rawalpindi, which had been in their family for three generations before they were forced to abandon it during Partition. After leaving it, they were never able to return or retrieve any of their belongings.

In the small back corner room, his father, Akal Singh, curled up on his side. His bony limbs peaked out of the border of the quilt. The room reeked of menthol, urine.

"Papa-ji," Harjeet began. "It's me. Your son, Harjeet."

His eyelids stretched open, fixed on the ceiling. "It's been such a long time, my son. I didn't think I'd see you before the end."

Harjeet sat on the edge of the bed. A pale light shone on

his father's face. His jowls hung on either side of his neck like chicken giblets. His breath was short, ragged. He'd lost weight, gained creases around his eyes. His beard was solid white.

End stage heart disease, his nurse had told Harjeet over the phone.

"I should have visited more often," Harjeet said. "I'm sorry, Papa-ji."

When Harjeet and Chandani married, he told her point blank he was never going to return to India. She could go by herself to see her own family in Amritsar, and both families would be welcome in their new home in the United States, but he couldn't spend another minute on the same subcontinent that robbed him of his beloved Simran. For the most part, he had kept his promise, only returning to say goodbye to Lacchman.

"Harjeet," his father said. "Why did you come now?"

Harjeet shifted his weight, folded his hands. "You were a good father. You took such good care of us after bhenji died. I should have taken better care of you."

"I had help from your aunts and uncles, Harju. I never had to do it alone. But this is not the real reason you came to see me."

Harjeet spent all of his adult life away from Papa-ji. And yet, his father could see right through him. Distance and time were inconsequential. If Harjeet had learned anything as a child, it was how to be a respectful, obedient son, how to show up for the man who raised him, no matter how much time had passed.

"Help me sit up, my son," Papa-ji said.

He gathered his father under his arms, hoisted him higher on the bed. He fit two pillows behind his back.

"Do you know what I remember most about Simran?" his father asked, anticipating Harjeet's question.

"No, Papa-ji."

"I remember the day you were born, how after your mother passed, Simran held you in her arms and rocked you to sleep. I remember the way she looked into your eyes, how she whispered that she would always take care of you, that she would never leave your side. That's what I hear in my dreams. Your sweet sister making that promise to you."

"I didn't know that, Papa-ji. Thank you for telling me. "

His father reached out his trembling hand, laid it on Harjeet's knee. "I'm so sorry about that night, my son. You'd already lost your mother. You needed your bhenji."

"It was my fault she died," Harjeet said. His throat tightened on the words as they left his mouth. This was a confession he'd been holding in his entire life, the guilt that kept him from returning to Amritsar. He had been running away from this truth, and in the decades since, it had eaten away at his very soul.

The screams from that night—they never left him. They invaded his dreams every night for years. Had one of those screams been Simran's? Could he have rushed down from the hill to save her? The day after the raid, the train never came. Papa-ji and Lacchman had to drag Harjeet through the desert for several kilometers until a military bus agreed to transport them to Amritsar. Harjeet pled with them to leave him at the camp with Simran, to let him die with her.

"If I hadn't gotten sick, we would have left to Amritsar a few days earlier," Harjeet added. "We would have made it safely. We wouldn't have spent the night at the camp. Simran would have lived."

His father's mouth dropped open. "Is this what you've thought all these years, my son?"

Harjeet turned away. He spotted a small rosewood bench wedged against the wall. A faint memory came to him then, of him and Simran playing hide and seek in their old home, her hands covering her face, him crouching behind a similar bench, the same hiding place he used every time, her pretending she couldn't find him anywhere, pretending to cry over his continued absence, giving up, collapsing on the bench, him springing up behind her, giggling.

"Of course, Papa-ji," Harjeet said. "It was my fault.

His father covered his eyes. A low moan escaped his lips.

"Are you in pain? Shall I call the nurse?"

"Harju, is this why you've stayed away from all of us these years? From India?"

The circumstances of his sister's death had weighed on Harjeet with each of Simran's birthdays, each anniversary of her death, each anniversary of India's Independence, each memory of his bhenji that gradually faded over the years. Harjeet's guilt and grief had been one in the same, entwined so intimately he couldn't tell where one emotion ended and the other began. When Chandani finally got pregnant, after years of trying, he prayed for a daughter to name after his sister. A part of him felt Simran's loss all over again when Kush was born. He loved his son but wanted so desperately to see his sister again, to see any semblance of her in a daughter.

"I should not have stayed away," Harjeet said. "It was selfish of me to act as if I was the only one in pain, as if only *I* had suffered. Please forgive me, Papa-ji."

His father slowly shook his head. "You are wrong. I am the one who needs *your* forgiveness. I am the one responsible for Simran's death. No one else."

"You couldn't stop the raid, Papa-ji."

"That's not how your sister died," he whispered.

"Of course it was."

His father fell silent. He shut his eyes. "I woke in the night to chaos, Harjeet. I told Lacchman and Simran to stay put while I found out what was happening. You were still sleeping. I didn't want to wake you—you'd only be frightened. Outside several Sikh men huddled together, frantically exchanging information. Invaders had started setting fire to the tents on the other side of the camp. They were slaying people, taking the women and girls."

"We didn't have enough weapons to fight," Papa-ji continued. "One of the elder Sikhs suggested we martyr our women and girls while we still could. He called for them to be brought out of the tents, to kneel in a straight line, for each of the men to take a turn with the sword. I couldn't bear the thought! But Simran ran to us with the other women. She hugged me and said she was ready to go be with God. I told her to run. She refused! She knelt down with the others. Then came my turn with the sword."

Harjeet felt sick. He could hardly breathe. He had heard stories like this one, some of the darkest chapters of Partition, where husbands, brothers, and fathers killed their own wives, sisters, mothers, and daughters, for fear they'd be kidnapped, raped, and converted.

He never imagined this was his own family's story too.

"Simran was so brave, Harjeet!" His father's voice livened. "Lacchman saw with his own eyes how courageous she was. She did not cry. She was not afraid. She put her hands together and began praying. With one slash of the sword, your bhenji was with God!"

The room spun. Harjeet stood, stumbled toward the window. He tried to push away the image seizing his mind, the sharp blade of the sword slicing through his sister.

He covered his face with his hands. "No...no...Papa-ji, we could have hid Simran somewhere!"

"She was right to do what she did, to become a martyr instead. She died a righteous Sikh woman!"

A rage filled Harjeet. "How could you let that happen? How could you not protect her?"

His father's eyes went wide, and when they did, Harjeet could see death gazing back at him, his mother's death, his sister's, Lacchman's, and now his father's own imminent end. Papa-ji had been a fool, a fool who believed there was a difference between martyrdom and murder, a fool who believed that fate demanded such brutality from a father's own hands.

Harjeet released him. Without another word, he backed out of the room, down the hallway. When he reached the bathroom, he splashed water over his face and sunk to the floor.

It wasn't his father's confession that sickened him so. It was Harjeet's realization that even when he was a little boy, he knew, deep down, that there was more to the story of what happened to Simran. It was one of the reasons he moved to the United States, to the opposite side of the earth. And by doing so, he'd become complicit in the lie too.

Harjeet pulled himself up, exited the bathroom. The nurse greeted him in the living room. She wore a stethoscope around her neck, was holding a blood pressure cuff. "Sahib, are you feeling ill? Will you be joining your father for his tea?"

He glanced one last time around the main room, a place where he once sat on Papa-ji's lap, took sips from his chai, listened to his stories about their Simran, their former lives in Rawalpindi. The stories of their happy life covered up a horrific truth.

"No," he finally said. "Please tell my father I said goodbye. I'll be on the next flight out."

CHAPTER TWENTY
Atlanta
Later, April 15, 2017

I t was the first really warm day of spring. The oval table
sat in the shade of an oak tree. The breeze ruffled the
buds of tulips not quite fully opened. Chandani removed
her sunglasses, let the sunshine wash over her.

Something was on Shan's mind. She could barely look
Chandani in the eye, shifted several times in her seat. She
stared at the menu in deep concentration, hummed.

"So many great choices," Shan said. "It's going to be hard
to decide what to get."

"I'm in no rush," Chandani said. "Take your time."

Their evolving friendship was an odd one. What forty-one
year-old wanted to spend time with a sixty-five-year-old? Since
Shan's miscarriage, Chandani had come to believe an older
widow and a younger divorcée could have quite a bit in common. They were both trying to figure out who they were without their long term partners and how to stand on their own two
feet again.

For Chandani, it was nice, this allegiance. Their friendship made her feel useful for the first time since Harjeet's death. Shan had found in Chandani a conduit for her culture, her heritage, for the country of her family's origins, and Chandani found in Shan someone who took great interest in her memories of her childhood and young adulthood in India. Not long after Chandani told Shan that Harjeet's sister died in a refugee camp raid during Partition, Shan revealed that her father moved to India in 1981 to search for his own father who disappeared during Partition, and more recently, that her estranged grandmother had written a book of poetry under a pen name and dedicated it to Shan's missing grandfather.

Funny, wasn't it, how one person could unlock the mysteries of another like the combination on a safe?

There was something about the age of forty, that sort of midway point of life, when people started to feel the need to be connected to the generations before them. Last night, Kush called. They had a long talk. It was the best conversation they'd had since she moved down to Atlanta. He told her he was planning this fall to go to Kolkata with Physicians Abroad for six months. He'd take a side trip to Amritsar to visit members of the family he hadn't seen since he was a small child. She didn't know what compelled him to do this, after so many years of distancing himself from his heritage. But it appeared that at age forty-two, he was going to search for his own roots, much in the same way Shan was now searching for hers.

A waiter approached the table, took their orders. They handed over their menus, sipped on their waters.

"Thanks for meeting me," Shan said.

"I love this place," Chandani said. "They make the best samosas in town." Her first meal in Atlanta was here, at this Indian restaurant. It was also her first meal in a restaurant since Harjeet died. The rest of the food was so-so—she could get far better Indian food in New Jersey. But the restaurant had come to symbolize something for her—taking that first scary step in a new life alone. She was glad this time to bring a friend.

Shan nodded, pulled the sleeves of her long-sleeved shirt over her thumbs, glanced down in her lap.

Chandani noticed that Shan had finally gained back some weight since the collapse of her marriage. Her skin glowed. Her hair was shorter, chin length, in soft layers around her face. A faint sheen of gloss coated her lips, a silver square pendant hung around her neck, a chunky ring with a stone, tiger's eye, replaced her wedding band. There was a spark to Shan that Chandani hadn't seen before.

Shan swirled her glass. The ice clinked against the inside. She stopped, watched as the ice stilled. "Chandani, I'm going to the Netherlands. I think I know where Deepa is. She used to teach at Amsterdam College."

"Really?" Chandani asked.

"I pulled this up on my walk over here. Take a look." She tapped a few times on her phone, turned the screen toward Chandani. It was a website for the college with a list of upcoming events. Shan's finger pointed to one event in particular.

Retired poetry professor Kavita Grover will be reading new work, as well as poems from her collection, Exodus.

"It's in a few weeks," Shan said. "She's the featured reader."

The server set their appetizers in front of them. Chandani shook out her napkin, laid it on her lap. "Have you thought about calling or emailing her first?"

Shan picked up a wedge of naan, took a bite, chewed slowly. "I could, but I worry she'll just ignore my messages. Besides, I need to talk to her face-to-face. I've learned some more information about her life, Chandani. I think I've misjudged her. I should have tried to reach out to her years ago."

Shan told Chandani about the Partition Project, a website archiving survivors' testimonies, and Deepa's account about how her parents died.

"I knew that Deepa's parents died tragically," Shan said. "Until I came across this website, I had no clue how. I also didn't know Deepa was with them when they died. That she tried and failed to save them."

"My God," Chandani said. "That's truly awful. I'm so sorry to hear it." She wondered if her relatives in India knew about the Partition Project, if they'd ever tried to record their memories, anywhere, of that terrible time. Chandani's aunt, Ekta, passed away ten years ago. No one ever talked about her infant son's death during Partition. In another generation, Geet and his short life would be forgotten about completely.

Shan cleared her throat, set down her spoon. She wiped the corners of her mouth with her napkin. "There's something else, Chandani. Right before coming here, I ran a different search on the same website. And I found a video of Harjeet."

Chandani's spoon was midway to her mouth. She set it back in the bowl. "You found a video of *my* Harjeet? Are you absolutely certain it was him?"

Shan nodded. "The photo next to the link is the exact same photo from your pooja room. I watched the video. It's his story. It was posted on February 4, 2015."

Chandani sucked in her breath. Her elbows slipped off the edge of the table, knocked over her glass. Shan reached over quickly, righted the glass, and grabbed a few napkins to soak the spill up. She then reached across the table and took Chandani's hand. "Chandani, are you okay?"

She nodded, cleared her throat. "Harjeet...he died on February 25, three weeks later," she said. Her palms suddenly felt cold, clammy. Her chest felt tight, as if her ribs might crack.

He hadn't left a note. There had been no final confirmation that he loved her, that she made him happy, that he was sorry for leaving her. No goodbye, after so many years together. She had deserved one.

She pushed her chair back, slung her purse over her shoulder. "I have to go, Shan. I...I need to see the video at home, for myself. Alone."

Shan signaled the server for the check. "Let me just get this and I'll drop you off at home," she said.

Chandani left Shan at the curb and rushed inside. She didn't look back, didn't thank her for lunch. There was a burning in her to see her husband, to hear his voice. She had to get to him.

She sat down at her desk, opened her laptop. As Shan promised, an email with a link to his story was waiting in her inbox. She tapped the touchpad. A still frame of his image appeared before her. It took her breath away.

Her Harjeet. Her handsome, lovely husband. Oh, how she'd missed that sweet face, those eyes, a deep brown, so expressive, those eyebrows, dramatic, his perfectly manicured beard, and the feel of it between her fingertips.

He was sitting on some sort of a stool. She didn't recognize the room. It looked like a classroom. She tried to think back to the day he recorded it, where she might have been, how he might have gotten away from the house without her knowing. He'd rarely left the house the last twenty years of his life.

She pressed play, leaned closer to the screen.

His low, husky voice resounded in the room. It was as if he was sitting right in front of her. She reached out, touched him. Her finger met only the hard surface of the screen. He was steady, calm, as if reading from a teleprompter. He talked briefly about the few memories he had of living in Rawalpindi, mentioned his mother's death soon after his birth, and then began recounting the day they left their homeland.

Harjeet then recalled the train ride, the unexpected stop in Attari, and the harrowing night in the camp. He had not spoken to Chandani about it for decades. Hearing it again, so fresh and vivid in his mind, seeing it on his face, in the tone of his voice, reminded her how deeply and how heavy this trauma and grief had weighed on him. Had she *really* supported him in the ways he needed her to? Were there moments when she had chosen to look away from his pain, when she should have done more to carry it with him? She now didn't know. Truthfully, she could have been a better wife. She could have extended her Harjeet more grace, compassion, and patience. She should have done *more*.

After he relayed learning about his sister's death, his image froze on the screen. The clip had finished.

She collapsed back into her chair. Her chest heaved. She placed her hand on it. She was about to close her laptop, when the video continued.

It was Harjeet again in the same room. He was no longer wearing his blazer. He slumped lower in his chair. A glass of water now sat on the table next to him. His eyes appeared moist. He sniffed.

She inched forward, turned up the volume.

"That was the story I was told about my sister, Simran." His voice cracked. He turned his head to the side, pursed his lips, swallowed. "It was all... it was all a big lie. I saw my father last in 1996, just before he died," he said. Harjeet lifted the glass, brought it to his lips, sipped. "The Sikh women at the camp were not murdered by the raiders. The Sikh men decided... decided to... martyr their own women and girls."

He glanced at the ceiling. The camera zoomed closer on his face. His head dropped. "My father killed my bhenji."

"Oh, no," Chandani gasped. "No, no, no."

A hand appeared at the bottom of the screen, offered Harjeet a tissue. He took it, pressed it against each of his eyes, folded it in one of his hands.

"Ever since my father told me this, I haven't been able to...I have had great difficulty getting out of bed. I've been in therapy, on antidepressants, sleeping pills. I can't...I can't seem to get the image out of my mind. It's...it's killing me."

He regained his composure, looked once more directly into the camera. "That's all I wanted to say. Stop recording please."

The screen went black. Chandani laid her hands on her chest, closed her eyes. The day Harjeet returned from India after his father's death, he looked as pale as a ghost, said he picked up the flu. She cared for him those first several days, brought him his tea, cooked simple rice dishes, kept the blinds closed, his room cool, just as he asked.

She never believed his flu story. She figured he was grieving his father's death.

But her Harjeet never got better. He slowly shed his business clients, told them he was semi-retiring. He quit coming to the phone when Kush called from college. He was no longer interested in their after-dinner walks to the local park. They used to take breadcrumbs to feed the ducks at the pond, would sit together on the bench and watch the sunset before heading back home. He quit wanting to host dinner parties and stopped cooking altogether.

She could never have imagined that the man she dropped off at the Newark airport for a trip to Amritsar would return to her such a different man. That he would spend the last third of his life battling such demons.

Three weeks after the time stamp on the video, she went shopping with her girlfriends to Manhattan. When she returned, she found him lying in bed next to three empty pill bottles.

She stepped away from the computer, curled up on the sofa. Goosebumps budded along her skin despite the warm air. For twenty years, she blamed the wrong ghost for her husband's depression. It wasn't Simran who haunted him all these years. It was his father.

Guilt and grief had not killed her Harjeet. The revelation of a horrific truth had.

CHAPTER TWENTY-ONE
Amsterdam
April 3, 2017

The sky was gray but bright, as if at any moment a slice of light would cut through its opaque layer. A gust of wind ruffled Shan's hair, chilled her neck. She pulled her collar up around her ears, regretted leaving her scarf behind at the hotel. Jetlag had turned her thirty-minute catnap into three hours of deep, dreamless slumber. She was running late.

This plan of hers was absurd. So absurd, she didn't tell anyone beside Chandani about the trip. What was the point? She would be gone for four days. If Deepa refused her, she'd just take in the Van Gogh Museum and the Anne Frank House and call the trip a post-divorce vacation.

A young woman wearing a knit cap passed by her.

"Excuse me," Shan said. "Where can I find Andersen Hall?"

"In the languages building around the corner, first one on the left," she said. "Can't miss it."

"Thank you," Shan said. She plunged her hands into her pockets, scooted down the pathway.

Her life in Atlanta felt so distant, and not just in miles. One year ago, she was married and pregnant, working in a competitive, prestigious career, living in a beautiful, single-family home she owned. Now she was a single, childless, unemployed renter chasing a virtual stranger on the other side of the Atlantic Ocean.

Last week, while they were perusing books at the local bookstore, Chandani asked Shan whether she was happy. It was a question Shan hadn't asked herself in years. On the outside, she possessed all the markers of a tragic individual. She was still very sad about the miscarriage but she wasn't *un*happy anymore. Amid the pain, she had found a way to be content. The two greatest stressors in her life, her job and her former husband, were gone. Maybe that's how the state of happiness manifested for adults—autonomy and the ejection of toxicity.

The door to Andersen Hall was propped open. She stepped inside. It was an intimate room with dark, wide-planked hardwood floors, cream-colored drapes. The early evening light bled through the crack between them. Three antique sofas lined one wall. Wood chairs with low backs and armrests formed semicircles around the makeshift stage.

Students in long flowing dresses and blazers milled about. Wine glasses and longneck beer bottles dangled from fingers. Four silver platters overflowed with sausage rolls, croquettes, cheese balls. Shan picked up a dish, piled on a few bites from each platter, hid in the corner. On the plane ride over, she thought about where she should position herself during the reading, wondered if, after thirty years, Deepa would even recognize her.

The size of the crowd decided it for her. She had no choice but to stand at the back, camouflaged by other attendees.

A young man in dreadlocks and a dark suit walked to the center of the room, stood behind the microphone. The audience hushed. "Welcome students, faculty, and members of the community to our fourth poetry reading this semester." A side door opened as he spoke. Two men entered the room followed by a woman with a shock of white, waist-length hair dangling past her bottom. She wore flared, silky pants, a loose-fitting sweater with a wide collar. Glasses perched on the top of her round face. She flowed into the center of the room, studied her seating options, chose the far end of the sofa. She crossed her legs at the knee, laid a book with a few loose papers on her lap, rested her glasses on the tip of her nose.

Thirty years ago, at their first and only meeting in London, Deepa's stark black hair had been pulled back so tightly from her face, the roots tugged her skin toward her ears. She seemed stern, cold, had reminded ten-year-old Shan of Cruella De Vil. Would Shan have viewed her differently, would she have extended her grandmother more compassion, if she'd known Deepa had watched her own parents die in a burning building and had been separated from the boy she loved? Deepa's face had a softness to it now. Shan hoped that meant she had found some semblance of peace.

The emcee introduced the evening's readers, read a brief bio about Kavita Grover. The pen name had become her real name, her real identity. Perhaps one that let her forget her tragic past. Deepa rose, approached the microphone, thanked the audience for coming. She shuffled the pages of the book, landed on one, flipped to another. She pushed her hair behind her ears. A slight tremor moved through her hand.

"This poem is from my book, *Exodus*. It's called 'Child.'"

Your searching soulful eyes are
beams of a lighthouse.
You don't know enough to forgive,
wrestle with demons you never wrought,

carry a legacy, a burden that isn't yours,
that flows through your blood.

Shan closed her eyes. Her head rested against the wall. Deepa's voice inhabited a color, a texture, a rhythm that Shan hadn't sensed when she'd read this poem silently to herself.

She read four more poems after "Child"—all new work from a new, soon to be published book. She stepped back from the microphone when she finished. The audience broke out into applause. She bowed ever so slightly. A smile appeared on her lips, her first of the evening.

The audience thinned out quickly afterward. Deepa clasped her hands, greeted stragglers who seemed to hang on her every word. They handed her pens so she could sign their copies of her book. Shan hung toward the back, placed her empty dish on the table, pretended to look at the paintings on the walls. When the last student departed, Deepa scanned the back of the room.

Her gaze fell on Shan. She squinted. A glint of recognition appeared on her face. She looked away, swiftly exited room.

Shan grabbed her bag, rushed out after her.

Night had fallen. The moon's glow glistened across the pebbled sidewalk of the courtyard. Deepa's silhouette perched at the edge of a stone bench. A gas lantern cast a light on her profile. She opened her purse, pulled out a pack of cigarettes, tapped one out. Her body curled over it. She lit it with cupped hands, released three puffs of smoke. Her legs extended out from under her. She gazed out into the twilight.

Shan took a few steps, lowered herself to the far end of the bench, dropped her bag on the ground between her knees.

Deepa kept her face forward, took another drag on her cigarette. "You look exactly like him. Seeing your face is like seeing his ghost." She tapped off the dangling ashes. "I've smoked for over fifty years. You'd think I would have died first." She brought it to her mouth again, inhaled. A few cinders splintered off, the orange glow grew fainter.

Shan didn't know what to say. She had not expected this flood of regret to suddenly pour out of her estranged grandmother. "I miss him too."

Deepa nodded, as if she had needed this confirmation, as if all these years she'd been wondering this very same thing—whether her son's daughter had been as affected by his death as much as she had. Either her grandmother was the most callous person Shan had ever met, or she was so mired in her own grief she couldn't see past it to anyone else's.

"Why didn't you ever try to find me?" Shan said. "Why didn't you want to know me?"

Deepa tugged her dupatta over her shoulders. "It seems so simple to you, doesn't it? Whatever this is that you feel—my rejection of you—it's bigger than that. It's not personal."

"How is it not personal? My father went to Delhi because of you," Shan said. "He died there, alone, without the family he left behind. It's hard not to take that personally."

Deepa stared at her hard. "I never wanted Vijay to move to India. He moved because I finally gave in to him and told him his father's name." She took another puff, fumbled with the pack in her lap. "I shouldn't have done it. I regret it more than you could ever know."

"Just his name?" Shan asked. "Did you tell him anything else?"

"I didn't know Amir for long. I didn't even know his birthday. All I knew, all that I remembered, was that Amir had a sister named Laila, that their family's name was Rahim, and they moved to Lahore after Partition."

Lahore, the same city her father had planned to visit before he died. "Amir had a sister?" Shan asked.

"Yes. She was younger."

"If Amir and Laila were in Pakistan, why would my father move to Delhi?"

"That's where Vijay found a job. But he wasn't just searching for Amir. He also wanted to find my parents' clinic in Delhi and talk to anyone who might have known them. He wanted to find my school teacher, Madam Grover, who I lost touch with soon after moving to London to see if she ever heard from Amir. Your father did, eventually, plan on making his way to Lahore."

"Did *you* ever try to find Amir?"

Deepa lit another cigarette. She brought it to her mouth. It shook in her fingers. She let it drop to the ground and stubbed it out. "I was living in London with a new baby, taking care of my godmother when she was diagnosed with cancer, and then my godfather after his stroke. I didn't even know Amir's parents' first names, or the name of the aunt they were staying with in Lahore. But I did write multiple letters to the government in Pakistan and to refugee organizations. No one could find them."

"I couldn't find Amir in the Partition Project," Shan said.

Deepa pursed her lips, blinked her eyes several times. The full understanding of how Shan found her seemed to dawn on her. "Laila isn't in there, either. I had searched for her too."

"What was he like?" Shan asked.

"Who? Vijay?"

"My grandfather, Amir," Shan said. "What was he like?"

Deepa paused. "Handsome. Kind. He used to write me these little notes. He folded them into shapes. Origami. He made them for Laila, and then for me too." Her eyes shone in the moonlight. There was a glimmer of something in them, a hint of what kind of life she had before Partition, a childhood of innocence, of laughter. Love. It had been many years, perhaps decades since she had known that kind of joy.

Deepa glanced away. "So many people died during Partition. Over a million," she said. "Amir and Laila probably died too."

"You don't know that."

"I know some things. I lost my parents, my adoptive parents, Amir, Vijay. When my son died, I knew I couldn't blame Partition for everything. I'm tainted. Her head dropped to her chest. "That's why, after Vijay died, I stayed away from you too."

Shan's mouth fell open.

In the days after the miscarriage, Shan wondered whether her son could know what she had felt, worried he might have sensed, during those first few weeks, that she hadn't wanted him at first, that she had scheduled an abortion. She feared this rejection of him might have seeped into him somehow, and ended his brief life. A part of her still believed this to be true. She still carried around the guilt of not being a good enough mother to him, a good enough person.

Guilt seemed to burden generations of Khannas.

Shan opened her purse, rummaged through it. She found an old receipt, wrote down the name of her hotel, her room number. "My flight leaves tomorrow evening," she said. "If you want to meet for coffee or lunch beforehand, please let me know. And here's my email address and phone number, in case you want to get in touch after I've returned home."

She handed it to her grandmother, stood.

Deepa closed her fingers around it, stared at her fist.

"Deepa," Shan said. "I'm so sorry about what you have gone through. I wish I could have been in your life to help you. None of it was your fault. I hope you understand that. And even if you didn't need me, I needed you. I still do." She didn't wait for her grandmother to respond. She turned away, headed down a cobblestone sidewalk, through the courtyard, the light from the moon guiding her path.

❃

Deepa called first thing the next morning and asked to meet. "I have something I want to give you," she said.

Shan jumped in the shower, turned the water hot, let the steam fog the inside glass walls. She threw on a shirt, twisted her hair tight in a bun. She hadn't expected to hear from Deepa, certainly not while she was still in Amsterdam. She pulled on her boots, rushed out of the room. She had six hours before her flight.

Deepa had beaten her to the café and snagged a table. A cup and saucer sat in front of her, the tea already half drunk. She opened her hand. A yellowed paper crane, no longer than Shan's thumb, sat in its center. Ink was smeared over a few of the folds.

"It's all I have of your grandfather," Deepa said. "I want you to have it."

"Are you sure?"

"I'm a very old woman, if you hadn't noticed. I won't be able to hold on to it forever."

Shan gently picked it up, cradled it in her hand. She imagined her grandfather's fingers, folding and creasing, writing neat letters hidden inside. She imagined a girl, a boy, falling in love through art.

"There's something you should know," Deepa said. "Before he died, Vijay had made a decision to return to the States, to Seattle," Deepa said.

Shan leaned forward, certain she hadn't heard her correctly. "Dad was coming home? When did he decide this?"

"During my last conversation with him, a few weeks before he died, he told me he was going to forget about visiting Lahore. That he was no longer going to search for Amir or Laila. He said the time he spent looking for his father wouldn't make up for the time he was losing out on with you."

Shan set the crane on the table. Her mind rewound the time to the end of their India trip. At the Seattle airport, after her father delivered Shan safely to her mother's arms, he leaned over, kissed her cheeks, and told her something she didn't fully understand, but never forgot. "I'll see you, kiddo. Maybe sooner than you think."

"I wish I'd known," she finally said. For years, she had wondered what she'd done to make her father leave. If she had known he was coming back to her, it would have meant everything.

"I need to go now," Deepa said. She picked up her bag.

"Wait," Shan said. "Your poem, 'Child,' the one you read last night. It's about my father, isn't it?"

Deepa looked down, touched the blue veins that ran over the top of her hand. "I wrote 'Child' in August of 1985. It was the last poem I wrote for the collection. It wasn't about Vijay."

She rose, walked back through the café between cramped tables and chairs. The tails of her trench coat blew back behind her like a train. She opened the door, paused in the doorway, glanced back once more at Shan, before stepping outside.

An image flashed through Shan's mind from the very same month: ten-year-old Shan exiting Deepa's London apartment with her father, the awkward hug she shared with her grandmother in the dim light of the hallway, her gaze, which held something. Sadness? Pain? Confusion? Regret? She couldn't put her finger on it.

The poem, "Child," was about her.

CHAPTER TWENTY-TWO
Atlanta
May 10, 2017

When Chandani went in for her standard manicure, Margaret, her usual manicurist, flattered her about the shape of her fingers, the strength of her nails, tried coaxing her into forking over twelve extra dollars for the French tips. Chandani was inclined to get her regular trim and shape, either her Red Raven or Pale Peach polish (she alternated between the two), but something had been begun brewing inside of Chandani. She wanted something more.

She had cried for days after watching Harjeet's video and rarely answered the door when Shan came by to check on her. At first, she was so angry with her husband for not sharing the truth about Simran's death after he returned from Amritsar all those years ago. Then she was angry at Harjeet's father, Akal, for his confession that sent Harjeet into a tailspin from which he could never recover.

But then Chandani thought more about Harjeet's final, selfless act. He had shared his story with the world. He had given his voice to one of the darkest and most painful chapters of Partition. And he did so with such love, compassion, and honesty. His testimony was a gift. It was now a part of a permanent archive that would ensure that this history was never forgotten. Her husband, as it turned out, was as brave as any of the long line of soldiers in his family. This fact made her swell with pride.

She finally opened the curtains again in her home. She took a long, hot bath. Peace, a peace she hadn't known in so long, returned to her. Kush had sensed her metamorphosis over the phone.

"Mom, we've been wondering for almost twenty years why we couldn't help Dad get better. I blamed him. You blamed yourself. But for him to live with this kind of agony for twenty years, and choose to stay with us for as long as he did, that's the deepest kind of love, isn't it? That's true courage."

Chandani smiled. She held out her hand, tilted her head. She would get the French tips. Might as well live a little. Margaret had told her, after all, that her fingers were made for French tips.

Back at home, light streamed between the plantation shutters of her living room. She picked up the laptop, brought it outside, settled on her porch swing. Late May in Atlanta bloomed in every patch of grass, every garden, every tree. A carpet of white and pink impatiens formed a perimeter along the porch, lined the walkway to the mailbox. The pastel petals of her tulips were weighted with ripeness.

Yesterday's soaking rains had washed away the last remnants of pollen from the car, the mailbox, the pickets of her white fence. The air had a lightness to it again, a buoyancy. She slipped off her slippers, stretched open her toes, felt the air rush between them.

She opened her laptop. She was not the most computer literate person in the world, but she had volunteered at her local New Jersey public library for fifteen years, was accustomed, and quite adept she might add, at finding a needle in a haystack.

After several weeks of online research, calls to the Partition Project and two refugee organizations in Lahore and Delhi, and a useless experience with a private investigator who did nothing but try to extort money from her, Shan was on the verge of giving up her search for her grandfather and great-aunt. She was ready to throw in the towel.

This saddened Chandani in a way she hadn't expected. Shan had discovered Harjeet's story.

Returning the favor, Chandani thought, was the least she could do.

She first considered what, if any stones, had been left unturned. There were two primary barriers to the search. One, Amir's and Laila's first names and surname were some of the most common. Two, their advanced ages meant that their internet footprints, if they had any, would be minimal. Assuming they were still alive, they were not likely expounding on social media about their latest vacations, or what they ate for lunch. If anything existed about them online, it would be in the form of their obituaries.

Laila was ten years younger than Amir and more likely to still be alive. It made the most sense to exhaust the search for her first.

Chandani ran through several pages of entries for *Laila Rahim Lahore*. She came upon dozens of Facebook and Instagram accounts with fresh, young faces, teenagers making the peace sign, wearing large dark sunglasses over half their faces, tattoos on their upper arms, the low parts of their bellies. Apparently, the name "Laila" inspired reckless abandon.

She typed, *Laila Rahim Partition.*

She paged through the enties. None were relevant.

She sighed, cracked her knuckles, pushed back again in the swing, typed in *Amir Rahim Partition.*

The search unveiled actors, doctors, television commentators. No one appeared over the age of forty.

She shut the laptop, slid her feet back in her slippers, swung the door open to her house. She scanned the kitchen, the living room. Shan's copy of *Exodus* by Kavita Grover was sitting at the end of her piano bench. Shan had lent it to Chandani a few days earlier. The horror, the despair, the fragility, in the years since the British drew a line that ruptured a people embodied every verse of *Exodus*. Deepa had put in words so much of what Chandani had heard from her relatives who were old enough to remember that time.

She moved to the sofa, folded her legs underneath her, opened her laptop again. She pulled up the Partition Project website and Harjeet's photo.

Deepa and Harjeet had one thing in common. They eventually felt compelled to come forward and tell their stories. Deepa had taken a more circuitous route. She first adopted a pen name and published a poetry collection anonymously, but it was still all there, years before she submitted her story to the Partition Project. Harjeet had held it all in, where it festered, ate him alive before he finally gave himself permission to release it in the form of a video right before his death.

She opened her browser, ran her fingers along the keyboard. When Chandani was still living in Jersey City, she used to read "Missed Connections" on Craigslist for the New York area. Oh, the poems, the haikus, the romantic monologues written from one stranger to another! Those smitten by chance encounters had taken such pains to personalize their searches, to fashion particular details of their brief, magical exchanges. In Shan's search for her grandfather, Shan had not considered how *he* might have gone looking for Deepa.

What would Amir's search have looked like?

There was something in the way people communicated their feelings in a blossoming love. On his good days, Harjeet used to leave Chandani post-it notes stuck to the refrigerator every morning before he left for the office. She'd come across them when she made coffee. *Back by 6, My Love.* Or, *Low on milk. Will pick up more on my way home.* They brightened her every morning, but she hadn't saved any of them. What she wouldn't give to have some of those notes back, now that he was gone.

Chandani removed her glasses and wiped them with the bottom of her shirt. She set them back on her face.

The paper crane. Shan had shown it to her when she returned from Amsterdam. *Amir used to write love notes to Deepa hidden in origami.*

The origami was the means for their communication, the medium for their love. If Amir was looking for Deepa, perhaps that's how he would have gone about it.

Chandani typed, *Amir Rahim Partition Origami.*

The third entry caught her eye. She clicked on it. It was a newspaper article published in the *Lahore Daily* only four days ago.

Laila Rahim's 'Departures' to open at Lahore Museum of Contemporary Art

Lahore sculptor Laila Rahim, age 76, will present 'Departures,' the story of flight, loss, and adaptation to a new homeland in the aftermath of Partition. At age six, Laila fled from Delhi to Lahore with her parents and brother. Rahim, a metals sculptor, welds giant sheets of copper, tin, and bronze into origami. The show will open next month and run for six weeks. Rahim will give a lecture at the museum about her exhibit on July 3 at 7 p.m.

Laila Rahim. Seventy-six years old. Origami. A brother. *My God*, thought Chandani. *I've found them.*

CHAPTER TWENTY-THREE
Lahore
March 22, 2016

From the balcony of her flat, Laila watched as dawn illuminated the tin rooftops of the market. Their ribbed tiles appeared like ripples in an ocean. Three vultures with hooked necks darted from side to side, scanned the ground for fresh corpses. Disappointment flashed in their black, beady eyes. They spread their wings, one after the other, lifted off into the air, their barbed talons retracted tight into their bodies.

Below, vendors rolled their carts and wheelbarrows into place, kicked down brakes, unveiled produce and trinkets in neat, compact rows.

Her tea had long gone cold. She tied a dupatta over her shoulders, extended her legs, rotated her feet at the ankles to coax blood flow. She rose, leaned over the railing. A breeze tickled her ears. Crisp air coursed through her lungs. She spotted the blue awning of what was once their very first silk shop, now her studio. During the early years, she and Mahad spent sixteen hours a day operating the business. She worked behind the counter, adduced the luster of the cloth, the slight slubbing of its hand weaving, the intricacy of patterns.

Mahad had manned the back, handled the books, filled orders for weddings, maintained the once dilapidated building. She worked at the counter, helping husbands treating their wives, mothers doting on daughters. She and Mahad had made excellent business partners. He joked with her often in front of all the customers. *I'm the luckiest man in the world. My wife is the brains* and *the beauty.*

They closed the shop for three hours in the middle of each day, same as the other shops, and walked back to their flat. Mahad would nap on the sofa with a newspaper spread open on his chest. She'd prepare lunch and keep chai simmering on the stove so it would be warm enough for him when he drank it later. She'd fall in love with her husband all over again while listening to his light snores.

Theirs was not a perfect marriage. They had experienced their share of heartache too. For years they tried to conceive. Letting go of the dream to start a family was crushing. But Mahad didn't do what many men she knew did. He didn't discard her. In fact, he did the opposite. He told her that without children, he could now devote more time and attention to her.

Forty years into their marriage, years after their one shop spawned six other silk shops all over Lahore, Mahad was diagnosed with early onset Alzheimer's. When dementia began clouding his mind, he confused Laila with his beloved mother, his sister, even his grandmother. Yet he continued to be so grateful for the meals she cooked, the baths she prepared, the reminders of how to use a toothbrush, and he told her so, almost every day. Up until the end, when he could still speak clearly, he asked her if he was being good enough to her.

His death last year had torn Laila to pieces. She closed the silk shops temporarily and took some time to mourn and think about what she now wanted for herself.

And then the visions came, first at night, and then even during the day. They presented a series of images to her, and eventually a narrative took shape. Steel. Metal. Bronze. She saw the sheets of hardness bend, fold, ruffle, sharpen, reflect. She'd spent so many years caressing the soft, slick fibers of silk, and yet, her mind pointed her to other more durable, unyielding, textures.

She sold six of their seven silk shops to one of her managers. She kept the original and, with the proceeds from the others, purchased the entire building and the one immediately next to it. She tore down the dividing walls and the ceilings in between floors, added floor-to-ceiling windows, the counters, and painted the cement floors to create a large, airy main room.

She started collecting scraps of wire and sheet metal. For the first few weeks, she took the time to familiarize herself with her new materials, examined their weight, their mass, their sharp edges, noted their pliability, their sheen.

She liked the sound a hammer made when it pounded metal, how the vibration traveled up the handle, up her arm, like an electric shock. She couldn't get far with only a hammer, though. So she bought a welding machine, an electrode, a chipping hammer, a set of electric shears, a guillotine, tin snips, and a welding helmet. She learned how heat melted and shaped copper, tin, and steel from a local welder. She studied the force of sparks grinding off the metal. There was a sense of risk to her newfound medium. A power. An invincibility she'd never known.

Her ringing phone jarred her out of her thoughts. It was a sound she didn't hear often. Her dearest friends, in their old age, had moved into their children's homes in nearby towns, a few all the way to Karachi. Her building now burst at the seams with young families. She knew them enough to smile or make small talk while passing in the hallway. She doted on the children, offered them lollipops. But the community she and Mahad had known over the course of their lives had moved to quieter, smaller towns.

The phone rang for the fourth time. She was tempted to stay put, but something told her to answer it.

"Hello?"

"This is Dr. Enami. I'm following up after our meeting last week."

"Oh, yes, of course," said Laila. She took a deep breath. "It's so good to hear from you."

"I'd like to talk to you about showing your work at the museum. I'm thinking summer of 2017. I was so impressed by your pieces. You have a strong point of view, a powerful voice, and a unique perspective on Partition. Let's set up a meeting next week at my office to sort out the details for your debut."

Laila sat down slowly as if trying not to break the spell. She was not expecting this news. Last week, she had spent all morning scrubbing her studio from top to bottom, washing the floors, tilting her pieces just so to capture the natural light. The museum director, Dr. Farah Enami, hadn't said a word when she toured Laila's studio, didn't ask a single question, didn't write anything down, snubbed Laila's offer of snacks, addressed her directly only upon leaving, by simply wishing her a good day.

She didn't expect to hear from the director again, assumed that at Laila's age it was too late for her to begin a new career as a sculptor. She didn't give a public showing of her art another thought.

"I can't believe it," Laila whispered. She puttered around the flat in a trance. She searched for paper, popped open drawers, lifted magazines from the coffee table. When she came upon an old envelope, she jotted down the names and dates Dr. Enami rattled off for the duration of Laila's show. She could hardly take it all in, thanked her profusely before hanging up.

Day had begun burning the chill off the earth. Sunlight seeped through the crevices in the curtains. Laila set the phone down, examined her fingers and the blunt, unpainted nails of a sculptor. They were almost unrecognizable to her now. When she worked with silk, she spent hundreds of hours soaking, filing, and painting her nails so that when she laid them against a swath of silk, they magnified its opulence. Her nails had lost their luster working with metals.

But they had gained strength.

She dumped the remains of her tea in the sink, picked up her purse, slipped on her shoes. This was a rebirth, a new life, so far along into her old one. During her lowest moments, in the months after Amir left, the years of infertility, and caring for her beloved Masad in his final, heartwrenching years, she never thought a day like this would come.

And yet, here it was.

CHAPTER TWENTY-FOUR
Lahore
July 1, 2017

Allama Iqbal International Airport buzzed with activity. Newly disembarked passagers stretched their arms and retied their shoes upon emerging from gates. Parents secured their children in strollers. Teenagers texted furiously on their smart phones.

"I can't believe we're finally here," Chandani said. "It feels like a dream." She had slept most of the flight from London to Lahore, woke up an hour before they landed, freshened up in the airplane bathroom, fixed her hair in a tight bun. She looked like she just stepped out of a spa after over twenty hours of travel. Shan could do nothing to tame her static-filled hair or reduce the swelling under her eyes. She settled for brushing her teeth and reapplying deodorant.

They collected their baggage. The line for customs was fairly short. They declared nothing, continued on to baggage claim. The *click-click* of their rollerbags' wheels traced their footsteps. Outside, locals shuffled along roped-off areas, squeezed among one another to get the first look at the parade of travelers, called out the names written on their white cards. Children ducked and chased one another under the rope.

The hot air hit them like a slap. Shan's throat felt gritty. She brought her water bottle to her lips, sucked it down. They made their way to the curb where a taxi driver loaded their luggage into the trunk.

It appeared to be rush hour. Motorbikes thrummed between autos, buses spewed exhaust, groaned in acceleration. Passengers clung to the doors, held tight to their briefcases. Men and women walked along the road wearing business suits, abayas, jeans, salwar kameez. Street vendors hawked fried foods.

Chandani removed her camera from her bag and leaned out of the window. At every intersection she took at least a dozen photos. *Click. Click. Click.* She focused the lens. "I'd forgotten what this was like."

"Forgotten what?" Shan said.

"I'd forgotten what it was like to use a camera to see the world, how a lens illuminates the beauty, and forces you to see the details you might otherwise miss in order to appreciate the nuances of that which seems ordinary." She snapped a few more photos, looked over her images. "Such a beautiful city. This is my first time in Lahore too."

Shan leaned her face into the breeze. It ruffled her hair, kissed her cheeks. An elderly man with a cane meandered across the street. He appeared to be in his eighties, about the same age as Deepa, the same age as Amir. She strained to look for any resemblance to her or her father, but saw none. No matter. It still gave her great comfort to be in the city he once inhabited, to be able to imagine what he might look like today. Chandani pulled the camera back inside the car, glanced over to Shan as if she'd just read her thoughts. She reached over, patted her knee.

"Shan," she said. "It won't be long now."

❀

The next evening at the hotel, Chandani picked out one of her own sari blouses, a lavender one, looped it through Shan's arms, fastened it along her bare back. Shan had packed black pants and a pale yellow blouse for the event, was surprised at Chandani's insistence she wear a sari. The blouse was a little tight on her shoulders, but it otherwise fit. The sari was a deep eggplant with orange embroidery along the trim.

"But I've never worn one before," Shan protested, the irony of her statement obvious as soon as the words left her mouth. She was half Indian, yet had not worn any type of Indian clothing in thirty years. There was never a reason for her to. She would have felt like an imposter. And yet, here was Chandani, encircling her with cloth, tucking the folds in the front of Shan's petticoat.

"But how will I walk?" Shan asked.

"I haven't amputated your feet," Chandani said, laughing. "You'll walk exactly the same as you always do." She studied Shan tenderly. "What's the matter? Are you nervous?"

"Maybe a little." She was so nervous. This was the end of the line. She had exhausted all other leads. If this sculptor was not Laila, there was probably no other route to Amir. She had kept this trip a secret from Deepa. She had wanted to wait until she could be sure this Laila was *the* Laila.

Shan's search had kept her anchored, given her a purpose. She wanted to find Amir, but she also wanted something else— the feeling of interconnectedness between her family members, between the generations, the knowledge that she was a part of a larger story of the people she loved and their histories. This mattered to her too.

"It's going to be fine, Shan," Chandani said. "I just know it." She positioned Shan in front of a mirror, laid her hands on her shoulders. "Come," she said. "It's time for us to go."

❀

A glass building sat at the corner of an intersection. *Lahore Museum of Contemporary Art* was carved in a large slab of blue stone. A white sign draped above the door. *Laila Rahim's* Departures, *now through August 31.*

They exited the auto. Shan scanned the area, took a few deep breaths. Chandani came to her side, looped her arm through hers. Shan hoped she hadn't dragged her dear friend halfway around the world for nothing.

"Don't forget to breathe," Chandani said. "It's the most important thing."

They approached the entrance. Two women in salwar kameezes chatted on the steps. Shan hiked up her sari skirt, paused in the arched doorway. "I wish my father was here," she said.

Chandani leaned close to Shan, squeezed her arm. "He is," she said.

The hallway burst with patrons. Conversations bounced off the high ceiling. A man behind a counter in a dark suit asked for their tickets. "The lecture is in Shah Hall, right next to the gallery." He pointed off to the side. "You can enter the room any time after eight p.m."

"Is she here yet? The artist?" Chandani asked.

"Not yet," he said. "She'll probably come right at eight."

A sign directed them to *Departures.* They followed the stream of visitors through a wide hallway with floor to ceiling mirrors. Shan almost didn't recognize herself in her reflection, her more steadied, assured gait in a sari. She straightened her posture, angled her head, tried to fake whatever elegance she could muster.

A doorway was draped with a black sheet. "Wait here for one moment," a young woman told them. She spoke into a microphone clipped to her collar. "Okay, you can enter now." She held open the drape. "Enjoy the show."

They stepped inside.

In the center of an otherwise dark room was a shimmering light. Shan blinked, unsure of what was before her. The shapes gradually came into focus. Hundreds of shiny, copper, palm-sized sculptures hung from the ceiling with clear wires, eye-height. They had wings, elegant necks, beaks pointed like tiny arrows. They lined up in neat rows, wing tip to wing tip. Origami cranes. Gears in the ceiling conducted their movement. They rose and receded like waves.

A sign against the opposite wall caught her eye. She edged around the perimeter to read it.

Laila Rahim was six years old during June 1947, when she and her family fled to Lahore. For Departures, *her artistic debut, she melds steel, bronze and copper sheets into origami, the art of Japanese paper-making. Flight, escape and creation were important themes for her. 'Origami signifies the kinds of transformation that refugees must make to start a new life. They must create something new, something beautiful, from a blank page.'*

Below the statement was the title of the piece.
CONTINENTAL DRIFT.

Shan and Chandani wandered to another room with much larger sculptures. Some were smooth like glass, others dimpled, corrugated, charred. A crow, a hawk, a rose, a lotus. In the very center was a life-size bronze gondola. A woman's multicolored silk shawl draped over a seat in a striking contrast.

"Stunning," Chandani whispered.

They approached another piece entitled BROKEN. Two jagged pieces of a heart hung against a wall. Red paint ran along each side of the aperture. Shan's hand floated toward it.

A man with a thin mustache stepped forward. "Please, no touching."

"Sorry," she said. "Do you know anything about the artist? Do you know whether she has family attending tonight?"

He shook his head. "I don't."

Shan and Chandani perused the exhibit for another hour. Chandani peered through the lens of her camera, snapped photos where allowed. At a few minutes before eight, guests began funneling down the hallway back through the foyer, toward the reception hall. Shan and Chandani joined them.

Thick, wood doors opened to a large room. Ivory linens draped long tables. China platters overflowed with samosas and kebabs. Roses spilled out of crystal vases. A small stage was centered in the front of the room. A black podium and two chairs sat at the center. Patrons mingled in suits and ties, long, flowing skirts, high heels—professors, critics, or perhaps Lahore high society. They imbibed glasses of champagne distributed liberally by servers.

Shan scanned the room for the woman she traveled over eight thousand miles and ten time zones to find.

"Do you see her anywhere?" Shan asked Chandani.

"No. But let's grab seats near the front."

At fifteen past the hour, a woman in a silk suit and short cropped hair approached the podium, tapped twice on the microphone. "Please, if I can have everyone take a seat for our guest of honor. We're about to begin." A hush fell over the crowd. They set their empty goblets on tables, made their way up the aisle, filed into empty seats. She read Laila's bio. "It is a great honor to welcome her here tonight," she said. "Please give a warm welcome to the artist, Laila Rahim."

Shan pivoted in her seat.

Laila floated down the aisle in a black hijab, a startling red salwar suit, heels that clicked on the floor. She climbed the stage, shook hands with her introducer, and whispered something in her ear. She moved behind the podium, lowered the microphone. It amplified her breath, the crinkling of papers. "Thank you so much, Dr. Enami, for that lovely introduction. And thank you all for coming. It feels surreal, this life of mine, that I'm able to share my art with our nation at this late age. It is a privilege and an honor for which I am immensely grateful."

Shan scrutinized Laila's full face—her wide-set eyes, her dimpled cheek, her mannerisms—for any sign of their relation. She found none.

Laila cleared her throat. She took the audience through her process—how she acquired her materials, how she welded them together, why she'd chosen to work with metals. "There's something primitive, something empowering about them. Ages ago, metals comprised the first tools, the first weapons in civilization. I wanted to pay homage to the confluence of their ambition and their function, to the relationship between strength and beauty." She talked about how origami became the inspiration for her form, the means to implement her vision. "I've loved origami since I was a child. It's playful, functional, yet mysterious." Her explanation was devoid of a more personal connection. She didn't mention a brother.

Shan's heart sank. Perhaps this *wasn't* the right Laila.

The applause afterward was hearty, prolonged. Laila appeared surprised by it, bowed twice. She stepped off the stage quickly, walked briskly back through the aisle. It was only when she reached the end that Shan realized she was leaving the room, skipping out, it appeared, on the reception.

"I'll be back," Shan told Chandani.

She hopped up, adjusted the pallu of her sari, scooted down the aisle, wove between the guests now rising from their seats. In the hallway, she looked right, then left, caught a glimpse of the back of Laila before she disappeared around the corner. Shan caught up and followed her into the women's restroom.

The soft glow of sconces lit pale green walls. White hand towels trimmed with lace lay next to each basin. Laila leaned over one, splashed water over her face. She dabbed her face with a towel, nodded to Shan when she saw her.

"Are you okay?" Shan asked.

"I'm fine. It's just stage fright, I suppose." She laughed. "It's a little late in life for me to learn how to speak in front of a crowd."

Laila folded the towel, tossed it in a bin. She leaned against the wall.

"I thought you did very well," Shan said. "I was so moved by your exhibit, especially 'Continental Drift.' That was my favorite. I almost couldn't tell whether the room was moving or the cranes were."

Laila sat down on a small stool, kicked off her heels. "Thank you," she said. "That was the idea. You're American, is it?"

"Yes, I am. I guess that's pretty obvious."

"Hmm."

"I was just wondering," Shan began, "whether you're related to an Amir Rahim. He was originally from Delhi and moved to Lahore sometime in the summer of 1947."

Laila's eyes narrowed. "Why do you ask?"

"He's my grandfather."

"Oh, you have the wrong person then, dear."

"Amir Rahim is my father's father. And Deepa Khanna is my grandmother."

Laila's eyes widened. "Deepa? Your grandmother is Deepa?"

"Yes she is."

"I remember a Deepa Khanna from Delhi. But Deepa and Amir didn't have children. My brother died at age sixteen, a few weeks after we moved to Lahore."

A weight crushed Shan's chest. "I'm so sorry to hear that. I didn't know he'd passed away." Her grandfather had been dead for seventy years. He had already been dead for decades when her father began looking for him in India. Here she was, searching for a man she hoped would be in his eighties, and yet, he'd never made it out of childhood. "But Amir *is* my grandfather. Deepa became pregnant with his son, my father Vijay, right before your family left for Lahore."

Laila shook her head. "How can that be?"

"Let me show you something." Shan reached into her bag and took out the origami crane that Deepa had given her in Amsterdam. "Does this mean anything to you?"

Laila brought it close to her face and gasped. "This is Amir's handwriting!"

"Amir promised Deepa he would return for her after taking you to Lahore," Shan said. "But after her parents were killed, she was forced to move to London. She wanted to wait for Amir. But she had no choice."

Tears sprung to Laila's eyes. "Oh, my child, he tried to go back to her! A few weeks after we reached Lahore, he secretly boarded the train back to Delhi. When my father discovered his plans, it was too late. The train had already left the station."

"What happened?"

Laila removed a tissue from her purse, patted her eyes. "They call them ghost trains. Shortly before they crossed the border, either to or from India, the conductors, who had been bribed, would stop them, jump out, and run away. Before the passengeres realized what was happening, a mob would descend upon them. Amir's train was attacked like this. He didn't survive. I don't think anyone on his train did."

"Oh, no," Shan said.

"That day was the worst of my life," Laila said. "For a long time, I was so angry at him for leaving me. But then I realized that that was who Amir was. He would never break a promise he had made. Is Deepa still alive?"

"She lives in Amsterdam. I didn't tell her about this trip. I wanted to be certain that I had found you first."

"I still have the very last note he made for her," Laila said. "I kept it all this time. It was my inspiration for this show. I was supposed to mail it to her, but after Amir's death, I lost Deepa's Delhi address. I was just so young too."

Shan sat down next to Laila and told her about her father's move to Delhi with the hopes of one day finding Amir, and his sudden death in his thirties. She explained how she came to find Deepa, and then how she found Laila through an article about her exhibit.

Laila touched Shan's shoulder. "You and I are family. What a gift this is for the both of us! What a journey you've had to make so that we could share in this magical moment. I am your great-aunt! You are Amir's granddaughter! But I don't even know your name."

It was such a simple, straightforward question, one that Shan now found herself having difficulty answering. What *was* her name? When she'd shortened it as a child, she scrubbed her father, his legacy, from her identity as if it was a pesky stain. She had been Shan for so long, she thought she knew who she was as Shan.

"Shanti," she finally said. An image returned, of her and her father walking toward the Taj Mahal, of the way he looked at her when he said it. His voice from years ago echoed in her ear. "My father called me Shanti."

"Shanti means peace," Laila said. "Did you know that?"

"I do," she said. "I do."

CHAPTER TWENTY-FIVE
Lahore
September 3, 1947

S oon it will be dawn. From the front bedroom, Amir
can barely make out the low voices in the kitchen. His
parents and aunt and uncle have been up the whole
night talking. *Arguing.* His aunt complains about the financial strain of keeping their family. His father ensures them
they won't stay much longer. They'll find a new home soon.

Laila's snores whistle from her side of the bedroll. Her eyes
twitch twice, still. The curling tendrils of her hair wind tightly
around in her fist. He crawls to her, rests the side of his face
against her back, listens to the thrum of her beating heart. His
head moves with the undulation of her breath.

He rights himself, removes the envelope from the pocket of
his shirt, checks the contents—a letter to his parents explaining
where he is going and why, a letter to Laila promising he will
write to her often, will visit her soon. And finally, a paper lotus.

Amir lights a candle, locates a pen. On the back of Laila's
letter he adds a request, one he hopes his sister will never have

to fulfill. *Should anything happen to me, I need you to find a way to get this lotus to Deepa.* He writes down Deepa's Delhi address. He then inscribes four words underneath the petals of the lotus: *Forgive me, my wife.*

Amir places it, along with the other papers, back into the envelope. He props it up against the candle. He then opens his knapsack, removes several dozen folded hearts and encircles them around her sleeping body—a halo around her head, a carpet at her feet. He extinguishes the candle's flame.

He rouses when the adults finally retire to bed. On the other side of the wall, his mother releases a few muffled cries. His father offers a hush. Amir places his palm against the grainy surface separating them, as if to comfort them through the concrete. They hate it here in Lahore. Delhi has always been their home.

He hopes, someday soon, that Ammi, Abba, and Laila will be able to forgive him. That they will still accept him as their son, even though he is abandoning them when they need him most, even though he is marrying a Hindu girl. He will work hard to send back money to them so that they can find their own place to live in Lahore.

He pushes himself to standing, picks up his knapsack from the corner of the room, runs his fingers through his hair. He opens the bedroom door slightly, peers out. Remnants of smoke from incense sticks migrate toward the ceiling. A cricket hops along the floor. His family's chappals mingle with those belonging to his aunt and uncle. Amir slips on his pair.

Outside, the air is thick with a smog that coats him like a second skin. A sleeping dog startles at his appearance. Amir freezes. Its bark will call attention to his escape. The dog thinks better of it, stretches, makes its way farther down the road.

Amir sighs.

His vision takes its time adjusting to the darkness. He lifts the strap of his bag higher on his shoulder, rubs his face in the crook of his elbow. His feet kick up clouds of dust. He retraces his steps back toward the train station where his family arrived three weeks earlier.

A faint glow begins to penetrate the darkness. A crowing rooster signifies the imminence of dawn. He begins a slow jog. If he doesn't catch the first train out, his family will have time to read the notes, to search for him at the railway station. He imagines his mother's shock at his absence, her wails, his letter falling from her hands.

He stops, glances back down the road toward his aunt's house, wonders if there will ever be a world in which he can have both his family and his wife. He doesn't want to choose one or the other. But for now, he must choose his wife.

The tattered brown roof of the station comes into view. Rows of men, women, and children slumber in heaps along the edge of the street. Babies bury themselves in their parents' sides. Piles of bags, tin containers, encircle their feet. A faint fire burns itself out.

He turns a corner. The railway station looms larger. A signboard reads LAHORE in four languages. Lines snake from the ticket booth. Passengers congregate, talk in hushed tones. Others wander aimlessly through the growing crowd. A coil of barbed wire separates the Hindu section from the Muslim section on the platform. Amir wears a button-down shirt and slacks, nothing to identify himself as Muslim on what will be a Hindu-filled, India-bound train.

He touches his shirt pocket, traces the outline of the ticket the servant boy purchased for him two days earlier. He weaves through bodies, makes his way to the front. His toes teeter off the lip of the platform. In the distance, a tower of billowing smoke appears. Elbows and knees jostle forward. People call out to one another, scoop up belongings, hoist children onto their hips. The crowd sways forward, fills the empty spaces, thrusts Amir closer to the edge. He extends his arms to maintain balance.

The locomotive roars around the bend. The stench of burning coal fills the air. A bump sends him careening onto the tracks. His head slams into one of the rails. His vision blurs. He slowly raises his head. It feels as if it's cracked in two.

"Help the boy up," a woman shouts.

A dozen hands thrust toward him. He scrambles to his feet, grabs a hand, rolls back onto the platform. A few men clap his back.

He touches the back of his head. His fingers moisten. He brings them to his face. They are covered in blood.

An elderly man offers a handkerchief. "Apply pressure," he says. "You can keep it."

"Thank you," Amir says.

The train slows. As it pulls along the platform, before it even comes to a complete stop, the crowd surges forward, fills the doorways, climbs through windows, scales the sides to the roof. Amir is still disoriented from the fall. He hesitates. No matter. A surge carries him into the train car. His feet barely touch the ground.

He finds himself an empty bench, settles in. Within seconds, three others squeeze in on a seat meant for two. He looks out the window. Not even half of the travelers are able to make their way onto the train. He sees a thin, frail woman left behind, the pallu of her sari hanging off her elbow. She brings her hands to her face, cries. She has been separated from someone.

He wants to offer his seat, to climb onto the roof so she might have space in the car, but he's trapped. A small little girl in a pink salwar kameez, her hair in two messy braids, now sits at his feet, eyes him expectantly. She is about the same age as Laila, and this realization makes him ache for his sister. *Temporary*, he thinks. *Their separation will be temporary.* As soon as he reaches Delhi, he will write his sister a long letter begging her forgiveness. As soon as he earns money, he will mail her a gift.

The little girl appears to belong to no one. Her eyes are locked on him. He smiles at her, pats her head.

The train heaves away, builds speed. Each meter brings him closer to his wife. He thinks about her waiting for him at her home, pacing the floor, crying out for her parents. These last three weeks must have been terribly difficult for her. She must be so afraid. Maybe she doubted his intention to return. But he is coming for her. He is on his way, at last.

The little girl rests her head on his knee. He lays his hand on her damp cheek, leans back, feels the warmth of the rising sun on his face. The train rocks gently from side to side, lulls him to sleep.

He wakes to the little girl's screams.

CHAPTER TWENTY-SIX
Amsterdam
July 2, 2017

Above the Amstel River, Caspian gulls circled and swooped, sliced through the orange glow of the sunset with their wide wingspans. The moon's reflection grew larger against the water's rippling surface. Deepa rose from a bench, meandered through the cobblestone streets. Her favorite cheese shop, the bakery with the moist scones, loomed in the distance. At the curb, a line of bikers zoomed past her. The gust of wind in their wake cooled her face. The bikers here reminded her of India, where bicycles and bike rickshaws once ruled the roads.

India. She imagined how much it had changed in seventy years but had never returned to see those changes herself. The very thing that kept her away, her grief, is what drove her son to it. How ignorant she had been to keep Amir from Vijay, to pretend she could be enough for her son. Gertrude had been right all those years ago. Vijay needed to know about his father. He had a right to know, a right that superseded her right to keep Amir's identity from him. What good did she think could come of denying Vijay? She had been wrong. She wished he was alive so that she could tell him how sorry she was, could beg her son for forgiveness. She had been wrong, too, about staying away from his daughter. Death had turned her into such a hardened old woman. She missed the Deepa she once was, the school girl surrounded by her parents' love.

On the other side of the street, a kit of pigeons pecked near the base of a trashcan. She opened her purse, tossed the remains of an oatmeal cookie she'd tucked away. They fluttered their wings, attacked the bounty. She watched them until the last crumb disappeared, boarded the next trolley home.

Her keys jostled in the doorknob to her building. She kicked the door open, leaned heavily against the banister, trudged up the long, narrow staircase to the second floor. She'd fallen in love with the eaves of her apartment, the high, slanted ceiling, her stunning view of the Rijksmuseum, its majestic red façade, its towers. It had reminded her of another view—the one of Agra Fort from the western side of the Taj Mahal, the place where she first spoke to Amir.

The apartment had been a foolish choice for a home. She'd not counted on how quickly her joints would deteriorate in her eighties, how difficult climbing steps would become. Her chest heaved as she mounted each landing.

The waning sunlight washed her living room in an orange glow. Her money plants stretched their stems along the windowsills of the dormers. She kicked off her shoes, sunk her toes within the cool threads of her shag rug, collapsed into the cushions of her sofa. She loved her apartment in Amsterdam. It felt like the closest thing to a home since her parents' home in Delhi.

Of course, she loved London too. But Nora and John's premature deaths ruined that city for her. It was as if the string of tragedies that began in Delhi had followed her across the Himalayas, the former Persian Empire, the Mediterranean Sea, the European continent, and the English Channel. Gertrude had eased this pain some, had been a lifeline for both her and Vijay. If Deepa had one regret (though certainly, there were too many to list) it was ending her friendship with Gertrude and taking her son away from her. He had needed her. They both did.

Shan and Deepa had spoken several times since she returned to the United States. Her granddaughter was persistent and stubborn, and reminded Deepa of herself. She wouldn't wait for Deepa to return her voice mail messages. She kept calling, day after day, until she eventually caught Deepa at home. Now when more than a few days passed without hearing from her, Deepa found herself on edge. She worried about her. She missed her.

The phone rang. She pulled it out of her purse.

"Deepa? It's me," her granddaughter said. "You're not going to believe this. I'm calling you from Lahore."

"Lahore?" Deepa said. "You're in *Pakistan?*"

"I have some amazing news. Are you sitting down?"

Deepa didn't know what sitting down had to do with anything. "Yes, what is it?"

"I found Laila, Amir's sister. She's alive and well and an artist. She's been living in Lahore this whole time! Can you believe it?"

Deepa closed her eyes. Laila, sweet Laila, skipping through the marketplace with a basket of flowers, her arms encircling Amir's shoulders, her sticky, jalebi fingers.

"I can't believe it," Deepa finally said.

"I have very sad news too. Amir died only three weeks after you last saw him. He was on a train bound for Delhi. It was ambushed. Everyone on board died, including Amir. But he was on his way back to you."

Deepa dropped the phone. It smacked the floor like a brick hitting concrete, shot across the room. She lowered herself slowly to the ground to search for it.

In the seventy years since he last held her, since he departed from her parents' flat, she considered the possibilities: His parents discovered his plan, forbade him to return to Delhi; he couldn't find it in his heart to leave Laila; he didn't have enough money for a return ticket; his father was too sick for him to leave Lahore; he returned to Delhi and when he couldn't find Deepa, went back to Pakistan, and the saddest possibility she could imagine—his family never made it out of India alive, that they died, as so many other Muslims did, before reaching Pakistan safely.

She'd not considered *this*. That he boarded a train in Lahore and died on his way back to Delhi. Back to her.

She rolled to her knees, crawled across the floor. She found her phone under her kitchen table. She brought it to her ear again.

"Deepa? Are you there? Deepa?"

"Yes," Deepa said, breathlessly. "I'm still here."

Shan revealed the notes Amir left to his family upon departing Lahore and the last origami note he left for her, which Laila kept all these years. "It says, 'Forgive me, my wife.' He wanted you to know that if he didn't make it, he was sorry."

It was almost too much for Deepa to take in.

When Amir had not returned, she deprived her son of the few truths she knew about his family, abandoned her granddaughter, cut off Gertrude. She buried herself in her career, forged an existence in isolation, where she didn't have to rely on anyone to survive.

For so long she had felt nothing. She had buried her emotions so deep within herself, she wasn't sure she could feel anything again. Except for her poetry. She had allowed herself the luxury of honest expression through her words, as Madam Grover once advised her to do. But once she penned those feelings on the page, she left them there. She forbade herself from carrying those emotions around.

"My Amir. I loved him. I loved your grandfather," Deepa said. "Thank you for finding Laila. Poor Laila, to lose her brother so young. Please tell her I'm sorry, that I...that I wish things had been different."

"You can tell her yourself. Let me give you her number."

Deepa grabbed a pen and paper, took it down. She would call Laila first thing in the morning. It would be so good to hear her voice, to find out about her life. Laila had never departed Deepa's heart. And then Deepa would finally reach out to Gertrude, too, just as she promised. It was time.

Deepa set the phone down, made her way back to the sofa, opened a drawer in the coffee table. She removed an album with pictures of Vijay as a baby and child, had paged through it every single evening since his death. There was Vijay, lying on her chest soon after she gave birth to him, Nora holding infant Vijay in her lap, Vijay petting a cat in the courtyard, toddler Vijay and John sitting together on a bench, holding hands.

Her son looked so much like Amir. She wished he could have known him.

Exhaustion overcame her. She adjusted a pillow, leaned back, clutched the album to her chest. She stared at the ceiling, at the way the light entered the window, drew beams like arrows pointing, where? She didn't know. Her shoulders relaxed deeper into the cushion. Her breath took its time filling her chest cavity, expelled itself deliberately. Her eyelids twitched, lowered.

A grayness swirls in her mind. Hues emerge, like watercolors, forming a scene both unfamiliar and familiar. She is young again, strolling through the markets in Delhi. Her hair hangs loose, windswept. Amir walks alongside her cradling newborn Vijay in his arms. His smile is bright and wide. Vijay peers up at him as if he can read his father's thoughts, as if he's known his father for a long time, in some other life. Amir brings his son closer to his face, whispers in his ear, tells him a secret, something only a father would tell a son. Deepa rests her head on Amir's shoulder, feels his warm breath on her forehead. They gaze together at the face of their darling boy.

CHAPTER TWENTY-SEVEN
Agra
August 15, 2017

H er memory of the Taj Mahal had not faded in the slightest. Or perhaps the monument had frozen in time during the intervening years. In a life with interruptions, surprises, disappointments, the Mahal was the only true constant, the place where her great-grandparents, Manoj and Kavita, had mourned the division of India, the place her grandparents, Deepa and Amir, had begun their courtship, where her father Vijay had once pledged to be a better father to her. So many promises were made, so many hopes birthed on its terrace, so many dreams envisioned. It was, for all of them, a place of infinite beginnings, a fitting place for Shanti to begin again. And it was the perfect day to do so—the seventieth anniversary of Independence.

Sunrays glowed along the white marble of the terrace. Tourists milled about. Selfie sticks bisected the air, their owners jostled and angled to get the perfect background shot, to relax their smiles into something that felt a little more natural.

"Over here," Laila called. She raised her sunglasses, squinted. Laila had not been to the Taj Mahal since she was six years old. She was not certain she could accompany Shanti on this trip. But a local university in Agra had invited Laila to speak to their history department about her art and helped to arrange her visitor's visa from Pakistan.

Shan walked to her aunt's side. Chandani, who had been snapping photos of the exterior, soon followed. Laila led them both to the northwest side overlooking the Yamuna River and Agra Fort. She set her hand on the railing.

"This is the exact spot where I first met your grandmother," Laila said. "It's one of the first memories I have as a child. I remember, so vividly, how Deepa and Amir looked at each other, the rhythm and beats of their conversation, the slight variations in their expressions, their demeanors, the intentions conveyed so seamlessly in the silences." Laila sighed. "I wish Deepa could have been with us here now."

They both felt her absence acutely. But a reunion was forthcoming. Next week, she and Shanti would travel to Amsterdam together.

"Aunty, I know this spot," Shanti said. "My father had brought me right here to look out at this same view." She leaned over. She peered down below to the Yamuna River, tributary of the Ganges River, which started in the Himalayas, flowed through Delhi, eastward into Bangladesh, and emptied, eventually into the Bay of Bengal. One body of water joined another and then another in an endless cycle that would continue long after they all departed this earth.

When her father brought her here thirty years earlier, she sensed the immortality of this place. There was a timelessness to it. And today, the link between her father, her grandparents, and her great-grandparents seemed stronger than ever, present in ways she couldn't explain.

"Turn around, you two," said Chandani. "We need to memorialize this."

Shanti and Laila smiled. After Chandani snapped a few photos, Shanti wrapped her neighbor in a tight embrace. "Thank you, Aunty. Thank you for giving me back my family. I would have never found them without your support."

Chandani touched her cheek. "Shanti, you are the one who gave me back my Harjeet by helping me understand the root of his pain. And now that you have, my wounds can begin to heal."

When Shanti and Laila continued to Amsterdam, Chandani would be catching a flight to Amritsar. She had a sister, nephews, and great nieces and nephews to meet for the very first time.

Chandani slung her camera strap around her shoulder and squeezed Shanti's hand. "I'll meet you two back in the gardens. I want to get a few more shots from there."

A young girl wearing a light blue frock, about the same age Shanti was when she was last here, spun in circles on the terrace. Her braids flung in the air. Her face turned toward the sky. A man approached her, wrapped his arms around her, kissed her forehead. The doting father. He offered his bent arm, escorted her toward the steps to the gardens. Shanti once knew that kind of love, the love between a father and a daughter. She didn't have it for long enough. But now, in her forties, she felt it stronger than ever. She would hold on tight to it and never let it go.

Shanti reached for Laila's hand, the hand that, in some way, held a part of her father, her grandfather, and now a part of her too.

Laila looked up into her eyes. "How is it that I barely know you," she said, "but feel as if I have always known you?"

Shanti smiled. "And this is only the beginning." She opened her backpack and extracted a paper crane she had made on her own with nine words inscribed under its wings. *For Kavita, Manoj, Amir, and Vijay. Love always, Shanti.* She centered the crane on top of the railing and then wrapped her arm around her great-aunt. "Let's go," she said. "There's still so much for us to see." Together, they slowly walked back toward the mausoleum.

A breeze kicked up that shifted the crane slightly. Its beak, like the needle of a compass, now pointed in the direction of the Yamuna River, Agra Fort, and a horizon that seemed to stretch like a band around the whole, infinite earth.

ACKNOWLEDGEMENTS

Much gratitude to the outstanding folks at Hub City Writers Project who poured their hearts into this book, especially Betsy Teter and Meg Reid. Thank you for making all of my dreams come true.

Gayatri Sethi's scrupulous suggestions were essential. I am indebted to her not only for her investment in this novel, but also for her emotional investment in me as an author. Roohi Choudhry's keen critique guided me toward rounder, more fully realized characters. Tiara Bhatacharya's invaluable expertise on Partition ensured that the plot, while fictional, was as consistent with historical events as possible.

There are several institutions and organizations today that collect the stories of survivors from the Partition, including the 1947 Partition Archive and the Lakshmi Mittal and Family South Asia Institute at Harvard University. I am grateful to them for their scrupulous work, invaluable archives, and their tremendous support.

I wrote early drafts of *The Parted Earth* during my MFA program at Queens University in Charlotte. Many thanks to my workshop colleagues and instructors, especially Pinkney Benedict. I had the immense honor of attending writers' residencies at the Hambidge Center, Wild Acres, and the (no longer) Rivendell Writers Colony. I'm grateful to the staff for the space to write.

Much love to my parents, my husband, and my three children, who have endured this long road to publication with me and cheered me to the finish line. I could not have crossed it without their love and support.

I've dedicated this book to my grandmothers. I miss them more than words can say, but am grateful for my memories and their stories.

Paperback Extras

ABOUT THE AUTHOR

Anjali Enjeti is a former attorney, award-winning journalist, and political organizer. She is the author of *Southbound: Essays on Identity, Inheritance, and Social Change.* Her writing has also appeared in *the Boston Globe, the Atlanta Journal-Constitution, Al Jazeera, the Washington Post,* and elsewhere. She teaches in the MFA program at Reinhardt University and lives with her family near Atlanta.

THE UNBEARABLE WHITENESS OF MAINSTREAM, CANONICAL SOUTHERN LITERATURE

by Anjali Enjeti

The first white-authored southern novel I read when my family moved from Michigan to Tennessee was Olive Ann Burns's *Cold Sassy Tree*. It told the story of a preteen boy named Will Tweedy whose family is thrust into scandal when his grandfather, newly widowed, marries a much younger woman. The action takes place in the early 1900s in northeast Georgia, but the book was published in 1984, the very same year I officially became a southerner. Small-town gossip was still very much a force eighty years later, and that novel helped me understand the ways it traveled and changed narratives, especially in the Deep South.

In the vast majority of white-authored southern novels I read, nostalgia served as a harbinger for racism, and southern pride was a stand-in for white fragility. These books were tethered and intoxicated by a romanticized, anti-Black, and white-washed history of the South.

Enter Harper Lee's iconic *To Kill a Mockingbird*, first published in 1960. To use a term made popular by Spike Lee and sociologist Matthew Hughey, "It is the time-honored Magical Negro narrative."

Many of us who grew up in the South know this novel by heart. White attorney Atticus Finch of sleepy Maycomb, Alabama, represents Tom Robinson, a Black man who has been accused of rape by a white woman, Mayella Ewell. In the book we learn a good deal about Atticus, his quiet, moral manner, his tenderness with his children, his kindness toward their Black cook, Calpurnia, and the lengths to which he will go to seek justice.

He is our hero. He is our white savior.

We don't learn a whole lot about Tom. This is because Tom only functions as a device (a Magical Negro) to educate the white characters Jem, Scout, and Dill (as well as white readers) about injustice. We don't know much about Tom's family, his interests, his personality. All Lee needed from Tom was for him to be the victim, and for white characters to understand racism through his victimization. Hence Tom has no dimensionality or characterization.

To Kill a Mockingbird's descendent, John Grisham's 1989 book *A Time to Kill*, fails in a similar fashion. Jake Brigance replaces Atticus Finch as the white savior to defend a Black man named Carl Lee Hailey who is on trial for killing the men who gang-raped his young daughter in Clanton, Mississippi.

Carl Lee has a slightly meatier role in A Time To Kill than Mockingbird's Tom Robinson, but he is still a flat character whose primary function is to elevate the heroism of Jake Brigance and teach white characters about racism. Carl Lee's child has been terrorized and traumatized, but it's Jake who gets our attention. It's his fears and future that are centered in the story.

Both *To Kill a Mockingbird* and *A Time to Kill* fetishize Black pain to redeem white characters, and in doing so they also redeem the non-Black readers who can celebrate an ending where justice is (supposedly) done. These novels then feed into an equally racist meta-narrative whereby the mere act of reading these books transforms white and non-Black readers of color into less racist people.

The consumption of these books is wholly performative. It affords readers the false sense that they've achieved a deep understanding about racist structures and racial distributions of power, so they can become the white savior in their own narrative about racism. I'm not like them. I'm not racist! I'm a good person! This frees them from more closely examining their own internalized racism and acknowledging their complicity in systemic racism.

I know this because I've heard non-Black readers say as much. In the 1980s and early 1990s, when I encountered these books for the first time, conversations with white southerners invoked a popular refrain. We need to remember our pasts. This ambiguous penance erased present-day racism and their own role in it. In the white imagination, the act of reading, followed by the act of remembering, served as the act of undoing racism.

This is the toxic life cycle that reading racist white southern literature continues to perpetuate.

Let me say here, briefly, that when I first encountered many of these texts as a teenager in the 1980s, I was incapable of parsing the white supremacy infused in their narratives. How could I? I was steeped in whiteness myself. All of my cultural references were white. My seemingly evolved white teachers, whom I loved, praised these books. I read *To Kill a Mockingbird* for the first time at age twelve, and it remained my favorite book until my mid-twenties. I devoured Margaret Mitchell's *Gone with the Wind* at age thirteen, and if asked, I would have likely deemed it the quintessential southern novel. After all, this is what I had been told.

Decades before movements like #WeNeedDiverseBooks and #OwnVoices, I believed that white southern authors who told stories about Black pain were performing a valuable service to the non-Black community.

So why shouldn't their books be celebrated?

In the summer of 1990, I read Melinda Haynes's debut novel *Mother of Pearl.* The book is set in the small town of Petal, Mississippi, in the 1990s. It tells the story of a friendship between a twenty-eight-year-old Black man named Even Grade and a fifteen-year-old white girl named Valuable Korner. The book has issues throughout, but the end in particular is wholly incognizant of the racist forces of the day. Spoiler alert: after Valuable dies giving birth to a son she names Pearl (whose father is no longer in her life), Even Grade decides to raise Valuable's white son as his own. Apparently the white baby's summer tan will cure anyone's suspicion about whether this white child belongs to a Black man. End of story.

Mother of Pearl was the first book that gave me pause about all of the white-authored southern novels I'd treasured before it.

When I learned that Oprah named *Mother of Pearl* as her next book club pick, I filled out an online form on her website to relay my sharp critique about the book. To my shock, a producer from the show called and wanted to hear more about what I thought. They were considering inviting me to be a guest on Oprah's book club show. A second producer called a few days later for a more extended interview.

I was no critic back then. I was twenty-five years old, one year out of law school, and a judicial clerk for two judges in Family Court in Delaware. I didn't possess the kind of language I have today to hone in on exactly why I found the book to be problematic. I fumbled for words and repeated myself. The best I could do was describe the book as "unrealistic." But even that word seemed wholly inadequate for the issues I found in the book.

Unbelievably, the producers found my responses worthy. They flew me to Chicago to discuss *Mother of Pearl* with Oprah herself, Haynes, and a few other readers. The limousine ride from O'Hare to the hotel downtown was my first ever.

Oprah is as luminous in real life as she is on television. After we situated ourselves on sofas, she breezed into the studio, sat on a sofa next to Haynes, and proceeded to conduct the conversation with grace and wit. At one point I managed to express my disappointment with the end of the book in a way that was more gentle than in my interviews with producers— Haynes was sitting right there, after all—but before I could fully state my case, Oprah interrupted me and moved on to another part of the book. That short clip is pretty much my only contribution to what later aired of the book club show. The producers wanted an episode that praised Haynes and the book, and that's exactly what they got.

I flew back to Philadelphia wondering, for the first time ever, what it was that I loved so much about white southern literature.

Much has been said about Kathryn Stockett's 2009 debut novel *The Help*, which has since sold more than ten million copies. The book tells the story of a white aspiring writer named Eugenia "Skeeter" Phelan who attempts to improve the lives of Black maids in 1960s Mississippi, specifically those of Aibileen and Minny, by literally telling their stories in a book titled Help that Skeeter hopes to sell to a big New York publishing house.

In summary, a white author (Skeeter) mines the voices of Black maids (Aibileen, Minny, and several others) to sell her own book (Help), much as Stockett herself mined the voice of the Black maid who raised her (Demetrie) to sell her own debut book (*The Help*). By writing the book, Stockett herself becomes the white savior in her own real-life narrative where her debut novel rids the world of racism. And by embodying the voices of Black maids, she carries with pride the torch that Harper Lee and John Grisham have passed to her.

I'll defer to the wise critics—that is, the Black critics—who vigorously and justifiably skewered *The Help*. Roxane Gay's brilliant 2011 essay in The Rumpus, "The Solace of Preparing Fried Foods and other Quaint Remembrances" (which focused on the movie as opposed to the novel), challenged the absurd fascination with a book and a movie that tried, and failed, to narrate racism: "In *The Help*, there are not one but twelve or thirteen magical negroes who use their mystical negritude to make the world a better place by sharing their stories of servitude and helping Eugenia 'Skeeter' Phelan grow out of her awkwardness and insecurity into a confident, racially aware, independent career woman. It's an embarrassment of riches for fans of the magical negro trope."

White critics, though, heaped praise. I will never be able to scrub my mind of the headline of one review in *USA Today*:

"Good 'Help' Isn't Hard to Find, Thanks to Kathryn Stockett." *The Help*'s white critical acclaim catapulted the book into the zeitgeist, spawning what I'll call *The Help* Effect. White readers, white critics, and white media anointed Stockett as the voice of the South. Her book gave the white savior / Magical Negro trope a shiny updated best-selling exterior.

Interviews with Stockett saturated the media. Many were nauseating. In *The Guardian*, Stockett described the Black maid who raised her. "Yes, she was called Demetrie. I started writing in her voice because it felt really soothing. It was like talking directly to her, showing her that I was trying to understand, even though I would never claim to know what that experience was like. It's impossible to know what she felt like, going home to her house, turning on her black-and-white TV. And I'm not saying I feel sorry for her, because she was a very proud woman."

The interview becomes more unbearable as it goes on. When asked whether President Obama's election is a sign that racism has decreased, Stockett turns to the theory of color-blindness. "I think if you're president, color goes away completely: you're president and it doesn't matter if you're white, green or purple."

This was not an isolated sentiment. It embodied a new, post-racial South, one that white southern readers were more than ready to pounce on.

There is an enormous range and depth of Black southern authors, and it is these authors who deliver, time and again, authentic, riveting stories about the Deep South. When I read Alice Walker's *The Color Purple*, I recognized something in that book that I couldn't articulate as an eighth-grader—that unlike white-authored novels I'd read, this novel didn't exist to teach or show or prove anything to me. The same can be said about my first time reading Zora Neale Hurston's *Their Eyes Were Watching God*. Janie's fierce independence and her unwillingness to conform to societal norms went against every stereotype I held about women in the Deep South. And after I first discovered Maya Angelou's *I Know Why the Caged Bird Sings*, I fell in love all over again with language. I carried that book around in my backpack for months.

What I didn't realize in childhood that I can see more clearly today is how southern literature has always been a genre of exclusion. Identity determines an author's southern-ness more than the setting itself.

According to the 2000 census, fifty-five percent of Black people live in the southeastern United States. Yet there are not nearly as many Black southern authors as there should be, and white southern authors all too often pen southern stories that belong to Black people.

The Deep South first belonged to Indigenous people. Yet too few southern Indigenous books have been published. "It's important that people in the South realize that they are living on Native land," said Choctaw Nation author LeAnne Howe in an interview. "By ignoring or not knowing or never having thought of Indians before, you've really cut yourself out of hundreds and hundreds of years of experiences of the people that came before."

I can only imagine the number of Black and Native writers querying agents and editors with their southern stories. Or, for that matter, the number of Cuban American writers in Mississippi. Or Cambodian writers in Louisiana. Or Venezuelan American writers in Tennessee. Or Iranian American writers in Texas. The South has always been far more racially diverse than southern literature has reflected.

For years I pitched a novel about an Indian immigrant family who ran a gas station in a small North Georgia town. The family's lives were tangled in secrets dating back to a tragic accident a decade earlier. The book was about the bitterness that comes from unfulfilled dreams, the isolation one can feel when living far from a major urban center, and the toxic small-town gossip that can shape a family's narrative. The novel was as southern as a southern novel can get.

I submitted the book for many years. Several agents said they weren't sure how to sell it or didn't know who the intended audience was. I had grown up surrounded by southern books. This was an authentic southern story, I myself was southern. Why couldn't they sell it as such?

A few years later, a white southern author published a novel that featured white characters and wove in elements of Hindu mythology. The book embodied the perfect formula for the white gaze, southern sensibility, and a dash of Indian garnish to deem it both marketable to white readers and exotic. Here I was, an Indian southerner trying to sell a southern story about Indian southerners at a time when no other Indian southern author was publishing novels about the South. And a white southern author beat me to it.

In 2019 my reckoning took the form of another novel by another Indian American author from the South, Devi S. Laskar's poetic debut *The Atlas of Reds and Blues*. Though she now makes her home on the West Coast, Laskar grew up in North Carolina and spent several years in Georgia working and raising her children.

The book tells the story of an Indian immigrant known only as Mother who is shot by law enforcement and bleeding in her driveway in a suburb of Atlanta. As Mother's life slowly drains from her body, scenes flash before her shaped by the region where she and her family have made their home, a region that has never welcomed them, where they are seen as foreign, where they are watched and surveilled. "From the periphery of her eye she makes out the women, white on white and peroxide blond glistening in the Monday sun, aviators reflecting as they stand guard over the clipped grass and pressure-washed concrete, chess pieces waiting for the next move."

Atlas is a reminder that there are many stories about the South that have yet to be told, and that the South is far more racially and ethnically diverse than the publishing industry has ever perceived it. It is a region rich in history, in people, and in the stories Indigenous, Black, and other writers of color are feverishly writing every day, waiting, hoping, that they will someday see the light.

ANJALI ENJETI TALKS WITH
ANITA FELICELLI

Anita Felicelli: I enjoyed the cultural complexity of *The Parted Earth*. It's rare to see this degree of conscious global awareness in an American novel. How did you cultivate that awareness in your fiction?

Anjali Enjeti: Well first off, thank you for such a lovely compliment.

Many of the most difficult chapters of our world history have a global and generations-long impact. Survivors of the Partition dispersed all over the world, as did survivors of the Holocaust, the Vietnam War, the Rwandan genocide, and the Somali Civil War. The trauma and the stories from these events traveled with them and shaped the places they settled and the people that formed their communities. Partition happened in the subcontinent, but its legacy can be felt everywhere today.

While human struggles can be intimate, personal, and unique, they're also universal. So much of what we endure as humans is interconnected, and this is a theme I wanted to emphasize in the novel. I say this not to essentialize events in history but to observe how they shape us in similar ways.

AF: I like how you describe mixed identity in *Southbound*: "Mixed people are oftentimes not seen as wholes, as authentically belonging to any race, culture, religion or ethnicity. We are aberrations or unicorns, rumors whispered among nosey neighbors." What difficulties and/or benefits have you found in writing and organizing with a mixed identity?

AE: Goodness, I find it all so difficult. As a mixed person, I oftentimes feel as if I'm sucking too much oxygen out of the room while also erasing crucial aspects of my identity. And how I feel about being mixed is complicated and evolving. How I saw myself as a mixed-race brown woman five years ago is different than how I see myself now, and how I will see myself five years from now.

I want to tell stories from an authentic lens, and I want to organize without centering myself, but I also feel I need to be inclusive in order to reach as many people as possible. In organizing, we talk about meeting people where they are, and this is what I hope to achieve as an author. This means I write the story I'm compelled to write, but also give enough background and context for readers who are not familiar with the kinds of narratives I'm writing. In organizing, I have to work with people every day with whom I disagree on some issues, because I have to build a coalition with them. We either sink or swim together. So if I'm not actively working to create a space that we can both enter, safely, to commune with one another, I've failed.

I'd like to think my mixed identity makes engaging with others, whether as an author or an organizer, more natural for me, but it's not. I'm a work in progress. I'm as flawed and fallible as the next person and oftentimes feel as if I'm holding my hands out in front of me in a dark room and searching for a light switch.

AF: What responsibility should a writer have to his or her own community? To what extent do you believe it's part of a novelist's work to try to influence her own community to do better with regard to Islamophobia, for example? What is the role of politics in fiction?

AE: We have a huge responsibility to our own communities, whether we are writers or not. We need to encourage our own folks to do better and unpack their own biases, whatever those biases may be. Writers, especially, know how to communicate well and effectively and have a pretty good idea about how to bring up and dissect tough issues. We should, I feel, be at the forefront of doing this work.

I've written many opinion pieces about white supremacy, xenophobia, and Islamophobia. They will pass right over the heads of some people who read them, including those who truly believe they're not engaging in bigotry. But some people can more easily see the truth of how they marginalize others in fiction, because it's more subtle, not so didactic, and they're not being directly called out for their problematic beliefs. In a novel we're saying, "Look, here's a serious issue. How did we get here? What part do we all play?" Fiction can open the eyes of readers who are otherwise resistant to seeing what they need to see about themselves. So yes, to answer your question, I do think politics play an important role in fiction.

AF: The story of Harjeet, a Sikh man migrating with his family during Partition, is violent and intense. It's brief, only two and a half chapters of the novel, but it's going to stay with me. What was your thought process for writing such a sensitive, potentially controversial storyline for a character with whom (I believe) you don't share an identity?

AE: That's correct, I do not share an identity with Harjeet. His story reflects one of the darkest chapters of Partition, and it was not uncommon. Folks from every ethnic/religious group on the subcontinent participated in it. It's based on firsthand testimony I uncovered during my research. For a long time, I wrestled with whether or how to tell his story. The last thing I wanted was for a survivor of Partition to read this novel and think, "This is tragedy porn," or to feel as if their community is being maligned.

I did a few things to make sure I got Harjeet and his family right, as well as the other characters, including Amir and Laila, who are Muslim. I hired two authenticity editors with similar racial/ethnic/religious backgrounds. These editors' ancestors had also survived Partition, and they knew their stories. Even after I worked through suggested revisions, I worried about whether the book would cause harm. So I also hired a historian who collects and archives Partition accounts to read all the parts of the book that take place during Partition. I'm glad I did. She made suggestions to alter crucial details that I'd not uncovered in my own research.

I could not, nor would not, write an entire novel about Harjeet—I'm not capable of it. Nor could I have written an entire novel about Amir or Laila, from their points of view. The presence of these three characters loom large throughout the book, and their roles are vital. But their actual appearances are limited, and that's intentional. I know my limitations as a writer.

I also did not presume I could write Deepa's story any better than Harjeet's, Amir's, or Laila's simply because my identity is a (slightly) closer match to hers. I was just as scrupulous about how I portrayed her. I've never really believed, actually, that shared or partially shared identities automatically confer accuracy, authenticity, or truthfulness in character-building or storytelling. *The Parted Earth* revolves around Shan, whose father is Indian and whose mother is white, and my own father is Indian, and my own mother is mixed-race but white passing, but I could have just as easily gotten Shan completely wrong. I'm no authority on writing biracial or multiracial characters just because I'm multiracial.

Writing any characters well, I believe, comes down to approaching the subject and characters humbly, with great intention, understanding the risk of harm to marginalized communities, interrogating internalized biases, and collaborating with professionals to catch what you will inevitably miss as a storyteller. Paranoia, doubt, and the fear of not getting it right are healthy and helpful emotions when we're telling tough stories.

AF: I found the role of Gertrude in *The Parted Earth* intriguing. From Southbound, I know that Gertrude was the name of your grandmother who grew up in Austria during the era of Nazi Germany, whose father was turned in for betraying the Third Reich. The character Gertrude tries to be a good friend to Deepa, the initial protagonist of the novel, and her small son. And yet she finds herself overstepping. It read to me as a blunder that is common among people who are trying to be allies. What do you believe the role of an ally is? How do we show solidarity without overstepping?

AE: Yes, Gertrude is loosely based on my real grandmother of the same name, and in *The Parted Earth*, the fictional Gertrude confuses her love for her dear friend Deepa as having the right to do what she thinks is best.

I find questions about allyship and solidarity so difficult to

answer, though, because while I actively interrogate my internalized bigotry and try to change my problematic behavior, I
still have a lot to learn. Generally speaking, I think of solidarity
as a verb, an active state of awareness, action, and being. More
often than not, allyship feels performative—it's more about
how our actions appear to others rather than whether these
actions can effectuate change.

Here are some of the questions I regularly ask myself while
engaging in this kind of work: Who do I consider "my community," and who and why are some folks excluded from this
group? Am I spending the majority of my time amplifying the
words and actions of marginalized folks, or am I centering
myself? Am I accepting credit from others instead of diverting
or at least sharing the credit with folks who have been doing
the same work longer and more effectively? Do I need to have
my voice in every conversation about justice, or am I helping communities more if I stay silent, listen, and then work to
change my behavior? And above all else, am I bringing others
along on my journey of learning?

AF: In order to organize, you have to be able to call people
in. How did you think through the political critiques you levy
in *The Parted Earth* and Southbound? For instance, there are
Indian Americans that support the RSS, the far-right paramil-
itary organization, yet also support causes progressives support, such as environmental causes. They might feel defensive
about critiques of India and Hindu nationalism and shut down.
Did you worry about how the Hindu American community or
any other community might receive the novel? How do we
build coalitions and also critique?

AE: I have been trolled, harassed, and threatened as both an
activist and a writer based on what I've said about the RSS,

Prime Minister Modi, and the BJP, so much so that I now do a fair amount of self-censorship online. But we all have very important work to do as a community to dismantle the belief that far-right extremism has anything to do with any religion or any nation. The critique of far-right extremism, how it operates, and who it affects the most isn't a critique of a faith or a people. It's a critique of institutions, governments, and bad actors in power who weaponize their ideology to commit violence against minorities. In the case of Hindu nationalism, it's a critique of how some Hindus weaponize Hinduism against Muslims, Dalits, and other minorities. And it's everyone's responsibility, whether Hindu, non-Hindu, Indian, non-Indian, to call this out—no matter what continent it's happening on.

In organizing, we talk about how important it is to abstain from judgment and not denigrate folks just because they're not as far along in their understanding of equality and justice. But it's very difficult to begin these conversations when people refuse to see the hypocrisy involved in supporting progressive causes and condemning discrimination in one country but not in another. And people are dying from far-right extremism. This is a dire situation. We don't have the luxury of time to teach or explain why views are harmful to the people holding them. To be honest, at times I feel like throwing my hands up in the air and giving up.

Anita Felicelli is the author of Chimerica: A Novel *and the award-winning short story collection* Love Songs for a Lost Continent.

PARTITION READING LIST

What the Body Remembers by Shauna Singh Baldwin

The Other Side of Silence: Voices from the Partition of India
by Urvashi Butalia

Victory Colony, 1950 by Bhaswati Ghosh

Midnight's Furies: The Deadly Legacy of India's Partition
by Nisid Hajari

Sunlight on a Broken Column by Attia Hosain

*The Pity of Partition: Manto's Work, Life and Times Across
the India-Pakistan Divide* by Ayesha Jalal

The Great Partition: The Making of India and Pakistan
by Yasmin Khan

In Freedom's Shade by Anis Kidwai

Partitions by Amit Majmudar

Mottled Dawn by Saadat Hasan Manto

Tamas by Bhisham Sahni

A Suitable Boy by Vikram Seth

Salt and Saffron by Kamila Shamsie

Mandalay's Child by Prem Sharma

Cracking India and *Ice Candy Man* by Bapsi Sidhwa

Train to Pakistan by Khushwant Singh

The Dog of Tithwal: Stories by Saadat Hasan Manto, transl. by
Khalid Hasan, Aatish Taseer, Muhammed Umar Memon

DISCUSSION QUESTIONS

What character did you most identify with over the course of the novel?

What knowledge did you have about the Partition of the Indian subcontinent before reading this book, and what have you learned after reading the book? If you did have previous information, how did this book change your feelings?

At its core, this novel is about generational trauma through history and personal tragedy. What does Shan learn from Deepa about herself and her ancestry?

Chandani tries to be a friend to Shan, but she often oversteps because of their generational difference. How can we learn from their relationship?

There are moments of silence in this book when a character does not speak up for themselves or a loved one. What moments stuck out to you and how did they function in the novel?

How does the theme of generational grief and trauma affect the characters of Deepa, Vijay, and Shan? What decisions do you think they made because of this trauma?

The COLD MOUNTAIN *Fund*
S E R I E S

NATIONAL BOOK AWARD WINNER Charles Frazier generously supports publication of a series of Hub City Press books through the Cold Mountain Fund at the Community Foundation of Western North Carolina. The Cold Mountain Series spotlights works of fiction by new and extraordinary writers from the American South. Books published in this series have been reviewed in outlets like *Wall Street Journal, San Francisco Chronicle, Garden & Gun, Entertainment Weekly,* and *O, the Oprah Magazine;* included on Best Books lists from NPR, *Kirkus,* and the American Library Association; and have won or been nominated for awards like the Southern Book Prize, Crooks Corner Book Prize, and the Langum Prize for Historical Fiction.

The Crocodile Bride • Ashleigh Bell Pedersen

Child in the Valley • Gordy Sauer

You Want More: The Selected Stories of George Singleton

The Prettiest Star • Carter Sickels

Watershed • Mark Barr

The Magnetic Girl • Carter Sickels

PUBLISHING
New & Extraordinary
VOICES FROM THE
AMERICAN SOUTH

FOUNDED IN SPARTANBURG, South Carolina in 1995, Hub City Press has emerged as the South's premier independent literary press. Hub City is interested in books with a strong sense of place and is committed to finding and spotlighting extraordinary new and unsung writers from the American South, our curated list champions diverse authors and books that don't fit into the commercial or academic publishing landscape.